Wyld Dreamers

Pamela Holmes

urbanepublications.com

First published in Great Britain in 2018
by Urbane Publications Ltd
Suite 3, Brown Europe House, 33/34 Gleaming Wood Drive,
Chatham, Kent ME5 8RZ

A CIP catalogue record for this book is available
from the British Library.

ISBN 978-1-911583-04-2
MOBI 978-1-911583-08-0

Design and Typeset by Michelle Morgan

Cover by Michelle Morgan

Printed and bound by 4edge Limited, UK

urbanepublications.com

To my father, Richard, who spent happy boyhood summers on a Rhode Island Farm

PART ONE

Chapter One

1972

All her life, Amy Taylor has been a dutiful daughter. She still wakes early, anxious there is an essay to finish or a deadline looming or an exam she has missed. Then the smell of furniture spray and the drone of the hoover remind her that her school days are over. Jubilant, she springs from her bed. She will take the next step, even if she does not know where it will lead.

'Julian lives there with his father,' she told them.

The lie slipped out easily. As she watched her father digest the information, it occurred to her that if she had been economical with the truth more often, things would have been easier. He closes the doors of the cabinet behind which sits the television. He flicks on the electric fire and settles in the comfy chair that he always chooses. The BBC news has just finished (he does not approve of ITV). They will now discuss Amy's proposed holiday.

Her boyfriend, David Bond, sits on the sofa next to her mother, the foam cushions dipping so that he must concentrate on stopping his body from rolling into the woman he is trying to impress. Amy's father pours the tea and they are, for a moment, mesmerised by the brown liquid that streams from the spout, grateful for the delay in starting what will be a difficult conversation.

'Sugar, David?' says Shirley. Her pearl necklace matches the pearly shine of her nails, both worn for the occasion.

Her boyfriend's insouciance is only partially tamed by the ironed shirt and tie. It makes David look at the same time both younger and older. David, the first man Amy has ever lain alongside in a bed, skin to skin, gripping him with shy fingers and hot thighs, feeling the choking desire she had read about in books. It shocks her that now he seems almost a stranger. But they had agreed when he came for tea he must look as respectable as possible, not wear his loon pants and tie-dyed t-shirt. When her parents ask about the arrangements for sleeping - which they will - they must be able to believe what David says. Being dressed smartly will help. Her parents must feel assured that what they cared about more than anything, their daughter's virginity, will be protected.

The proposal is that Amy accompany David to spend a month on a friend's farm in Somerset.

'My friend Julian Stratton has asked me and another friend from university, Simon Webster, to stay with him this summer. We're going to help rebuild a cottage in the grounds of his father's farm. A working holiday really, while we all decide what we're going to do now we've graduated.'

'It's meant to be lovely countryside around there,' says Amy, passing the plate of biscuits to their guest. 'I'm sure we'll get a chance to visit Exmoor.'

Amy does not know if it is beautiful in Somerset. But her father, who spends his evenings in the small square garden behind the house tending the vegetables that the family eat at every meal, will be pleased to think she has an interest in nature.

'But what help will you be?' John finds it hard to accept his shy daughter has become this confident young woman. He remembers the trembling toddler, the cautious schoolgirl.

'I'm strong, Dad, I can work,' Amy protests.

'I haven't noticed you doing much in my garden,' her father

replies curtly. He is more annoyed than he should be. He senses he is being manipulated but cannot see how.

'The boys will be doing the heavy work, Mr Taylor,' interjects David. 'Cigarette?' He stretches forward with a lighter. Neither man speaks while they inhale. 'I don't know if Amy has mentioned it. Julian's father is a well-known photographer, Seymour Stratton. I suspect you know his work?'

Both parents nod vaguely; Amy knows they are lying.

David continues: 'Fashion, the arts, royalty I think, sometimes. But Mr Stratton is taking time away from London to rebuild this cottage. He'll be there with us. It's a smallholding really; some grazing land, a few acres, some outbuildings. Amy will do some of the lighter work, painting perhaps. There'll be paid labourers, too.'

Amy wonders how David knows this. Then she remembers a piece of information that will elicit sympathy. 'Julian's mother is not alive,' she says.

'Isn't that terrible? Poor boy,' Shirley says. After a pause, she adds: 'So you can do the cooking, Amy. I've taught you a few dishes and I can lend you my Marguerite Patten recipe book.'

It was her mother's habit, when uncertain, to thrum her fingers on her bony clavicle. Sometimes Amy wonders if one day when her mother is agitated whether her fingers might leap up and wrap themselves tightly around her throat to strangle her.

'That's what I was thinking, Mum. Look, you could always phone up Mr Stratton and talk to him if you're worried? Dad, why don't you do that?'

It is a gamble worth taking. Seymour Stratton is unlikely to be at the farmhouse to take the call. He is rarely there, according to Julian, preferring to remain in London with his friends and work. Often works abroad, Julian explained, photographing models in exotic destinations. It would probably be Julian who answered the phone or perhaps the housekeeper.

Amy predicts the call will not be made for it would imply her parents do not trust their daughter.

Shirley says hurriedly: 'I don't think we need to bother Mr Stratton, do you, John? It sounds like a lovely holiday for you both. A month in the country, isn't there a book by that name? And then, of course, you start the secretarial course in September.'

'Yes Mother,' Amy nods. 'I can't wait.'

*

Only economical with the truth, she tells herself the next day as she packs her contraceptive diaphragm into a bag of clothes and clambers on the back of David's motorbike, waving goodbye to the small place where she had once been happy and is now desperate to leave. Any residual guilt is blown away by the wind that flattens her eyelashes and the rain that whips her blond hair into damp spaghetti. Her boyfriend's greatcoat is as soft as a downy pillow. She presses up against him, comatose with joy.

On the ride, it rains almost constantly. Once they stop to buy petrol and the owner, taking pity on their blue lips, offers them sweet tea. They sit by the electric fire in the smoky office, blowing warmth on each other's fingers, tingling with expectation like children with sweets.

'Julian's girlfriend will be there; Stella, a girl he met in London. I called him last night. His father is bringing Simon down in the car in a day or two,' David says.

'I can't believe we're on the way,' Amy is almost breathless. 'We're free! A whole month. I was convinced Father wouldn't let me go. Can I drive the tractor? How much further is it?

Does Julian have a dog? I love dogs, always wanted one. I'm so freezing, so happy…'

The road from Taunton streams out behind them. Lampposts and traffic signs and letter boxes flick by. The road heaves over the spine of a hill, arching them towards the sky. Now they are racing across the Brendon hills. Fields and trees and vast views of landscape flash past. Sometimes a gust of wind catches the bike and it skitters. For a moment, they seem to hang suspended. Then the wheels hit the tarmac and they are off again. She is not afraid.

Lulled by the miles, David almost misses the turning. He pulls on the brakes just past a line of white cottages. The force of the deceleration presses her forward; the damp of her shirt is freezing. They turn down a steep lane. Twisting and turning the bike plunges into a dark, narrowing tunnel, the rumble of the engine dampened by the moisture-laden undergrowth and over-hanging branches. Finally the lane levels. A few minutes later, they ride on a track along the edge of a field and pull up in a farmyard.

David cuts the engine. Thick silence presses in. Across the yard she can make out the shape of buildings. Her feet squelch in her boots as they hit the ground.

'Come on,' David says. Like bow-legged cowboys, they waddle towards the house. The front door opens. There is Julian with a glass of whisky in one hand and a big towel in the other. Behind him rolls out the pounding cry of Eric Clapton for love and Layla.

'You're both soaking,' Julian beams, 'come and get warm.'

Wrapped in towels while their clothes steam on the Aga, David and Amy devour bread and cheese and slug wine from a bottle. Julian watches them with amusement. His girlfriend Stella, her mouth fixed in a permanent pout, appears indifferent. As she drifts in and out of the kitchen to change the record, her beaded kaftan tinkles as it trails behind her.

Julian is more at ease than the few times Amy has seen him before. Fetching another dry towel, asking if they've had enough to eat, he is the perfect host, regaling them with a story of a brilliant record shop in Notting Hill. Nothing like the mysterious person David talked of, the one who missed his essay deadlines and was hounded by hangovers.

Amy glimpses around the kitchen. It is the exact opposite of her mother's carefully cleaned melamine laboratory. The walls are painted like cloud-filled cerulean skies. A romantic *trompe l'oeil* landscape covers the wall behind the Aga. A wooden table that could seat twelve is scarred with initials. Around it cluster chairs painted in primary colours. A pine dresser is chock-a-block with jugs, cups and bowls in assorted sizes and patterns. A deep stone sink. The casual glamour of the place is irresistible.

It feels awkward to ask but she must pee. Julian says there is a loo in the boot room. She had never been in a room called that before. Over dusty linoleum she picks her way between shoes, wellingtons, coats, an odd sock, a coil of wire and a sleeping dog she later knows is called Pilot to a door behind which there is a toilet. The sink has not been cleaned.

Sitting on the peeling wooden seat, the chain flush and porcelain handle dangle by her ear. Her mother has always sung the praises of her avocado bathroom suite. She would not understand what her daughter is doing in a house where nothing matches. Her daughter grins.

Amy peeks into the room from which the music plays. In front of a large fireplace three saggy sofas cluster like knee-splayed old ladies on deckchairs. Stacks of books are piled on the floor. Along a shelf between chest-high stereo speakers is a long line of records. Stella is flicking through them. She sees Amy and returns to searching. Amy returns to the kitchen.

'Dad won't mind,' Julian is saying as he passes David a half full bottle of gin. They pull their chairs close to the Aga.

Julian will show them the cottage in the morning, he explains. He is pleased they have come to stay; there is so much fun to be had.

As the men talk, Amy's eyelids dip. Drowsiness presses like a heavy blanket. Next thing she knows, David is shaking her shoulder and telling her to come to bed. Too sleepy to speak, she trails after him and Julian up the stairs; Stella has disappeared.

Julian gestures at one of the doors. 'Take that room if you like. Any room really, except that one over there. It's Seymour's.'

In their room there's a high wrought iron bedstead. Though she can barely summon the energy, she peels off her underwear and hauls herself up, unwashed and unbrushed. Pushing David's hand away, she falls into a dreamless sleep.

Chapter Two

Shirley Taylor dries the breakfast things and puts the tea towel in the twin tub. The nylon sheets crackle as she pulls them off Amy's bed. Her daughter left this morning. It is hard to find sufficient energy to breathe.

She sits on the carpet, scratching through its tight pile hoping to find a little piece of Amy, a strand of hair or a flake of skin which she could slip into her pocket. She runs her fingers lightly along the mattress and over the side table, lets them drift across the jewellery box with the ballerina on top as if to absorb traces of her daughter.

She crawls to the wardrobe, straightens her daughter's sandals and shoes again, breathes in the tiniest whiff of feet. Slowly, tentatively, she pulls open a drawer to rest her hand between a jumper and a blouse, imagining she can feel the heart that once beat there. When she cannot feel it, she sits back on heels gasping.

Shirley climbs onto the mattress, clasps softly to her chest the cushion Amy embroidered in Year 7 and recalls the first time she saw her tiny and bawling daughter. How her heart swelled as though it would burst from her chest in a great arc of love. Proudly showing Amy to the midwives as though they had never seen a baby before. Memories of the toddler digging in the garden for worms. The schoolgirl frustrated when her socks pooled around her ankles because her shins were so skinny. The careful student who left her O level revision notes on the bus. The truculent streak that blew in as she blew out the candles on her fifteenth birthday cake and her behaviour became volatile.

But even when sharp words were exchanged and doors slammed, it was never more than a day or two before the girl sidled back to her mother's side. The slight of a friend or an outbreak of spots, something would shake the girl's universe and she'd be there, quarrel utterly forgotten, seeking solace. With her daughter's head in her lap, Shirley would caress the proffered cheek, marvelling at the freckles that sprinkled her cheekbones like demerara sugar. Teasing the tangles from her daughter's silken mane, massaging her scalp to chivvy off knotted thoughts, she and Amy breathed in tandem. Precious times, known and accepted, always and for certain, to be numbered.

'She got away alright?' John asks his wife that evening.

'Yes, fine,' Shirley replies.

She puts his supper plate on the table. She does not mention the change of plans, how David explained his parents could no longer lend their car so the only option was for him and Amy to travel by motorbike. John would never have agreed to his daughter travelling this way; he would have locked her in the house and ignored the howls of fury.

She does not tell John that Amy hitched up her long skirt, clambered up on to the back of the motorbike and wrapped her arms around David's waist. Or how with a single wave, their beautiful daughter roared away. And she does not admit, even to herself, that somewhere deep inside the thought of riding on a gleaming machine like that makes her breathless.

John touches her hand. 'Shirley, are you alright?'

'Yes, I'm fine. It seems quiet somehow, knowing she's not here. I didn't say, John. Amy called from a petrol station, somewhere along the way. Everything is fine, she said. She'll call again in a few days.'

Shirley carries the empty plates to the sink, washes the pans and carefully wipes the worktop. She watches her husband hoe the neat rows of vegetables, finding weeds where none grow, knee-deep in the foliage like he is wading in a green sea. And she knows he is as miserable as she.

CHAPTER THREE

Her watch says ten o' clock when she wakes next morning, dry-mouthed. 'Here Comes the Sun' is playing at full volume and The Beatles are right. Dim light filters through rents in the red satin curtains making the room glow rosy-pink; how can David sleep?

Amy is washed with cheerfulness. Their high bed stands in the middle of the room. Against the wall is a wooden chair that reminds her of school; there's a chest of drawers half-painted in gold. She slips down, not from under sheets and blankets as she is used to but a puffy eiderdown. Her bare feet hit bare floorboards. Taking a dressing gown from the back of the door, she tip-toes along the thread-bare carpet looking for the toilet. Stella appears in a floor-length nightdress and disappears into a room. The sound of splashing.

Amy sits on the toilet. The room swirls with dotted light from the stained-glass mobile that hangs like a mushroom above her head. On the door, a framed poster for an exhibition shows a half-naked man on a green bed. No carpet, no neatly stored bottle of toilet cleaner, no toilet paper. Luckily there's a used tissue in the pocket of the dressing gown. She washes her hands and face in the cracked sink. Back in bed, her cold feet wake David. Feigning fury, he rolls over to cover her with his body. Pinning her down, he blows kisses on her neck. She is jubilant.

Half an hour later, Julian kicks open the door and comes in carrying mugs of tea. He is dressed in what looks like a woman's nightie; his hairy legs stick out from the bottom. 'No time for all that now,' he says, 'we've got to get going. Seymour is arriving soon with Simon. Let's go see the cottage. Find yourselves some boots, it'll be damp.'

Cutting through a gap in the hedge into a field of chest-high nettles and hummocky grass they find it, a dilapidated two-up two-down stone building with a brick lean-to on one side. Slates are missing from the roof and parts of the building's exterior reveal what looks like straw and mud walls.

'Someone lived here until just before Seymour bought the place,' said Julian, water pooling around his boots. 'Pipe cracked last winter, that's why it's soggy here below the window.'

He shoves his shoulder against the front door. The wood resists briefly, then gives way. They dip their heads to step inside. A steep wooden staircase leads up from the hall. There is a sitting room with a fireplace and beyond it, another smaller room with a set of backstairs. The ceilings in both rooms are bowed, the walls streaked with dirt. There's a lean-to kitchen and bathroom. Mould grows on the walls. It smells damp.

Julian nods as Amy starts up the stairs. 'Yes, have a look. Stairs and floors are safe, that's been checked.'

'Needs just a little bit of attention,' she hears David and Julian jeering.

None of the three rooms upstairs are large. The middle one has windows on both sides. How pretty it once might have looked. She wonders who might have slept here. Had a baby been born, had someone died, perhaps? Would the ghosts fade once it was painted?

Brushing away cobwebs, she works at a window latch. She can see the farmhouse where she slept last night. Built from stone, the square building has windows on either side of the grand front door, a grey-slate roof and big chimneys. Hard to believe that she, Amy Taylor, is staying in such a place. She brushes away the thought that she lied to her parents to be here.

In the cottage garden, Stella is sitting on a branch of a tree. Her long dress spreads around her like a sail. The girl could be a model from the magazines that Amy sometimes flicks through in the newsagents. She exudes an untouchable air of exotica even in the way she breathes. Amy feels a flash of envy: why can't Stella wear trousers and an anorak like she does? Amy chastises herself for being small-minded. Stella simply suits the surroundings better than she does.

In the single room at the far end of the cottage, there's a set of wooden stairs to the room below. Picking up a brown curl of newspaper from the floor, she sees a story about 'a Country Show in 1959'. She waves it at David.

He is craning his neck to look up the chimney, trying to look as though he knows what he's doing or what he's looking for. She touches his shoulder. He turns and taking her in his arms, rests his chin on her head. 'Amazing place, eh?'

'Seymour talks about doing the place up. Though who'd want to live in this dump, I can't imagine,' Julian jokes.

'It could be made lovely, surely?' Amy looks around.

'For spiders perhaps. Want some?' Julian offers her a joint.

She shakes her head and wanders outside. Someone had once tended the garden here for there are the remains of a broken path and rose bushes and a plant she recalls her father called 'a butterfly bush'. How pleased he would be to know that she remembers something he taught her. She tugs a plant she thinks is a weed.

Stella brushes past. Barely glancing at Amy, she murmurs; 'I can hear a car coming up the drive. It's probably Seymour. Tell Julian I've gone to meet him.'

Amy goes back into the cottage. The boys are larking about in the kitchen. 'I think your father's arrived, Julian. Stella says she's gone over to meet him.'

'Right-o. Okay you two, prepare to meet Seymour Stratton.'

On the drive is a white Jaguar car. A man is reaching into the boot and pulls out two bottles of wine. It's Simon Webster, a university friend of Julian and David's whom Amy once met on an anti-war march in London. He has those angelic boyish looks that won't change much with age, fair hair and a shy smile. But it's the leather-jacketed man in his late forties whose she's more interested in. This must be Seymour, Julian's father. Wild curls and a pointed nose, his heeled boots make him only an inch or two taller than Stella. The woman stands next to him shaking her hair like a starlet preparing for the camera. A delicious wave of schadenfreude. Stella reveals overly large teeth when she smiles.

Amy and David follow Julian.

'Julian, my boy, how are you doing?' Father and son grasp arms. 'So these are the friends you've been telling me about.'

'Hallo Seymour, meet David Bond. He and I were on the same degree course.'

It is an accurate statement. Whether they will both graduate is not certain. David would be content with a second class degree but Julian, who spent much of the summer term away due to poor health, isn't confident he will pass. No one is quite sure why he was away so much. They sense it is a subject he prefers not to discuss.

Seymour and David shake hands. 'And this is David's girlfriend, Amy Taylor.'

'Hallo Mr Stratton, pleased to meet you. Thank you for inviting us to stay here with Julian. You have a beautiful place.'

'Hallo. Like it, do you, Amy?' Seymour's gaze seems to pin her to the spot. 'It's a bit tatty round the edges but yes, a certain charm. Julian, can you take the camera from the car? And the bag of food on the back seat. Would you mind bringing it in, David? Simon, those bottles must go straight into the freezer. Mrs Morle looking after the place alright, Julian? And how is our feisty Lynn these days?'

He leads them into the house, calling for Pilot, and asks someone to lay the table, to fetch glasses, to put music on. A Little Feat album plays while foods she has never seen or tasted before are spread across the table. Smoked salmon, the thinnest slivers of meat, olives fat with anchovies, roasted peppers sprinkled with herbs, a smoky green dip pungent with garlic. They rip pieces of bread from baguettes; the drink makes her tongue sing.

As they eat, Seymour tells them what he's been up to. People he has photographed that week, names she has seen mentioned in newspapers, exotic and eccentric people of note. He tells a story against himself, a gaff he made with someone famous and it's very funny. It all sounds unreal, too strange for her to envisage, the opposite of the life she has shared with her parents where routine prevails; jobs and homework and meals and washing up. The wisps of her hangover disappear.

'Let's have a toast,' Seymour says. 'To the summer. To you all.' He pushes back his chair and stretches out his arms in a grand gesture. 'Have you had a look around the place yet? What do you think of my escape to the country? I'm thinking it could become an artist's retreat, somewhere people can rejuvenate the creative juices and have fun. Just needs a few improvements, here and there, and that Julian could run the place, perhaps. That's all in the future. We're just glad you're here now to help us get our little dream going.'

Amy is a bit drunk. A song floats round her head, Dusty Springfield's 'I Only Want to Be with You'. She is sure it will be somewhere in the snake of vinyl in the sitting room. What if the boys scoff at her choice?

She puts on the record. It was playing the first time she saw David in the Student Union bar. Her brother had invited her and Mary, her school friend, to the 'Spring Bop'. The students, mostly men as far as she could see, were much older than she and Mary. They were arranged like skittles around the football table, shouting as they whacked or watched a tiny ball race up and down a table between the legs of plastic figurines. They clasped pints of beer. In the corner was a student with a different style. A cigarette clamped between his teeth, one booted foot resting on a stool, the man with long nut-brown hair, a stubble-coated chin and a Led Zepplin t-shirt lazily strummed a guitar. She was mesmerised. A girl with long hair parted in the middle joined him to share a joke. Amy felt jealous. Two months later, when she had kissed the guitar player, she was introduced to the girl. It was Maggie Bond, David's younger sister.

A ringing telephone brings her back to the present. No one, it seems, plans to answer it. So Amy decides she will. Down the hall she finds a room with a desk and on it, a heavy black telephone.

'Hallo? This is the, ah ... the Stratton family.' She stifles a snort. It is not her home but she answers the phone as though it is.

'Amy, is that you?'

Her mother sounds relieved.

'Oh, hallo, Mum! How are you?' Amy realises that her speech is slurred.

Her mother says: 'I've been calling on and off all morning, Amy, but there's been no answer. I've been so worried. You didn't ring last night to say you had arrived. Are you alright? Amy, are you there?'

'Mum, hi, sorry, I couldn't call last night. We got here really late.'

'You could have called this morning though.' No one else listening would know her mother is hurt, but Amy does.

'Sorry, Mum, I was waiting until one o' clock when it gets cheaper to make calls.'

'Amy, it's Saturday and calls are cheap all day!'

'Oh yeah, course. Sorry Mum. Yes, I'm fine. How are you?'

'I can hear music. Is there a party going on?'

'No, well, yes, just a few friends of the family have come for lunch with Mr Stratton. Dad alright, Mum? Look, I'll call again in a few days and tell you how we're getting on.'

Her mother does not reply.

In other moods, Amy might have persisted. But she wants to get back to Dusty and the smelly cheese. 'Mum, I said I'll call in a few days. Speak soon.'

Chapter Four

No one called her Lily, she told Mr Stratton the first time they met, well, that must be over ten years ago now. She had gone up to the big house after he wrote to her. The gentleman asked if she'd continue to work for him as the housekeeper, same as she had for the previous owner. She didn't like the man's look, not at all, and when he used her first name rather than her married name, she had to put him right, there and then. London ways he had, informal, not the way she wanted things done. She had drawn herself up to her full height, five feet three inches - only a little shorter than he - and addressed him sharply: 'I'll thank you to use my full name, Mr Stratton, and that's Mrs Morle.'

She sits by her Rayburn in her cottage just across the lane from Wyld Farm. The range is not fired up but its presence is a comfort and anyway, this is where she always sits. She puts her legs up on a stool; the cat settles in her lap.

She has been his housekeeper ever since he bought the place from the last owners, poor Mrs Clarke, God rest her soul. Went to stay with her daughter one spring, caught a chest cold and died in Southampton. Now Mrs Clarke had been a lovely lady; proper formal, always turned out nicely. Skirts and jackets during the day, always a dress for dinner. Mrs Clarke and Mrs Morle saw eye to eye on many subjects, none of which they put into words but was implicit in the way they were in the world.

Not like Seymour Stratton with his leather coat and flowery shirts. What did the man think he looked like? The only visitors to Mrs Clarke would be the family, her daughter or her son and his wife and his children who might stay at a weekend or at Christmas. Local friends might come for lunch or for tea in the garden in the summer. All regular and organised.

Not like Mr Stratton. He didn't come down often, weekends every so often, but when he did, he would bring friends and food and host parties. Guests arriving in their fancy cars; it could be hard to tell the girls from the men, they all had long hair and high-heeled boots. He would usually have telephoned to ask her if she was free to do extra work on those party weekends. And she would always agree. Extra money was welcome when you were raising a child on your own, wasn't it? Necessary even. The cost of shoes and the girl always wanting something and saving for the future.

So she'd tidy up on Saturday and Sunday mornings while he and his guests slept and the house was quiet, leave a cold lunch, then come back to wash up before supper. Once he asked her to serve drinks at an evening party, but she didn't like what went on; told him as much so he never asked her again and thank goodness for that.

She pushes the cat off her lap and heats some soup. Lynn will soon be back from work. Her daughter who makes the local boys stand up straight when she passes. Hair as dark as a blackbird's feathers and green eyes like her father. But while Harry was steady, his daughter is capricious. Whatever you told her, she would always check behind a closed door in case there was something she might want.

Mrs Morle puts sandwich spread on a piece of bread. She felt sorry for Seymour's son. Little Julian had come down on those post-party mornings, his father nowhere to be seen, sleeping with one of the women he'd driven down with, no doubt. He'd have wet the bed but wouldn't say; would leave the wet sheets stuffed behind a door as though they might disappear. The poor little scrap would sit near her as she worked, telling her about his favourite car or cartoon character. So many glasses to wash and polish dry, so many potatoes to peel, there was plenty of time for Julian to chatter on. He was a sweet boy and lonely, too, having to spend the weekend with his father's friends who, judging from the empty wine and whisky bottles left all over the house, drank a lot of alcohol at their parties. And from the strange smell of hand-rolled cigarette stubs left scattered, did other things unsuitable for a boy to witness. She did not like to think about it.

So much cleaning to do when they left. Every bedroom in the house used, and some sofas too from the bed linen that was strewn everywhere. Washing, drying, folding and tidying. Sometimes guests left a tip in the bedroom. The extra money was nice, but taking it made her feel like a servant. A difficult house to keep clean what with the crumbling plaster, draughty windows making the dust swirl, and dogs running in and out. But Mr Stratton never complained about her work or begrudged her the money she cost him.

She could never work out why but, despite his habits and the way he lives and the fact that she definitely disapproves of him, Mrs Morle likes Seymour. She sets the table. There is something about the man that is hard to resist. She can't put it any other way. He appreciates her as a woman. Every Christmas he gives her a bottle of scent beautifully wrapped in shiny paper and tied with ribbon. She savours every perfumed dab.

Now Mr Stratton tells her that Julian is going to live at Wyld Farm with some friends. She isn't sure how she feels about cleaning for a group of young people and anyway, shouldn't they be back at home with their parents and looking for jobs? How do these young people afford to live? Like that strange girl, Stella; as skittish as a racehorse. She must have parents? Aren't they bothered about what she gets up to, hanging around at Mr Stratton's house?

'How was today, love?'

The door of the cottage slams open as Lynn slouches past. 'Boring as usual,' is the reply, then the girl wearily climbs the steps to her room. A creak overhead suggests she has climbed into bed. There is silence.

*

The train pulls into the station. Maggie Bond catches the bus waiting outside. Almost immediately she falls asleep, rocked as it swerves along empty Sunday lanes. Mother has worn her out. She wakes up as it stops.

'Market Square.' The driver sounds bored.

On the steps of a fountain, two girls in heavy boots sit smoking cigarettes. Maggie gathers up her belongings, hoping her brother will turn up before she has to leave the safety of the bus. She is wearing the clothes she treasures most; a floor-length purple skirt and a cheese cloth top with lacy sleeves. Both items were from Kensington Market where her mother took her on a birthday shopping trip. She hopes people will think she is a hippy; they might even feel a little leery of her. The style detracts from her rounded tummy and large breasts, too; parts of her body that no amount of hatred can reduce. David assured her that boys liked girls with curves. But she loathes the band of flesh that rests on her thighs like a warm creature when she sits.

Maggie eyes the girls again, then with relief sees her brother in the driver's seat of a Land Rover that pulls into the car park. Beside

David she sees his latest girlfriend, Amy. Maggie has met her a few times before and wonders how long she'll be around. Maggie refreshes the red lipstick her mother hates her to wear, saying it makes her 'look like a tramp'. She puts on the divine floppy hat she had stuffed in her bag and inches between passengers towards the bus door.

David had phoned her at home two nights ago and invited her to come down to Wyld Farm. Their mother's pleas were easy enough to ignore, and anyway the chance to spend a free week in the country was not to be missed, even if Simon Webster would be there. David's friend had not replied to her letter despite leaving love bites on her neck after they had met at one of David's gigs last term.

Maggie had raided the savings box under her bed to buy a train ticket. She would get a holiday job and start saving up after her little holiday in the country.

'Hi little sis.' David tugs on her hat. 'Cool look.'

Though she bats away his hand as though annoyed, she is thrilled.

'So you managed to get away. How's it been at home?' He slings her bag in the open back of the vehicle behind a bale of straw. 'Get in, there's room for three in the front.'

'It's alright, the same really. Mother's going insane, so many questions. Wants to know how long you're planning to be here.'

'Yeah, I'll call her soon.'

Maggie slides in beside Amy and settles her feet among the rubbish on the vehicle's floor. Amy looks different somehow, Maggie thinks. Her dead straight blond hair is casually tied back with a piece of string; her jeans and wellington boots and what looks like David's jumper make her look glamorously boyish. 'Hiya Amy.'

The reply is cool as though Amy has given it careful thought. 'Yeah, hi.'

David starts the engine. 'So Maggie, just to warn you. Stuttering boy Simon is staying at the farm, too. I told you that, didn't I? '

Maggie flinches. How can he say this in front of Amy? Maggie looks for the door handle, wishing she could jump out of the Land Rover. But it's already moving along the road. She shrinks back against the seat. Surely David hasn't told Amy about her and Simon kissing? Or her humiliation when he didn't reply to her letter - to either of her letters?

Maggie glances at Amy but the girl is gazing out of the window as though in a trance.

'You're not going to believe the place where we're staying, Maggs!' David shouts over the engine's roar.

Perhaps her brother isn't teasing her? Her resentment melts as he rattles on: 'It's called Wyld Farm, it's practically a mansion. There's land around it, a few barns and this tumbledown cottage and two dogs and ducks. And this Land Rover to drive. Seymour, that's Julian's dad, a famous photographer, he says we can use it while we're staying down here. Amy, can you check the map? I'm not sure of the way back home yet ... '

'Oh David, you're hopeless at directions. It's this left here at the junction and then follow this road out to ...'

The town is left behind. The vehicle lumbers over a humped bridge and there's that delightful hollow feeling fluttering in Maggie's tummy that makes her cheerful again. A few miles later they turn off the main road and drive through a small village past a pub and a shop. A few miles after that, they follow an unmade track across a field. Weeds batter the wheel rims as they drive towards buildings. David parks the vehicle in a yard and a dog barks as she steps down, avoiding puddles. Music she adores, 'Bridge over Troubled Water', drifts from the open front door. A man closes the boot of a car. His expression is enigmatic.

'Come and meet Seymour,' says David.

It would have been awkward not to eat the chicken. Having only just met Julian's father, it is polite to muck in with everyone else, and the smell of roasting meat is irresistible. Crispy potatoes, carrots, peas and hot gravy persuade Maggie she'll be a vegetarian again tomorrow.

'Sit down, it's ready,' Seymour says. She's never been cooked for by a man.

Amy and David beckon for her to sit. As Julian carries a plate of carved chicken to the table, a woman appears at the door, flowers twisted through her curls like a Pre-Raphaelite muse.

'Stella, my dear, Scott McKenzie could write a song about you. Stella, this is Maggie.' The woman manages a brief nod.

Raising a glass, Seymour announces: 'You're welcome to stay for as long as you like, you know. Help out around the farm, start doing up the cottage, you'll be busy. We'd be grateful, wouldn't we Julian?' He taps his glass. 'Cheers!'

They start to eat. Someone has changed the record. The dreamy voice of Leonard Cohen drifts into the kitchen.

'Julian said you're about to go abroad?' David says to Seymour. She sees her brother is trying to impress their host.

'Yes, later tonight I'll drive back to London for a flight in the morning. A shoot in the Essaouira, Morocco. Have you been there?'

'Morocco? No, I haven't. I'd love to go.'

'You came with me once, didn't you Julian? How old were you?'

Julian passes a plate of chicken to Maggie. 'About thirteen. Don't you remember that weird French girl who you got to look after me? She got ill and you had to call the doctor. I remember being in a horse-drawn carriage and seeing a man on a donkey with a basket of cow legs.'

'Ah, yes, The La Mamounia Hotel with its fabulous garden and fresh oranges. The times I've had there.' Seymour sips his wine wistfully. 'This shoot will be routine. Winter clothes on the beach, fur meets sand, you can imagine the hassle we'll get. Fine if they send the right models and plenty of baksheesh for the local fixer.'

Seymour is easy to talk to. Amy mentions the short story competition that David won earlier that year. 'He wants to be a writer or a musician,' she says. She sounds proud.

'If you write another one, David, I've a friend who runs a literary magazine. I could send it to him, perhaps,' Seymour replies. 'And Maggie, you're going to be a nurse? Very commendable. I don't know how you can cope with ill people. Isn't it all a bit … depressing?'

'Our mother was a nurse before she got married so it's in the family,' Maggie says, looking at David for support, but he's too busy eating. 'I know it is hard work but I'd like to help people. I've got a place to train in a big hospital. It's a good social life and you can travel.'

'Absolutely. The whole world, you'll see it all. And commendable, too. I'm sure you'll be very good at it.'

Seymour turns to Amy. Maggie is relieved she is no longer the centre of Seymour's attention. It's like being caught naked in a beam of a strong light. 'And Amy, what are your plans? You've done 'A' levels and you're waiting for the results, I think?'

'I'm dreading bad news. I'm not sure they went that well,' the girl replies shyly. 'I start secretarial college in September. I need to pass both subjects to keep my place.' Her plans must sound mundane to a famous photographer.

'A secretary? I should have thought a smart girl like you might find that … a little dull? Anyway, there's plenty of time to think about what you want to do with your life.'

'Not really. I'd like to leave home, you see. So I need to earn money.'

'Yes, a dreadful business isn't it, money. Julian, time for pudding. Some chocolate tart in that tin, and where's that piece of brie that's oozing nicely? Now what will you have, Maggie?'

Chapter Five

He is easy with it, moves around the farmhouse and the land as if there is nothing unusual about owning a big property in the country. No space within Julian for impression; wealth has created a learned nonchalance. Stella too emanates assurance even in the way she gazes from a window. Tiny sighs slip between her lips at the merest hint of predictability.

It is not the same for the others. For them it is as though they have stepped into a magic land which shares only superficial aspects with the lives they've left behind. Few restrictions or routines and those which exist are governed by whim rather than will. Each day unfolds depending on fortuity, more often than not on Stella's dreams. They rise late, make food and wait for the evening to begin when they drink and smoke, talk and trip until the dawn chorus signals it is time for the party to stop.

It is a land of plenty. Thanks to the three-legged pot on the kitchen shelf there is always cash for food. Like the nursery story Shirley read to Amy of the pot that never stopped producing porridge, as much as they spend it miraculously fills with money. No one seems to find this unusual so she dare not ask how this happens. The privileged assume the world is beneficent, that someone else provides the wherewithal. Who would choose to appear gauche by mentioning reality? The four of them slip into an attitude of entitlement that Julian displays as normal. They are high on freedom.

The builder who is booked to begin renovations on the cottage does not show up. Amy overhears Julian talking on the phone to Seymour's secretary. He is flirtatious and charming. She imagines a girl with long fingernails writing down his message and giggling. 'Alright, I'll give the message to your father. "The builder for Bramble Cottage is a flaky toad".'

They mustn't worry, Julian tells his friends. Seymour will find another builder when he gets back from Morocco, if that's indeed where he is …

Julian shows them around Wyld Farm. Beyond the walled garden, he leads them across a boggy brook into an orchard. Between ripening apples and pears and peaches, David points to a tree covered with misshapen yellow fruits. 'What are those?'

'Quince,' Stella sighs as though David should really know this. 'It's cooked into a thick jelly that's eaten with Manchego cheese. Like in Spain last year …' She touches Julian's arm. 'Do you remember that lunch, Jules, by the pool? That delicious quince jelly, melting in the intense heat …' She runs her fingers up his neck, blows on his ear. 'Have you ever tasted quince, Amy?'

Stella, her hand still on Julian, stares at her. Amy jumps. The woman rarely addresses her directly. She shakes her head and wonders why she feels admonished.

Domesticity does not feature in Stella's lexis. When she dances, she loops around her boyfriend or sways alone as if in a trance. She is never impolite, will thank the person who brings her something but rarely reciprocates. If she does, the activity is orchestrated with a studied air as though accompanying spiritual practice.

But today something is different. A sheen of sweat coats the woman's pearly skin. A package addressed to her arrived that morning. Every day the postman walks a mile along the stream and through the meadow to bring the post.

'Thank you, Garfield, see you tomorrow!' Amy is about to accept the parcel when Stella's arm snakes from behind to snatch it from the postman's hands.

It contains pills that a friend of hers, a biochemist, created in a laboratory. Just a gentle hallucinogen, Stella says, holding out a pill to Amy. 'He wants them tested. You do take drugs, don't you?' She says, fixing her with a stone-hard stare.

Amy swallows the tiny pill quickly; there's hardly any taste. It can't have much effect, she hopes.

Julian announces he will take everyone on an adventure. They start in a wood that runs beyond the house. The canopy of trees is dense. Mosses and ivy form leafy jackets on the trees. Fluffy curls of grey-white plants dangle from branches like the beards of ancient men. It's as spooky as a fairy tale.

'Fancy yourself woodsmen? Seymour wants to open up this wood, fell a tree or two,' says Julian to David and Simon. 'He says it need more space. Who doesn't need more space, man?'

'Yeah, f-f-far out, man,' Simon giggles.

'Ever used a chainsaw? Throbs like a wild lover, makes a fantastic racket! I'll show you how it works, no hassle. We'll need the wood for the fire this winter.'

'Cool,' they chorus.

Amy nudges a fallen log with her boot. As it splits apart, woodlice swarm from the orange-cream splinters. Making her finger into a barrier, the hefty bodies clamber over it in synchronised waves. She cannot think about the winter when it will be cold, when they will sit together around the fire, but she will not be with them. A horrible feeling of dejection overwhelms her. She'll be studying at secretarial college so she can get a *job*. A girl like her does not have choices.

David touches her head. 'Alright?' he says.

She looks up. He towers over her; his face is fuzzy. She sees he is blowing her a kiss. It lands on her face as soft as butter. Her jaw trembles uncontrollably so that her teeth clatter against each other. David reaches for her hand and they follow Julian from the wood and into the light.

The six of them fan out across the field. Something catches her eye. As Amy turns to look, her brain knocks against her skull. Stella has draped a scarf over her head. It streams behind her like a glistening haze.

'You haven't met them yet, have you?' Julian says. 'In the field over there. Our sheep - Lunch, Dinner and Freezer.'

Her legs won't move any faster. Maggie pulls her by the hand. 'Come on!'

Julian says: 'I'm meant to come each day to check on them. But you know, I forget. It's a hassle and anyway, there are hedges. Where are they going to go? '

'Aren't they beautiful,' Maggie croons. 'Why do you call them that?'

'Their name gives it away, sister!' David teases. 'It's all in the name. Lunch, Dinner ...'

Maggie flicks out her hands as though to hit him, but he dodges out of the way, laughing wildly.

'We eat them, of course!' Julian says dramatically. 'A man comes in with a gun and he kills them. Bang, bang - and they're dead. Bang!'

'Bang!' 'Bang!' Simon and David mimic, then run about pretending to shoot guns.

'Oh god, no, that's awful!' Maggie drops to the ground, clamping her hands to her ears.

'It's the cycle of life, Maggie,' Stella murmurs sagely as she rustles past.

Amy hears a roaring sound and looks up expecting to see a plane flying low overhead. But the sky is empty. It's only the buzz of insects hovering over a patch of yellow-headed flowers.

The ground rises to a grand plateau. She marvels at the fields, a montage of red and ochre, saffron and aubergine, surrounded by hedges that resemble fat green serpents. A giantess might have dribbled nail varnish for here and there iridescent swathes of magenta sing from the landscape. Amy is about to tell David it's the flower Rosebay Willowherb but stops just in time as Stella rustles past. On the horizon is a lazy line of blue, the Bristol Channel.

'It's peaceful here, man,' says David. 'Let's chill out.'

The turf is sponge-soft. Julian and Stella lie down to wrap themselves in the scarf like a caterpillar in a cocoon. David and Simon, feet and arms in the air, pretend to be upturned beetles. A patch of daisies seems to beckon to Amy and she sinks to her knees as Maggie whispers: 'I can't bear to think the sheep are for the chop. I'm liberating them …' and disappears.

Every cell of Amy's body begins to stretch. Involuntarily she rolls onto her side and her mouth opens as wide as a cave. Gossamer strings of bile spew out to loop and hang from flower and leaf. The air crackles, but she is not sure if it is with sound or light. Her ear presses too hard on the ground, but she lacks the strength to lift it up. She drifts into a half-sleep.

Sometime later she is aware that Maggie is lying beside her. 'I have given them freedom,' she purrs.

Amy rolls on to her back. The sky is like a childish painting with puffy clouds of champagne and gold.

'Wouldn't you like to live here forever, Maggie?' she whispers. 'It's so peaceful, so far away from everything. Like a brand new world. What a dream, to escape … to share everything … we could grow our own food, have hens…'

‘As long as we don’t have to eat them,’ Maggie interjects and the thought strikes them as hilarious and they howl with laughter.

‘What’s the joke?’ says someone from far away.

A shadow blocks the sun. It’s Stella.

‘I’m getting bored,’ she says. ‘We’re going back.’

✷

‘Julian’s having an asthma attack!’ Amy and David are woken only hours after a long night partying. Stella is in their bedroom doorway, screaming, distraught. ‘David, drive him to hospital - now!’

Amy is on her feet before she’s fully awake. ‘Where’s his inhaler?’

‘I don’t know,’ Stella wails. ‘Can’t David take him?’

Sounds of wheezing from Julian’s room. Stella, in brocade dressing gown and embroidered slippers, vanishes inside. Amy hurtles down the stairs and begins to search frantically. The device is neither on the kitchen sill where it is often left nor in the office desk drawer. Then she remembers Julian using an inhaler when they were in the woods the previous day. In the boot room, she finds his waxed jacket and, in an inside pocket, the inhaler.

Heart pounding, she dashes back to Julian’s room. He is lying ashen-faced with his arms around Stella. He puts a finger to his lips. ‘I found it in my bedside table when I looked again. Poor Stella, I frightened her.’ His lips caress his girlfriend’s forehead.

Stella gazes back through half-closed eyes. ‘Oh, it’s you. I called Amy but you didn’t hear me. Where were you? It was too chilly to come and look for you. Hold me, Julian, I’m shattered.’

Amy is dismissed.

Chapter Six

Humming, Amy pins her hair up on top of her head. She wants to look her best on her last night. Tomorrow she will be on the train back to the place where she grew up. She can't call it home anymore. She is more at home here at the farm with her friends. Where she can be herself.

Amy winds a scarf around her waist, turning the lotus-strewn kimono she found stuffed in a chest into a garment that folds over her hips. She sneaks a look at herself in the bathroom mirror. For the first time since she's arrived here a month ago, she's appropriately dressed. It's absurd how good it makes her feel, this collection of cast-off items. Or does her change of mood have something to do with Stella? The woman left Wyld Farm for London yesterday.

It has been a perfect day. Picking elderflowers from high in the hedgerows in the field where the sheep graze, Amy laid delicately-scented flowers into her basket. Now the creamy-white lace heads dangle in sweetened water, floating with the grated rinds of orange and lemon and slivers of ginger. If only it could be she that would, in four days' time, complete the recipe's instructions. She delights in the author's name, Mrs Gennery-Taylor, imagines a tall woman with a fine bosom instructing her to strain the liquid, mix it slowly with sugar and yeast and then to watch the magic unfold as the cloudy mixture ferments into elderflower wine.

But Amy cannot do these things. She has to go home.

The kitchen sleeps in the heat of the Aga. Throwing open the back door, Amy sits on the step, hitches up her skirts to brown her legs and rolls a joint. Beyond a scabby lawn spanned by the washing line are the remnants of a kitchen garden. Lazy butterflies meander between bushes of sage and rosemary and thyme which struggle for space among ground elder and chickweed. There are cushions of comfrey and mounds of mint. The plant names float into her head without being summoned.

She wanders over to the greenhouse. Its cracked panes are smeared with dirt and cobwebs. The door buckles as she pushes inside. The air is dry and still. Leaves rustle as she moves between benches and upturned pots. A trowel lies in a quizzical tilt on a seed tray; a spider scrambles over it. How her father would have loved somewhere like this where he could raise seedlings! But he was a man who never got what he wanted, and she understood that this was the way he preferred to live; in a state of wanting. How could he waste his life like that?

Nearby, a head-high cage of saggy wire makes a canopy for fruit bushes. Pushing between the branches, she finds clusters of blackberries, tart-sweet redcurrants and fat gooseberries. Her skirt sags with fruit. Tonight they will eat berry pie.

The stone floor and marble shelves of the larder make it cool, the perfect place for pastry-making. In the half-light, rubbing lard into flour, she lifts her fingers high above the bowl as she sings 'All I Want'. Joni is a singer she adores but rarely dares to play when the boys are about. 'Squeaky girly voice … yuck,' they moan when Joni hits a wavering note.

Amy kneads the pastry. She's made most of the meals they've eaten since she's been at Wyld Farm. How will those lazy boys manage once she's gone? She rolls out the dough and sprinkles it with cinnamon and mace. As she slides the pie into the oven, the front door opens. Seymour comes down the hallway, his heels clicking on the flagstones.

'Amy, darling. How's life for our land girl?' He kisses her cheek and she is pleased to be splendidly dressed. 'London is simply too hot to survive.' He flings himself into a chair and beams.

Seymour has been down three of the four weekends she and the others have been here. He usually arrives on Friday evening, long after her parents would have gone to bed, with food, wine, a new record and stories of his frantic life. A life that sounds tempting, but he insists it must be escaped. On Sunday nights, he leaves late, seemingly unaffected by the drink he has consumed, or he bangs out of the house at dawn on Monday morning, whistling his goodbyes to Molly, waking them all, noisy and infuriating.

She grins back. 'We're fine. The boys are in the garage fixing the Land Rover. It was making strange noises.'

'Very good. Has the builder been?'

'He's been delayed again, he's coming next week.'

'What a sod. And how is the lovely Amy?'

'I'm fine, the weather's been wonderful. But you know, I've got to go home tomorrow.'

'That's nonsense! It's far too nice here and you're far too important to leave.'

'My parents expect me back. I've been here almost a month, Seymour. College starts in September.'

'Well, we need you to stay a bit longer. September is ages away.' He plonks his feet up on a chair. She has never seen a man look chic in sandals before. 'Call them. Tell them I insist you stay. Hey, we can't be inside on a glorious evening like this. I've brought food for a picnic. Why don't we eat outside? In the orchard?'

He opens the oven door a crack and there's a waft of spice and sweetness. 'Delicious, what a woman. I'll put some wine in to cool. We'll need plates and so on …'

The door slams as he disappears from the house. Molly follows him to the door.

No sign he has brought anyone else with him. She would not admit it openly but she's relieved. No Sophia with her fringe and obsession with the Bloomsbury artist Dora Carrington or Emile the long-haired French man who turned his bedroom into a meditation temple where he seduced Maggie, or William the physicist who smoked Gauloises and rarely spoke.

And no Coral. Last weekend Seymour brought a tall Afro-haired woman who evaporated upstairs without a word. Next morning, Seymour appeared in the kitchen in a dressing gown and bare feet, his toenails painted silver.

'Do we have any coffee? Not even milk? I must get you a cow!' He had winked at Amy, going back upstairs with black tea. An hour later, Coral sashayed down the hall in a tight orange dress to fold herself into Seymour's car. 'We're off to lunch, bye!' shouted Seymour.

In the scullery, Amy finds a basket for the cutlery, glasses and plates. Bizarre to feel so relaxed with Julian's father. But Seymour is nothing like her parents or their friends who seemed to regard life as a repetitive process that must be adhered to without interest or joy. Seymour knows more about what's going on in the world than anyone else she knows. And he's witty.

Anyway, he can't be that old. Seymour told them one night that he was only 24 years old when Julian was born. Unplanned, he said, reaching over to touch his son's shoulder. Unplanned and irreplaceable. Julian brushed him away.

It was time to call her parents.

'Hi Mum, it's Amy. How are you? How's Dad?' Amy clears a space on the office chair though she knows she won't speak for long.

'Amy, dear, hallo. How lovely to hear from you. Now tell me what time the train gets in. We'll meet you in the car.'

'That would be great, Mum, but I'm, um, not sure that I'm coming home tomorrow, after all. Mr Stratton says it's fine if I stay a bit longer.'

'Longer? But you've been there for a month already. You don't want to overstay your welcome, Amy.'

'I don't think I am, Mum. I am helping out, working and ...'

'And your college is starting soon, dear. You have to prepare. And your 'A' level results. Your letter will be sent here.'

'Mum, college doesn't start until September and it's only July. There's ages to go. And you can read my results out to me on the phone.'

'On the phone? But Amy, how long do you plan to stay?'

'I don't know, Mum. A few weeks more, perhaps ...'

'Weeks? I'm not sure what your father will have to say.'

There is silence. Then Shirley repeats: 'I don't know what your father will say, Amy.'

'I don't have to do what he says.' Amy's voice is almost inaudible. 'I'm enjoying myself. I want to stay.'

'Amy! What are you saying? That you will not abide by your father's preferences or what I want? It's not like you, Amy, to change your mind so suddenly.'

'It's not sudden, I've been thinking about it for a while.'

'Have you? Since when? I thought you were determined to ... I'm missing you, darling.'

'I know, Mum. I'll see you soon, okay. I'll write in a few days and tell you what I'm up to. Goodbye.'

She sets down the phone like it stings. Years later, on sleepless nights, she would remember the conversation, go over and over the kinder and gentler ways she should have spoken to her mother.

But that night all that is in her head is the thought that she can finish making the elderflower wine after all. She wanders into the sunny evening with the basket on her arm.

Chapter Seven

Amy's father is at her door just after 6am. He whispers loudly, 'are you awake?'

Lightly sleeping, her limbs began to twitch as his knuckles touched her door. Her eyelids open reluctantly. Like an automaton, she puts on her slippers, reaches for her dressing gown, ties the cord and follows him down the stairs. In step, father and daughter descend; tread by tread, heavy steps, heavy hearts. These early morning sessions began three days ago when she came back home. The thinning bald patch on her father's head glistens like luncheon meat. Pink and round, it bobs as he goes down the steps.

The kitchen table fits in the alcove. She slides into her chair, the one she's used since childhood, her back to the wall. She watches her father move about; reaching for the cups, finding the spoons, the feeling of loss filling her belly as he fills the kettle.

She dreads what is coming next but knows there is no way she can stop it. The chair creaks as her father takes his place opposite her.

'Had she written to you?'

'No, we only spoke on the phone. On Sundays. You were there in the background, I heard her speak to you, do you remember? She didn't call during the week, no.'

'How did she seem? What did she say?'

'You must have heard our conversations. She seemed okay. Fine. Said she was missing me, of course.'

'Did she mention feeling unwell?'

'Dad, no she didn't.'

'Nothing at all?'

'She never mentioned that, no Dad, she's never mentioned it. Why are you asking me these questions again and again? What does it matter now? It's not going to bring her back. And why, for God – for goodness sake, why are you whispering?'

She is shrieking now. She can't help it. There's a timbre in her voice, one she has never heard before, a dark tone. 'Why are we whispering, for fuck's sake, Dad?

'Watch your language, young lady. It's early morning Amy, it's …'

'But there's no one else in the house. Mum is dead, Dad! We can't wake her!'

It is as though this is the first time her father has heard the news. His face, purpled with grief, collapses like the bones are being sucked inward.

Amy feels her sympathy shift, watches herself coolly assess this weeping man; his scaly skin, his chin patchy with stubble, his tears which patter on the plastic table cloth. He leaves no space for her grief; he's consuming all the oxygen.

Her father stands up suddenly, swings around to reach into the cupboard for something he cannot need and a squeal slips from his lips.

'I've read your diary, you know,' he says, his back to her. 'And I know what you've been up to with that boy David.'

He spits the words at the rose-patterned side plates and tea cups. The crockery rattles with his rage.

She imagines using her fist to smash it into the back of his head, how the rows of china would jangle. Perhaps a cup would tip and break, pink and white fragments shattering like confetti. She is briefly horrified that she does not find this idea appalling. She leaves the room. She must grieve for her mother. But she can only do this alone.

*

People huddle like crows in the church. She and her father walk up the aisle arm-in-arm as though they are on the way to the altar. From the corner of her eye there are faces she recognises; a neighbour, a school friend, the owner of the bookshop, and others she does not. She avoids eye contact, takes her place in the front pew, dressed in her mother's black coat, the lamb's wool collar tight against her tightening throat. In the pocket, her fingers curl around a tissue. Some parts of it are soft, others lumpy. Little of the service or the hymns or the short tribute her father gives penetrates her misery. He had asked her if she would read an excerpt from the Bible. When she shook her head, he did not ask again. Her head is thickened by sorrow. She thinks only about the tissue, how her palm cradles her mother's dried tears.

The wake is held in a local hotel. Sandwiches and tea and condolences are offered in equal part. Amy and her father walk about the room, sometimes together, sometimes separately, accepting the murmured comments of support. She knows that she moves gracefully. People stop their conversations as she approaches, fashion their mouths into mournful shapes to say how sorry they are for her loss. The men hold glasses of whisky, the women suck mints; both smell terrible.

A woman she does not know pats her hand; it is all she can do not to snatch her hand away.

'A brain haemorrhage?' The woman's lips contort into a grimace. 'What a terrible shock it's been for us all. Strange in a woman so young. Do they know why?'

The funeral service was horrible enough but at least she had not been expected to say or do anything beyond standing or sitting at the appropriate time. The wake is excruciating. Accepting condolences, smiling with gratitude when she feels none: she has to hold herself back from shouting at them all to go away.

Amy cannot sleep. Her body is rigid though her feelings swirl. She wants to cry but the tears are locked in a part of her she cannot access and with a key she cannot find.

Chapter Eight

With relief she spots the Land Rover in the station car park. David is usually late. But there he is in the driver's seat, his face wreathed in smoke. Her heart skips. She's longing to burrow her head right under his chin and wrap his hair around her face so she can pretend she's stepping inside him. Skipping over to the vehicle, she spots Simon in the passenger seat, head nodding rhythmically. There must be music playing. She runs back into the station and collapses on a bench.

'Amy, there you are. Why are you hiding?' David finds her a few minutes later. He pulls her to her feet. Wrapping his arms around her, he speaks into her hair. 'What are you doing here? It's good to see you.'

He manoeuvres her onto his lap and offers her a lighted cigarette. 'How was it at home? How's your Dad?'

'I had to get away. I felt terrible leaving, but I think he's going mad, David. He can't accept that Mum's died. And he's going on and on about what I'm up to and everything. Wants me to start that secretarial course. Says I should do it in 'honour' of Mum.'

'Ames, he's bound to be freaked out. Hey, where's my smiling together lady? You're with me now. Come on, beautiful, let's get going. Simon's here. Let's go.'

He takes her suitcase and leads her to the Land Rover. Its dented misshapen body and mud-splattered wheels make her feel relieved. The passenger door opens. Simon slides down off the seat.

'Sorry about your m-m-mother,' he mutters sympathetically at the ground.

'Thanks,' she replies and climbs in.

Over the noise of the engine, David has to shout. 'Work's begun on the cottage, Ames. Soon there'll be no more leaking roof.'

On the phone, he'd mentioned a local builder and his girlfriend who came after meeting Seymour in a pub. 'Bob's a laugh, likes to party too. We're having a blast, aren't we, Simon?'

'We are, y-y-yes,' Simon calls back, nodding at Amy.

'Who else is …?' she replies, but David has switched on the radio. The voice of Aretha Franklin fills the vehicle as they set off for Wyld Farm.

'The moment I wake up, Before I put on my makeup, I say a little prayer for you …'

She's missed her friends. She hadn't realised just how much until they were splashing along the puddled track towards the farmhouse. Over the hedge, the trench by the front door of Bramble Cottage is now an area of freshly raked soil. Like a grave; she shivers.

She can't help feeling disappointed to see a car and a van, neither of which she recognises, parked in the yard. She'd hoped for a night with her friends rather than a party. Telling herself she's being uncool, she follows David into the hall. It's patterned with muddy footprints. David and Simon don't notice her hanging back. They disappear into the sitting room, Rod Stewart's voice fading as the door shuts behind them.

Squealing sounds in the office. Peering round the door, she sees chicken wire and wooden boxes have been fashioned into a makeshift pen. Three puppies nip at the jacket of a man who sits in their midst, apparently indifferent to the puppy mess littering the floor. The man is bleary-eyed. It's Gerald, an old friend of Julian's who lives nearby. When he drops into the farm which is often, he is either stoned or drunk; it's never clear which.

'Hi. Far out,' he says to her. 'Lovely pups, eh? Come and say hallo. I can show ...'

She shakes her head and carries on down the hallway; it's crunchy underfoot. She heads for the part of the house she's missed the most, the kitchen. Its soft-coloured walls, the patterned plates, the Aga purring like an over-sized cat.

It's more dilapidated and chaotic than she remembered. Furniture is scattered as though a gale has been through the room. The windows are smeared, the sink is piled with plates and there are dirty pans stacked on the floor. But familiar and oddly grand. She touches each surface: the grain of wood on the table, the smooth tiles round the sink, the soft cushions on the settle.

'Amy ...'

She is expecting to see David. But it is Julian, who is rubbing his mouth with his fingers, a habit he has when he's taken speed. It will be a late night then.

'How are you? Long time, no see,' he says.

'Yeah, ah ... fine, I suppose.'

He does not mention her mother's death and it feels awkward for her to do so. Instead she says: 'The puppies are lovely. Where's Molly, Julian?'

'Tied up in the barn. Her puppies are being weaned. They've been sold and are going to their new owners any day.'

'Oh really? No! I want to play with them. They're so adorable.' She's trying to sound jolly.

'We've got Pilot and Molly, that's enough dogs. I should have drowned the puppies really. It's been a hassle to get rid of them,' he says dismissively.

Halfway out of the door, he turns back. 'Ah yeah, there are some people working here now, Bob and Helen. Why don't you come and meet them, they're cool.'

'I will, I'll come in a minute,' she says, knowing she won't.

The door is ajar. The music has stopped and David is playing the guitar. People are talking.

She heads for their bedroom, pushes David's clothes off the bed and, miserable, falls asleep.

*

It takes Gerald a few moments to realise that the girl leaving the village shop is the same one he saw at Julian's house a few nights ago. Her name eludes him, Joanna possibly, he was a little inebriated. He swings his Mini onto the verge and winds down the window.

'Oh hallo,' he calls out as Amy walks by.

While of a mind to ignore her father's warnings about talking to strangers, Amy still looks warily at the driver of the car. She sees Gerald.

She's never had a conversation with the man, what would she say? She knows he and Julian were at school together and that Gerald lives on his parents' estate in a cottage. He doesn't seem to work; Julian mentioned an inheritance. Gerald is like a mysterious creature from another world. He often arrives with dope, a bottle of wine and once with half a fruit cake in a tin; peculiarly domestic, he cut them each a piece but left his own uneaten on a plate. Sometimes he stays the night if he's too smashed to drive home. Amy dislikes his crumpled body on the sofa but she isn't sure why.

'I'm going to the pub for a quick drink before chasing up to the house. Care to join me?'

'Yes, please,' she says, wondering why she's agreed.

There are three men at the bar and another group playing darts. She feels conscious of their stares as she sits at a table. Perhaps it's what she's wearing: dungarees, a skimpy singlet and boots.

'I'll get you a gin, it's a good sharpener at this time of day.'

She hesitates. She usually asks for cider as it's cheap. 'Really? Thanks.'

The men move aside to let Gerald in. Gerald's fingers stroke the head of Jackson, his greyhound. Elegant and aloof, the dog is always at his side.

'Here you are. Only a single. Cheers.' Gerald is still unsure of her name. 'I was born two drinks behind everyone else, so just catching up.'

He downs half a lager, then sips a gin. 'The first drink is bettered only by the second. So you're at the farm for the summer? Enjoying the scene, I trust.'

He opens a packet of Players cigarettes. 'Want one?'

'Thanks.'

Her lips form a soft moue around the cigarette. 'I'm staying a bit longer, not sure how long. It's such a beautiful place and, well, I've never lived anywhere with so much space and land.'

'So Julian's back down here again. The country can get dull without good chums. Never sure university suited him all that well. It's where you met him, I think?'

'My boyfriend David and he were studying at the same place.' Amy remembers her 'A' level results lie unopened in her pocket.

'I was never sure if Julian was cut out for the academics but he's bloody good with machines. He tells me Seymour wants to renovate that cottage. Can't think how long that'll take, isn't it a lost cause? But Seymour is a man with plans, that's one thing you can say about him. David and the other chap, what's his name?'

'Simon.'

'Yes, boy Simon. They've experience with this sort of thing, have they, building and all that?'

'Not exactly. But we can help, all of us ...'

'Course you will, I'm sure you'll make a good navvy. It all sounds like rather hard work. You just enjoy the summer. Seymour won't mind, he likes people to have fun. Let me get you another. Jackson, stay.'

Before she can refuse, Gerald is buying another round.

'I won't be staying beyond the summer,' she insists. Gerald pushes over a packet of pork scratchings. Suddenly she's ravenous. 'I've got to go back home. I'm starting a secretarial course in September and I need to earn some money before that.'

'Why? Is that what you want to do?'

'I don't know, I have to do something until ...'

'Until what?'

'Until I find what it is I really want to do.'

'Isn't it obvious?' Gerald downs the rest of his drink. 'To have as much of a good time as one possibly can in this strange old world.' He sucks hard on the cigarette, inhales deep into his chest. 'Shall we go to the farm now?'

Something happens that night and it's only partly connected with her results (an 'A' and two 'B' grades) and the gins. There are also the psilocybin mushrooms that Gerald gives out and the huge voice of Grace Slick calling for courage in curiosity. Amy flirts hard with her boyfriend, and gets everybody to join her frenzied dance. The drugs begin to work their magic. Abandonment rockets into elation. Lights trail from their fingertips. The walls ripple and breathe. Weaving as one through the long hectic night to escape the irrelevant past and to reach for a future of wild and wondrous dreams.

CHAPTER NINE

'It doesn't make sense, Mr Stratton is rebuilding that cottage. Surely it's more sensible to pull the place down?'

Mrs Morle chops fiercely at the onions and reminds herself again not to talk out loud. At least Lynn can't hear, not with her bedroom radio playing pop music at that volume. The girl had come home from work, closed up the chickens for the night and slunk upstairs without a word. Mrs Morle sighs. At least her daughter goes out to work, not like those layabouts hanging around with Julian.

Pulling on a cardigan, she goes to the shed. Dry and warm even on the cold days, it smells of sawdust and creosote and of her husband though he's been dead these last twelve years. It was Harry's domain, the nails on which he'd hung his tools still visible, spaces on the shelves for his brushes and tins, his workbench up against the wall. Big and solid, just like he was.

Harry never regained consciousness from the stroke he suffered one September afternoon. Grey-faced and mumbling, he lay where he fell on the sitting room mat, his lunch congealing at the table. Over an hour it took for the ambulance to arrive. By then he'd fallen silent, his face a congealed red. As the ambulance men struggled to roll him onto a stretcher, Lynn arrived home from school. Mrs Morle bundled her daughter up the stairs. She didn't want her daughter's final memory of her father to be his blank green eyes.

It's a wood shed now. Every so often, Mrs Morle gives one of the farm lads a few pounds to bring a trailer of wood sawn up into lumps suitable for the Rayburn. Tonight she'll stack up the stove so it gets hot enough for a big bath that she and Lynn can share. She'll dry the clothes too; it's the only heated room in the cottage.

'What you doing out here, Mum?' Lynn appears at the door. 'I'll bring that in for you,' and she hauls the basket of wood inside.

'Thanks, love,' Mrs Morle calls. She's a good girl really. 'It's your favourite for supper …'

Mrs Morle nestles two pieces of liver in a pan of browning onions and checks the potatoes. It's no business of hers what they get up to in the big house but now that-girl-Amy has returned those boys will be eating something more substantial than beans on toast.

That's what the boys lived on when that-girl-Amy was away, as far as Mrs Morle could tell from the pans and empty tins stacked in the sink. Apparently the girl's mother died a few weeks back. So why in blazes had she come back to Mr Stratton's, leaving her father alone with his grief? She'd come knocking on Mrs Morle's door yesterday asking for advice on making apple chutney. Didn't have a clue. Nice enough girl but never been properly trained.

Last weekend when Seymour was down he'd roasted a chicken. The bones and skin were left in the fridge. Mrs Morle threw the lot into a pan with some vegetables and barley and cooked them up to make a soup. Why not, when she was cleaning in the house anyway? Seymour blew her a kiss, cheeky man, when he left on Monday morning in his fancy car.

Lynn sits at the table. 'I'm starving, Mum. Something smells good.'

'Mr Stratton has got himself a builder. Apparently he wants Bramble Cottage doing up,' says Mrs Morle, putting down a plate of food.

Her mouth full, Lynn says: 'Tell 'im to get in touch if he needs supplies and what not. I'll get him a deal. Or perhaps I'll slip across and see him next time he's down.' She carefully piles greens and carrots on to her fork.

'Julian's going to be doing some of it.'

'Some of what?'

'The building work. What Mr Stratton's hired is a man to keep an eye on things, the tricky stuff like the roof and electrics. Can't understand it myself, why he wants to renovate that wreck.'

'Julian don't know how to build. He's soft, he's lazy,' scoffs Lynn. She pauses to take another bite. 'He's a bit weird, isn't he?'

'Just a bit lost, love. He can learn. It's those friends of his staying at the house. Ignorant lot.'

'They were in the pub last weekend. Clever types but don't 'spect they'll be able to lift a spade. Nice-looking, mind.'

'You watch yourself, young lady. I don't want you getting mixed up with that sort. '

'What sort is that?'

'Spoilt and posh. Don't trust them.'

Mrs Morle cleans the plates into the scraps bucket and opens a tin of pineapple. 'Serve this out, will you, Lynn dear. Here's some custard.'

'We celebrating, Mum?'

'No, love, just fancied a change. Everyone else seems to be doing it.'

Chapter Ten

When she touches Daisy's calf, Amy's fingers recall that her mother's forehead felt the same: like linoleum, resistant and stiff. It is unnerving to know with utter certainty that the cells of the skin beneath her fingers no longer hold the magic ingredient that is life. It's not the lack of warmth or pulse but an indefinable change to the texture and quality of skin. Death is not knowable. But it is touchable.

Like melting wax, she slithers to the barn's earth-beaten floor. For the first time since she's come back, the tears flow, proper tears that run down her cheeks. There's a relief and a comfort in her anguish. She gathers scattered pieces of hay into a pile and lays her head upon it, watering the dry stalks of grass. They soften. They absorb the moisture. They release the sweet smell of summer.

Daisy chews stolidly at the sinewy afterbirth that had slipped from between her hind legs. Her head hangs low as though in contemplation, the odd moan escaping her swinging jaw. Occasionally her long, rough tongue explores the body of her dead calf, tidying up the remnants of blood and gore on its coat. A fleck of blood sticks to Daisy's nostril. Her tongue darts out to lick it away.

If only Shirley had been laid to rest in such a place. Rolling on to her back, Amy surveys the massive wooden beams which span the ancient barn. Against the eaves lodge birds' nests and spiders' webs. The slate walls are pocketed with dirt in every shade of brown and grey, forming intricate patterns that make her gaze drift this way and that. Moss and mould bloom in muted greens and ochres. It is quietly beautiful.

By contrast, her mother lay in a glorified shed. Cheap carpeting and curtains with prints of mountain lakes could not disguise its origins. The sounds of the town leaked through the flimsy walls.

'I'm not sure you should see your mother, that's how you'll remember her,' her father had said not unkindly, but she had insisted. He arranged for them to visit.

After they had breakfasted, showered and dressed, he drove them the short distance into town. He parked the car near the library. A girl she'd been at school with was walking along the pavement. The girl saw Amy too but flinched and hurried away without saying anything.

'I will see her alone,' Amy hissed in her father's ear as they entered the undertakers.

'Mr Taylor, Miss Taylor, good morning, I am Mr Robinson of Robinson and Sons. Once again my condolences on the death of your wife and mother. Please sit here while I make sure things are ready for you. '

The undertaker indicated two chairs by a low table on which sat a bowl of fake flowers on a doily and a Bible. He disappeared behind a thin curtain.

'Was that Mr Robinson senior or junior?' Her father whispered.

The man was so bleached of colour, his manner so devoid of affect, that his age was impossible to discern. It struck Amy as funny that neither she nor her father had any idea of the man's age. She began to giggle. Before she could stop herself, her shoulders were shaking, more with the effort of concealment than the humour. She was horrified to find she couldn't stop.

'Oh for goodness' sake, Amy!' her father hissed.

Mr Robinson appeared from behind the curtain. 'We are prepared.'

'I'm seeing my mother on my own.' As Amy stood, her laughter drained away. Stony-faced, she followed the man into the garden shed. With each step, her mood darkened.

Shirley was sheeted so tightly in the casket that Amy had to fight the impulse to loosen the bedding. Her mother looked unlike herself. There were slight bulges below her mouth and her fringe was combed straight rather than swept to the side. Why had they changed her hairstyle? Sounds of a car horn and on the street outside, catcalls. Her mother might be disturbed, she worried, before remembering that Shirley was not sleeping. She was frightened to touch her mother but if she did not, she might forever regret not saying a proper goodbye. The pale lips might feel rubbery or worse, solid. Instead she put her fingers on Shirley's forehead and felt the unforgettable sensation of dead flesh. How do fingers know that the body they touch is no longer living? The question hangs, but the answer is irrefutable; they know.

'Hi Amy,' Simon's voice brings her back to the present.

The man is standing in the barn entrance, but it's hard to make out his expression; the fading autumn light casts shadows. A bird swoops in over his head.

She searches in her pocket for a tissue. She cannot do what the farm workers do; shoot the snot from one nostril while holding the other tight-shut.

'The calf is dead,' she gulps.

'Yeah, I h-h-heard.' Simon looks around. 'Do you think we could eat it? Seems a shame to w-w-waste the meat. Wouldn't it t-t-taste like veal?'

When she doesn't reply, he adds. 'Hey, Amy, anything wrong?'

'Nothing,' she says, wiping her nose on her sleeve. 'It's just sad when something dies.'

'Yeah, it is, poor little thing,' Simon says sympathetically. He crouches down and holds out a crumpled tissue. 'Clean-ish.'

She wishes fiercely he would disappear. 'Well, I'm not tempted to eat it,' she snaps.

Simon waves a book at her. 'It's all about s-s-self-sufficiency. But it only talks about killing c-c-cows, not eating the ones that die of d-d-death, if you see what I mean. '

Simon nudges the calf's body gently with the toe of his boot. 'Rigor m-m-mortis has already set in, that's quick. I've read you're meant to gut the animal and then hang it for a few d-d-days before it can be eaten. I'll go and find Julian, see w-w-what he says.'

'Yeah, see Julian, that's a brain wave,' Amy says snidely as he disappears.

Another bird flies in and vanishes in the gloomy upper reaches of the barn. She'd like to follow it, fly up to the highest beam and settle on a ledge to watch everyone below. Ruffle up her feathers and hunch up her wings while her friends try to find her. Would she be missed?

That night they sit by the fire and play music and smoke grass. At one point, Maggie waves a joint at David when it's snatched from her fingers by Simon. A mock fight starts. It ends up with Simon squatting on top of Maggie making her yelp with laughter. Julian puts *Sticky Fingers* on the turntable, announcing to the room that the album confirms The Rolling Stones as the best band in the world. David jumps up, declaiming that on the contrary *Sgt. Pepper's Lonely Hearts Club Band* will change pop music forever and The Beatles reign supreme. Amy's heard it all before. It's something they do when they're stoned. They find it hilarious; Amy does not. She rolls another joint.

The men protest when Maggie goes to the turntable, saying chicks can't be in charge of music. But when 'Eight Miles High' starts, everyone starts to sing and sway along to The Byrds. Everyone except Amy. She huddles against a chair hugging her thighs. It helps to quell the paranoia that is starting to bubble through her body.

'Come on Amy, dance with me!' David tries to pull her up off the floor.

'I'm not in the mood,' she says, shaking her head. If she can stay completely still, she'll be fine.

'I've missed you,' he insists. 'Come on, babe.'

He succeeds in hauling her to her feet and wrapping his arms around her, murmurs into her ear: 'Don't get all dragged down and depressed now, will you. You gotta handle this, yeah? Be cool.'

The remark crumples her heart. 'What do you mean?' she says, pushing him away. Why is he being so thoughtless?

'Don't get all … I don't know, weird or whatever. Pass that over, Simon.' He holds a roll-up to her mouth. The cardboard end is soggy. 'Smoke this …'

'I don't want that!' She shakes her head. 'You don't know what to say to me, do you?'

'What do you mean? My beautiful woman is with me again. I've missed her. What else is there to say?'

It feels as if she is watching from a great distance as the people she calls her friends sway around the room. Their faces are indecipherable. People can't talk about death or they don't want to; they don't have the words. Getting away is what she must do. Unnoticed, she slips from the room and climbs the stairs. Perhaps David's right – what is there to say? There's no heating in the house apart from the Aga so it's freezing in the bathroom. Ignoring the dirty sink and damp towel, she quickly brushes her teeth. Just as she's rifling through the airing cupboard for her nightie, kept there during the day to stop it getting damp, a bitter voice slams her against the wall.

It whispers cruelly that her mother's death might be her fault. She couldn't wait to get away, it hisses, she was even willing to lie just to escape to the farm with her boyfriend. Shirley wanted Amy to come home, but Amy ignored her wishes. Call herself a daughter? Maybe Amy's selfishness caused so much stress that the cells of her mother's brain burst? Does unhappiness makes cells leak? Her mother was very young to have a brain bleed …

The accusations hurtle around her head. The images of the lonely calf in the barn and Shirley lying in the undertaker's shed are terrifying. Amy grips the sink, forces herself to stand naked in the icy bathroom. Her teeth chatter with cold but guilt makes her shake, too. Staring back from the mirror, her eyes are bloody pits. She deserves punishment.

'Amy, what the hell's going on?' Suddenly David is in the bathroom and he is flinging his arms around her, subsuming her in his warmth. 'What are you doing, you crazy girl? Look, I've brought a hot water bottle for you. Let's get some clothes on you and …'

'David,' she wails, 'it's my mother, I'm feeling terrible, I wonder if it's my fault …'

'Don't be silly, darling Ames. Hold up your arm …'

'It could be, it could …'

'Come on, let's get you into bed,' he says, and bundling her into another jumper, drags socks up her frozen legs and half carries her into the bedroom.

The voice is stilled. The shuddering of her bones gradually wanes. But just before she drops to sleep, she is conscious of one last whisper, one last hiss. That though she may mourn her mother, no more is she bound into someone else's story of her life. Appalling to acknowledge, it jeers, but she cannot deny that there is a tiny pulse somewhere deep down in her being that is glad she is free.

*

It was raining when the vet turned up. 'I'm used to it, don't bother yourself,' he said.

But Amy insisted on joining him. In clothes more suitable for a scarecrow, she took him to the pen where Daisy was waiting.

'She's calm, is she? Give her some cow nuts. I need to establish why her calf was stillborn. I'll do a blood test of course, but I'll examine her too.'

The vet slipped on a thick plastic glove that covered his arm as far as his shoulder. 'She may have had milk fever or brucellosis though she's been inoculated so it's unlikely.'

He slipped his arm under Daisy's tail and pushed into the cow so deep that his elbow disappeared and his shoulder pressed against her hindquarters.

Amy winced.

'Feels alright,' the vet said, twisting his arm to reach for another area in the cow's vagina.

Amy wished he would move more slowly though Daisy didn't appear to mind.

Withdrawing his arm, the vet said: 'She's delivered the afterbirth alright. You can start milking her for colostrum now.'

'What's that?'

'The first milk that's usually left for the calf to feed on. Thicker, yellower than regular milk. I'll call you when the blood results are back. If nothing shows up, you can start drinking the milk. That's what Mr Stratton bought her for, isn't it? You know how to milk a cow I take it?'

He snapped shut his bag and took off his apron, then washed his hands in a nearby bucket. She wondered how clean they were.

'I'd call the hunt today if I were you. They'll come and take the calf away. It'll feed the hounds for a day.'

Chapter Eleven

Mrs Morle watches from her cottage window. Ever since that builder turned up, things have changed. That lazy lot, previously scarce until lunchtime, are now at the cottage by ten o'clock in the morning and willing, it seems, to take directions on digging trenches or laying pipes. Accompanied by not-infrequent laughter. Mrs Morle had not understood labouring to be fun.

Bob, for he'd come across to the cottage to introduce himself and shake her hand (and his were clean, she noticed) spent the first month re-tiling the cottage roof; he brought a lad to carry tiles and the flashing. Julian and the other boys he directed from the scaffolding. Helen, his wife or partner - one didn't ask these days - got one of the chaps to pick out old mortar so she could re-point the brickwork. Nimble-fingered, Bob said of her. And she got that dreamy girl, Maggie was her name, to strip the paint off the window frames. No doubt Mr Stratton would be pleased that his cottage might be watertight in time for winter.

The other girl, Amy, seemed to spend a lot of her time in the kitchen making the meals for them when she wasn't working in the garden. She'd dug the whole plot over, mind, spread it with muck from an old dung heap in the back yard and planted broad bean seeds. Even cleared a bed for asparagus. Fancy food. Mrs Morle doubted it would grow.

Seymour still employed Mrs Morle to clean each week. Good

job too, the place needed it. Amy, with a book in one hand and secateurs in the other, seemed oblivious to dirt. She crawled among the fruit bushes snipping the branches. Asked Mrs Morle not to chuck out the bottles anymore; the girl was going to make country wine from the fruits, she said, and rosehip syrup for sore throats. Mrs Morle tried not to wrinkle her nose.

Julian and his friends might be doing more work these days, but it didn't stop their parties. Sometimes when Mrs Morle woke in the night she could see lights in the house, even in the small hours, and when the wind was from a certain direction, she could hear music. How did they stay up so late and still get up in the mornings? Perhaps they didn't need sleep like normal humans or did it have something to do with that man Gerald?

He was there too often for her liking. She couldn't quite put her finger on it, but she felt in her water he was untrustworthy.

Gerald ignored her. Nothing new in that; many of Seymour's friends had done the same over the years. Took it in her stride. City-types, self-important and selfish, they couldn't see that anyone else mattered, certainly not the cleaning lady. But with Gerald it was more than that: he made her recoil. It wasn't that he looked scruffy, which he did, it was his expressionless eyes.

One time she'd come across him splayed across a sofa fast asleep, his leg sticking out from under a coat. She was tempted to lay a cushion over those line-scored cheeks, to press down on his pursed mouth. He was so still, she wondered hopefully if he was dead already. Unable to hear his breath, she flicked him with a duster. Not that she cared particularly, but somehow it seemed necessary that his body should be taken out of the house as quickly as possible if he had gone. But his eyes snapped open and she flinched, shocked to realise just how disappointed she felt.

*

Amy wakes with a jump. Her chest and neck are clammy, her heart flutters. A dream about her mother again.

She pulls open the curtain a fraction. A glimmer of sunlight touches the slope where the grass has been flattened by rain. Cold air streams under the duvet, making her skin sting.

She reaches for the towel she used last night to wipe herself after she and David had sex and notices with relief that it is streaked with blood. Although she is careful, even obsessive, David complains, about using the diaphragm every time they have sex, you can never be a hundred per cent confident of contraception. Peering down, she sees her nightdress is spotted red, too. It's a welcome distraction to deal with her period. Already the feelings stirred up by her dream are fading; her mother speaking to her soundlessly.

David rolls towards her and blows stale sleep breath into her face. She turns onto her side and stares out at the field now glowing in the light. He snuggles up to her, his erection pressing against her leg. 'I want you again,' he breathes into her hair.

'I've got to milk Daisy,' she whispers back.

'Stay for a little while, Ames, you know you want to.' He begins to pull up her nightdress.

'I can't, I've got to get up.'

'Don't be boring, Miss Amy Routine,' he taunts. 'Daisy can wait but I can't.'

Her rump is bare now and he strokes her buttocks, biting playfully on her neck.

'My period's started anyway.'

David pushes her away. 'You should have said,' he says, and rolls over as she slips from the bed.

Daisy is waiting patiently at the gate. She meanders along the path, following the sound of the cow nuts rattling in the bucket. She eats the nuts while she's milked.

Amy's wrists and hands are strong now, and she's come to love the rhythmic pull and squirt of the twice-daily task. Spreading her knees, she draws herself right up against the animal and rests her head on Daisy's scented flank. With alternate hands, she squeezes the milk down the rubbery teats until they flop like flat balloons.

Ten minutes later, the bucket brims with frothy creamy milk. Only a few weeks ago she was not so competent. One day Daisy kicked over the pail and Amy shouted in exasperation as the hard-won liquid trickled into puddles. The frightened cow hid at the end of the muddy yard as Amy found she was crying over the spilt milk.

But she couldn't help it. Ever since Shirley died, she has cried at the oddest times and without warning. The lyrics of a song, a dead mouse that Pepper leaves in the boot room, stones that sparkle in a stream, she can't predict what will set her off. David finds it exasperating.

Amy heaves the pail onto the kitchen table.

'Morning, milkmaid.' Julian eating cereal looks like Daisy does when she's chewing the cud. 'What the hell are we going to do with all this milk?'

Simon is putting bread between the hot plate and hood of the Aga. 'Do you want a p-p-piece of t-t-toast, Amy?'

Upstairs a door slams. 'Yeah, thanks. Well, I'll give some of the milk to Mrs Morle and Lynn and then …'

'That'll get you in her good books,' Julian teases.

'… and I'm going make soft cheese with herbs from the garden.' Amy pulls a recipe book off the dresser shelf and starts to flick through the pages.

'I didn't know we had herbs here. How very rustic. Pour us a cup of tea, will you, S-S-S-imon?'

'Yes, there's thyme and sage and mint. Found them when I dug over the ground. Here's a recipe. It says … "curdle the milk with lemon juice or vinegar. Once it's set, hang the curds in a muslin cloth over a bowl overnight and drip out the whey … flavour the curds, sweet or savoury." That's what I'll do then.'

'It sounds disgusting. Whatever it is you're making with rotten milk, I'm not eating it.' David comes into the kitchen. He's trying to sound cheerful, but she can tell he's irritated. 'Gerald's been sick in the bath, Julian. I've put him on your bed to recover and told him to clear it up.' He pours himself some tea.

'I think it s-s-sounds delicious, your herby ch-ch-cheese, Amy.' Simon watches her drop vinegar into a pan of milk. 'I'll eat it even if D-D-David won't. You're such a great c-c-cook.'

'Thank you.' She smiles up at him.

Half an hour later the kitchen is quiet. Amy arranges the clean bowls and tea cups on the dresser. She sweeps the floor of crumbs and the mud that's fallen from dirty boots; it does not, apparently, occur to anyone to remove their wellies before entering the house. Why does she feel it would be bossy to ask them?

In a large bowl, she sprinkles yeast onto warm milk that's sweetened with honey. She watches as the tiny granules bubble and foam into life, releasing the aroma she's come to crave. Stirring in wholemeal flour makes the mixture turn ropey. Dusting her hands, she kneads the swollen dough until it's as tacky as chewing gum. Making two loaf shapes, she punches them down in the pans and covers them with a cloth to 'prove'. The language of bread makes her happy.

She remembers the pleasure her mother took in household tasks and how she, Amy, would deride her for it. Now she too appreciates the comfort that domesticity can bring. How could she have been so unkind as to mock her mother about something she enjoyed? Emotions clog her throat like uncooked dough.

'Hallo.' Gerald is leaning against the kitchen door, dishevelled, but infuriatingly he looks composed. 'Good day. Are you alright?'

'You made me jump. Morning, Gerald, I'm just a little … it's nothing.' She resents being caught in a private moment.

'Is there any tea?' He looks around hopefully.

She resists the urge to fetch him a cup. 'Kettle's on.' Is her nose red from crying?

Gerald pours boiling water into a cup, then sloshes milk on the counter. 'Whatever it is that's getting you down, forget it, that's the way.'

As he cuts a slice off one of her loaves he sings: '*I beg your pardon, I never promised you a rose garden …*'

Spreading butter and jam thickly onto the bread, he goes into the sitting room. Amy puts the loaf back in the bread bin and sweeps the crumbs off the counter.

*

Maggie is squatting against the back wall of Bramble Cottage. She's meant to be scraping paint off the window frames. But surely it's important to start only when you're ready? Her hair needs plaiting or it'll get full of dust.

It's getting colder each day. At least the checked shirt and dungarees she found in the airing cupboard keep her warm and, cinched in with a belt at the waist, make her look like a proper farm girl. Digging into her pocket, she finds her tobacco and rolls a breakfast cigarette. Helen's out the front: Maggie can hear her calling to Bob, so she won't notice this slow start. Helen's amazing;

she knows so much about building. Bob confers with her on most decisions. She's strong too, lifting bags of cement just like the men. But has she forgotten how important it is to pace the day?

Maggie is enjoying life here. She's not a country girl, not like Amy, who delights in having dirt under her fingernails. But living in this group, practically a commune really, is a hoot. If it means you have to scrape paint, then so be it.

There's always new people staying, someone Seymour has suggested should visit, or Julian's friends, someone who's been thrown out of a squat or kicked off their pitch selling tie-dyed clothes in Portobello Road market. Sometimes people call to say they're coming, but more often than not they just turn up unannounced, saying they'll hang around for a day or two. They always end up staying longer. Usually because of the Wyld Farm jinx.

Cars which worked perfectly well on arrival succumb to the gremlin and die. Like Steve, the music journalist, with his shiny bomber jacket, tales of record company parties and passion for glam rock, the 'next big thing', he says. It took Julian days to fix his flash car. Marianne, who wanted to gather sheep dung for her collage, had to abandon her campervan and take the train home, dragging her sack of manure behind her. And Erica who arrived with her toddler Adrian (named after the Mersey poet apparently) and insisted on sleeping in a yurt in the garden. She would only eat raw food. Maggie couldn't remember how she finally got away.

Maggie sighs. It has to be said there is a shred of guilt that she didn't start the nursing course. It's never nice when your mother bursts into tears on the phone. But you have to make your own decisions about life and she doesn't want to be a nurse anymore. Staying here with everyone else feels *right*. Who knows? Take life as it comes. Julian and David were talking last night about staying on Wyld Farm for a year or two. Back to the land, get city kids to come and run a holiday scheme for them, teach them about farming …

That's when Maggie remembers the chickens. It's her job to shut them into the hen house every night.

'Shit!' She scrambles to her feet. 'Got to let the chickens out, be back in a bit!' she shouts to anyone who might be listening.

She heads for the orchard, grateful to escape the tedium of work, though she hasn't actually done any yet.

'I feel like a jailer when I have to shut the hens up in that tiny house,' she'd complained last night at supper.

Everyone's chairs were rammed up against the Aga; they were too fagged to make a fire. Someone passed her a joint.

'At least they've got their b-b-boyfriend, the big c-c-cock, with them. I'm sure they don't m-m-mind,' Simon joked.

Was he flirting with her? She hoped so. They'd slept together several times since she'd been here, but in the morning he would behave as though nothing had happened.

'Maggie and the c-c-cock keep the hens safe from the b-b-big bad f-f-foxes!'

She adored Simon's stammer. When he got stuck on a word, his eyes would fix hers. Resisting the impulse to say the word for him, she would gaze at him, mouthing it.

'I'm not sure there *are* foxes round here. I've never seen one,' she replied.

'T-t-tell that to the hunt!'

'I want the hens to be free, not locked up in the dark.'

'You think that if you b-b-believe something hard enough that it w-w-won't happen. That's k-k-kooky.'

'You're teasing me,' she pouted.

His grin made her lustful.

Maggie strolls past the farmhouse kitchen window and waves. Amy grimaces in reply; she's struggling with the mangle on the washing machine, wringing water out of a bedsheet. Such an old-fashioned contraption, there's no twin-tub here.

Maggie heads through the gate into the orchard. The fruit trees are bare of leaves now. She remembers seeing them for the first time when the boughs were weighed down with fruit.

It's then that she sees it - the hen house - flipped over on its side. Strewn across the grass, the headless bodies and bloody entrails of the chickens. Hand clamped on mouth, Maggie runs howling back to the farmhouse.

Chapter Twelve

With each station passing, the world looks more cluttered and less colourful. Shops and houses, roads packed with nose-to-tail cars, people everywhere and the only animals are dogs tethered to their owners. Amy already misses Wyld Farm and she only left an hour ago. She wonders vaguely if she is silly to miss a cow. Will Simon remember to milk Daisy?

Amy's teeth feel gritty. Her headache, caused in part by last night's party but also the thought of seeing her father again, is thumping in time to the train. The prospect of five whole days alone with him is not appealing.

Amy slips off her clogs and curls her feet up on the seat. Where will they open their presents? Sitting on her parents' bed on Christmas morning without her mother will be weird.

The ticket conductor examines her ticket. 'Going home for Christmas, are you?'

'Yes, I am.' Talking might calm her nerves. 'My father sent me the money for the ticket.'

'Did he now? That's nice of him. Mum and Dad want you home, I s'pect.'

His words hit like stones.

She imagines what Christmas Day will be like on the farm. Lunch will start as daylight fades. The kitchen will be candlelit and warm. Seymour will carve the goose and dig out the stuffing he made earlier, Julian will hand round bowls of vegetables and potatoes while Simon stirs the gravy. Stella will … Amy sighs. Stella will drift about in a splendid frock weaving mistletoe between the glasses and scattering holly berries.

How she wishes she could be there too! But there was no question of leaving her father on his own the first Christmas since Shirley died. The possibility had crossed her mind briefly, but she dismissed it as unkind when an envelope arrived with the train fare and a note from her father.

David and Maggie had been summoned home. Furious with them both for 'dropping out' as she called it, their mother had not sent them money for their fares, only demands. They had to borrow cash from Seymour. They were travelling home today, too.

Suddenly her heart leaps. At the end of the platform, Amy can see her mother surrounded by a crowd of people. Shirley is waving gently at a departing train, straining to be seen, her face lit by smiles.

Amy knows that it cannot be Shirley. Shirley is dead. But something primeval in her muscles and veins and nerves propels her to her stockinged feet. Even while her mind resists this illogical reaction, she finds she is dashing down the train, pushing past people struggling with cases and bags, and grabbing for the door handle to wrench it open.

A stranger stays her arm. 'Steady there, love!' urges the woman.

Amy forces down the window and cranes her head out. Tears whip away as the train gathers speed. Already the station crowd has merged into an indistinct mass and her mother, or the person she thought was her mother, has disappeared.

'You alright love?' The woman is still holding her arm. 'You got no shoes on. Where are they, love? Should I call the conductor?'

'No, no, leave me alone, will you? I'm sorry …'

Indifferent to the tears that are rolling down her cheeks, Amy makes her way back to her seat. On the way, she stops to help an elderly woman who is struggling to lift her case into the rack. Back at her seat, Amy wraps a jumper around her head and weeps.

Last night was bizarre. Seymour had arrived at the farm after nine o' clock, bags in one hand and a bottle of champagne in the other. He was trailed by Stella who was hidden by an enormous bunch of glitter-sprayed branches.

'We knew it,' Seymour said grandly. Plonking everything on the floor, he wriggled a thigh-high brass urn, a treasure from his great-grandfather's travels in the Far East, into the middle of the room. 'Christmas Eve tomorrow and the tree's still not dressed. Voila, decorations commence!'

Tiny golden bows had been twisted along the branches and glinted in the firelight. As Stella knelt to arrange them in the urn, her ruby-red dress pooled around her like blood.

'A modern version of Christmas! Isn't Stella clever? Now the whole room will be bedecked. Look what I've brought!'

Seymour whipped out boxes of fairy lights.

'Drape these lights anywhere you like, Maggie my dear. I'll pour us a drink.'

'I will … in a minute.' Maggie was drying her hair by the fire.

'You might have to tighten the bulbs to make them work,' he said, handing her a glass of champagne.

'I know what to do, you know. I have helped my mother decorate for Christmas before.' Maggie was irritated. The man always had to be in command.

Seymour ignored her. 'It's a great shame you won't all be here for Christmas. Now, where are the boys? It's time to celebrate!'

When Maggie didn't reply, Amy said: 'They've gone to the pub with Bob and Helen. Suspect they'll be back soon. You two must be hungry. Shall we eat? I've made some soup.'

'Sounds wonderful.' Seymour followed her into the kitchen. 'I've brought some Italian nibbles, if you're tempted. Prosciutto, salami, a piece of dolcelatte, focaccia and panettone … '

The boys had not returned by the time they'd finished eating. It briefly crossed Amy's mind that it would have been nice to spend her last night before Christmas with David. But Seymour was so entertaining with his stories of 'nightmare models' that she wasn't bothered.

After the second bottle of champagne, the four of them pushed back the furniture and started to dance. Maggie had recovered her spirits and flung herself about in her usual way. In a dramatic response to Marc Bolan's insisting they should 'Get it On', she accidentally knocked over 'the tree'. Insisting it was nothing, Seymour knelt down beside Stella to re-arrange the fallen branches.

That was when Amy noticed what the low light failed to hide and what she only remembered later when David woke her up as he crashed into bed. Seymour's hand under the sheath of Stella's hair, his fingers trailing softly down the girl's velvet-clad bottom. That was puzzling enough. What was even more perplexing was realising she felt a twinge of jealousy.

The train pulls into the station. Her father's car is parked by the kerb. He leans from the driver's seat to open the passenger door, just as he had in June when he picked her up here.

She would never forget his bizarre turn of phrase. As she'd settled in the car, he had taken her hand and said: 'Your mother has joined little Jesus.'

The way he told her that Shirley had died.

Gingerly she opens the door. He says: 'It's lovely to see you, Amy. How are you?'

He's wearing a shirt she's not seen before. He's had a haircut. She can smell he is wearing aftershave. He does not usually wear aftershave.

'Hi Dad. Good to see you too. You look well.'

'I'm fine, you know, considering. Train trip okay?'

'Yes, no problem. Thanks for the ticket money, Dad.'

He starts the engine.

'I was thinking, Dad, do we need to buy the food for tomorrow? We don't have to eat turkey if it feels a bit …'

'It's sorted, darling. I've bought the food and all the trimmings.'

'Really? Alright then.'

They do not speak as they drive home. In her family this is not unusual and it is something she appreciates today. The silence gives her a chance to prepare for arriving at the house, the first time she's been back since Shirley died. Will her father have put up a Christmas tree?

John does not take the usual route for that would mean going past the funeral parlour. Instead he drives by the common, a gorse-covered piece of land crisscrossed with footpaths. Sometimes she walked back from school that way. Memories of the pineapple smell of the flowers on early summer days flood back.

'Do you remember that incident, Dad, the man who flashed at a young girl walking on the common?'

'I do. He was caught by the police. Local, wasn't he? Your mother got worried about you walking home alone after that. Insisted you come home on the bus.'

'And that day she found mud on my shoes and accused me of walking on the common. And you stuck up for me. Do you remember?' Amy reaches over to touch her father's shoulder. 'I appreciated that, you know, Dad. But Dad …'

She is overwhelmed by guilt. 'I lied to you, Dad, do you know that? I lied! I don't know why, but I lied.'

He pulls the car over to the verge. Amy twists round in her seat to cry on her father's shoulder. Damp spots blotch his shirt.

'I'm sorry, Dad, I did walk across the common. Mum was right all along.'

For several minutes, he holds his blubbing daughter.

When she is calm, he says: 'Better now, Amy?' He starts the engine. 'By the way, I've got a girlfriend.'

*

Christmas Day is dominated by absent women; Shirley and her father's 'girlfriend'. Amy tries to imagine her mother is sitting at the table eating turkey and potatoes and stuffing. She thought people exaggerated when they said they couldn't remember what their dead relative or friend looked like – how could they forget a loved one's face? But now she knows it is true; she cannot summon Shirley. Instead the shadowy and nondescript presence of 'the other woman' is palpable.

'Look, I've found it!'

Her father's cream-coated fingers wave a silver shilling, the coin her mother hid in the Christmas pudding every year. It appalls Amy that he can take such pleasure in the absurd ritual, but she senses he wants to impress 'the other woman' even though she is not present.

'Where does Caesar keep his armies?' Her father insists they pull the Christmas crackers. Thankfully he ignores the paper hats. Amy assumes that's because he fears looking silly when he has his girlfriend on his mind.

'Go on, Amy. Where does Caesar keep his armies?'

'I don't know, Dad. Tell me.'

'Go on, guess,' he urges, starting to laugh. His mirth is unbearable. It suggests he is light-hearted; how can that be?

It was only later when watching Morecambe and Wise on television that her feelings turn to fury. She cuts her father a piece of the fruit cake she made. Every few days since November she has dutifully dripped leftover beer into holes made in the cake's surface. Now she can't stop thinking that while she was doing this, thinking about him, he was leering over another woman. Her mother's ashes were barely cooled. It is all Amy can do not to throw the cake at him. Instead she flounces off to bed. Despite her anger, she falls asleep immediately.

Her first thought on waking the next morning is that she's late for milking. Then she remembers where she is.

On Boxing Day, they eat leftovers for lunch, then walk in the woods. Afterwards, John leaves in his car without saying where he is going. She does not ask. At six o'clock the car pulls up at the house. She watches from her bedroom window as her father checks himself in the mirror, perhaps wiping lipstick from his collar. He springs from the car.

Later they watch The Old Grey Whistle Test on television, something she cannot do at the farm as there is no reception. His foot taps to the music.

The next day passes in a similar way. They have breakfast, take a walk, boil up the turkey bones for soup and eat supper. Then John leaves in the car.

Amy decides she will make bread. Searching in the cupboards, she finds the round baking tin Shirley used for baking birthday cakes. Squatting back on her heels, she examines its discoloured base. There's a tiny piece of burnt cake on the rim. She chips it off with her fingernail and lets the hard crumb dissolve on her tongue; it is still sweet.

All the cakes Shirley made for her over the years. Plain sponge with pink icing, chocolate cakes with cream filling, and once a fruit cake that Amy didn't like. She's ashamed to remember that she flew into a tantrum. And when she was fifteen, Amy put in a special request for coffee and walnut cake. It sounded so sophisticated and Amy's friends came and … Tears overwhelm her. Amy pushes the tin to the back of the cupboard. She and her father can eat sliced bread.

Later, she wanders into the back garden, but it's like a parade ground. Plants cut back hard like they've had an over-zealous haircut.

Her father arrives back before seven o'clock with takeaway rice and curry. They eat in front of the television. Amy goes upstairs to read. She can hear him downstairs, humming as he washes up the beer glasses.

On the fourth day, she blurts out at breakfast: 'I want to meet her.'

'Meet who?' her father says innocently.

'Your friend. What's her name?'

'Vi. But why do you want to meet her?'

'Because she's obviously making you happy.'

'Are you sure?'

'You *seem* happy.'

'I mean, are you sure you want to meet her?'

Amy does not answer.

Her father sighs. 'Have you got anything you could wear?'

He is irritating when he is not direct; she wishes he'd say that he hates her second-hand clothes bought at jumble sales, her 'granny dresses', her thick tights, her clogs.

'This is all I've brought. I don't have money for clothes,' she snaps.

'If you had a proper job, you would be able to afford them,' he replies coolly. 'What about your place at secretarial college? You've missed that for this year. Are you going to try again for the spring intake? I fetched an application form in case you want to complete it while you're home. ' He waves it at her.

'I don't want to.' She sounds like a petulant child. 'Alright, I'll look at it … soon.'

Outside, a young couple walk by. Their voices are animated, they are in a hurry. The woman wears a matching hat and scarf, perhaps a present from the man.

Her father is still talking. 'You'll need a job. You can't live at that farm for the rest of your life, you know. How are you going to earn a living? Is that David going to marry you? There's no talk of that, I suppose?'

'Drop it, Dad. We don't talk about that sort of thing. We're happy the way we are.'

'I bet he is. Living in sin. Gets just what he wants and no responsibilities. Just hanging about at that place. I'm not sure I understand what you're all doing there.'

'We're re-building a cottage and I'm growing vegetables and …'

'There's no future in that,' he shouts.

'And we're living the way we want to and it's different …' Her chin thrusts out, the force of her words making her shake. 'I don't want to be like you. I'm not like you, with your boring life and your television and your …'

He stands up. His face is flushed.

'If you want to come and meet my friend, get yourself into the skirt I bought you for the funeral. It's hanging in your room. And the top I gave you for Christmas.'

'Wear the clothes from Mum's funeral? Isn't that a bit *weird*?'

'I just want you to look your best when you meet her …'

'Then I don't want to meet her!'
But that wasn't true.

Chapter Thirteen

'Shit', Seymour pads into the kitchen, 'that fucking cat.'

The goose carcass is strewn across the kitchen, bits of skin stuck to the flagstones. The Minton china platter from which the bird was served yesterday at Christmas lunch lies on the floor, balanced on a roast potato and a rib bone. Though he has always found its flower-patterned border wearying somehow, he is relieved the dish remains intact. It holds memories from his childhood, both good and not-so-pleasant. The upturned gravy boat is coated in congealed fat.

'Why didn't they close the kitchen door before they went to bed?'

Seymour delicately lifts a piece of half-chewed meat from between his toes; he flicks it under the table. Someone else can clean up the mess. As he puts the kettle on the hob, he decides to return to London later that day. It's getting tricky here, what with one thing and another.

'Hi.' Stella is in the doorway in her nightclothes, her hair wild from sleep, her eyes ringed with make-up.

'Cat's been up to his tricks. He wasn't shut out of the kitchen last night,' Seymour replies.

'Don't fuss, darling.' She glides over to place a cool finger on his lips.

Strands of hair lie like fine spider webs across her neck. He ignores the thought of brushing them off her skin with his tongue and kissing the soft indent above her clavicle where her scent pools.

He steps backwards. 'Shit!' Mushy roasted carrot sprays over his foot. He wipes it back and forth across on the floor. 'I'm going back to London.'

'I'll come with you.'

'I've got to do some work.'

'I don't care, I want to be with you.'

'Stella, you should stay here with Julian.'

'I don't want to stay with Julian. There's a synchronicity between us that's irresistible.'

'Stella, you're going out with Julian. You're his girlfriend.'

'I'm sleeping with you.'

'Only a few times.'

'I want to be with you, Seymour.'

'Stella, our being together. It was … you know …' He watches her face fall. 'Of course it was wonderful. But you and I, we knew it was just a casual fling. Friends. Nothing more, you knew that. We discussed it.'

Her eyes are glassy like one of the dolls his sister had as a child. It's the look she has as she reaches orgasm. He takes a handful of her hair, as heavy as a curtain and tugs it gently. He won't leave this afternoon. He'll leave as soon as he's dressed. Alone.

*

Gerald swerves onto the verge just outside the village as Seymour roars by. The man didn't notice him. Parking his car in the farm yard, Gerald is relieved to have made it safely. In truth he's a bit too smashed to be driving. Luckily the roads are quiet on Boxing Day.

He weaves his way into the house, Jackson at his heel. No sounds of life.

'Jules?' he calls weakly.

He is the only person who uses this nickname and, though he knows his friend hates it, Gerald still uses it. Jules is quicker to say than Julian and anyway, the boy - for Julian is still a boy - should not be so precious. It's only nomenclature.

'Anyone here?' Gerald says again, but this time he expects no answer.

Gerald collapses on one of the sofas in the sitting room. It's cold. He pulls an abandoned jumper over his body. 'Jackson, up here boy.'

Both man and dog know this is not allowed but needs must. Gerald lights a joint and stares at the ashes in the grate as though with enough concentration the embers will spontaneously ignite. At some level, he believes it might just happen.

Minutes later, he is asleep.

The smell of smoke doesn't rouse them. If they stir, they will assume that Simon has lit a fire. Why would they get out of bed for that? Downers and dope have made Julian drowsy and Stella, propelled by confusion and misery when Seymour left the farm twenty minutes ago, had fled back to their bed and fallen into an unhappy slumber.

Jackson's barking woke them long enough for Julian to mutter: 'Stop that fucking dog's noise,' and for Stella to mumble back, 'It's your turn to make tea,' and for Julian to reply: 'We don't do turns, haven't you noticed,' before they both fell asleep again.

A strange smell wends its way through the house. Like cooking milk.

Earlier that morning Simon had been struggling to get any out of Daisy. Despite pulling and squeezing her teats, only a few drips plopped into the pail. When the animal stepped on his foot with her sharp pointed hoof, Simon bellowed. Milking was much harder than Amy had led him to believe.

'You need help.' Lynn was leaning against the shed, her eyes flashing with amusement. 'Just let me finish this.'

Taking a final hard suck, she stubbed out a cigarette, rolled up her sleeves and took his place on the milking stool. Her dark curls hid her face, but he sensed she knew he was mesmerised by her pale forearms as they moved up and down in a rhythmic dance.

Lynn sometimes came into the farmhouse to return something her mother had borrowed or to use the phone. Her tone was softly mocking when she asked permission to make a call. She would glance around dismissively as if expecting to see signs of chaos. Simon found her manner strangely erotic though he'd never admit this to the others. She was Mrs Morle's daughter after all.

Within minutes, the pail was full. 'I'll put it in the pantry,' Lynn said getting to her feet.

'There's no need,' Simon insisted, but she came anyway.

As soon they were inside the house, they could smell smoke and hear a dog's muffled growls. Hurrying into the sitting room they found Gerald asleep, oblivious to the smouldering sofa he sat upon and the nudges of Jackson who was trying to wake his master.

'For goodness sake!' With a disdainful and effective shove, Lynn sent Gerald sprawling to the floor while at the same time emptying the milk over the smoking sofa cushions.

By the time Julian thumped downstairs in his dressing gown, cursing and swearing, the drama was over.

'F-f-fucking Gerald must have fallen asleep,' Simon is ashen-faced. 'Dropped his j-j-joint or cigarette, I don't … If it hadn't been for L-L-Lynn, I don't know what I'd have d-d-done.'

Gerald looks up from the floor, bleary-eyed, and gives a weak smile. 'Hey what are you all doing? Jules, what's up, man? You look tense.'

Shaking his head, he seems not to know where he is. Meanwhile Simon has rushed back from the kitchen with a bucket of water which he flings over the sofa. Some of it sprinkles Gerald.

'Shit man!' he shouts.

'Seymour. Where is he?' asks Julian, blenching. 'He'll go nuts when he sees this.' He hovers his hand over the scorched area on the sofa seat. 'Is the fire definitely out?'

'Don't get hassled, man,' Gerald says hopefully.

'It's out alright,' Lynn says calmly. 'The whole sofa's soaked, mind and burn marks on the arm rest.'

'Fuck. I can't handle this, my head's banging. Shut up will you, Gerald? I need to think and I need tea and it is bloody freezing in here. Thanks Lynn, you're a star. You too Simon mate. It could have been a lot worse. Let's get warm in the kitchen and work out how we keep this from Seymour.'

Stella is in the doorway. She has found time to sweep her hair up with a clip. 'What's all the fucking noise?' she complains.

Julian says: 'Don't worry now babe, a small fire, nothing serious. Just got to keep it from Seymour.'

'Seymour's gone,' she says, disappearing back down the hall. Over her shoulder she calls: '… back to London.'

Five days later, Stella follows him by train. Not because Seymour encourages her. He does not return the messages she leaves at his studio or the notes she sends in the post.

The row that had been festering since Boxing Day finally erupts. The shouts and screams of Julian and Stella ricochet through the house. They bounce off the barn. Stella is short in stature, but she can produce an impressive volume of sound.

Lynn, hearing yells from the Morle cottage, sniggers. She wonders idly if the noise will put Daisy off her milk.

The trigger for the fight was after Stella and Julian did not have sex. He called her 'cold and unresponsive' as she wriggled to the other side of the bed avoiding his advances. She retorted that she'd preferred foreplay with his father. Incredulous, he asked her to repeat the remark. When she said that Seymour was the only man who understood her body and gave her intense orgasms, the row exploded.

Julian was in turn flabbergasted, disgusted, incensed and humiliated. Stella finally left the farm, dragging her beautiful and large carpetbag behind her. Ten minutes later she was back. The occasional buses which went through the village were not in service on New Year's Eve.

'I need a lift!' she demanded.

'Oh do you?' Julian replied.

'Do I have to ask again?' she sniped.

'You do. And you'll have to beg and you'll have to do it nicely,' he retorted.

'There is no one else to ask,' she spat back, 'and you aren't nice.'

Simon drove her to the train station. The men agreed to meet in the village pub on his return. The place was packed with local people drinking as quickly as possible before the pub closed at 11pm.

It was rumoured the landlord had 'lock-ins' but the Strattons had never been on that invitee list. The boys downed several pints before the barman called time. The New Year's Eve party planned to take place at the farmhouse with Seymour's friends bringing booze, food and possibly drugs, had been cancelled. It would now take place in Seymour's London studio. Julian and Simon were not invited. They would see in the New Year together.

'Christ, can't tell you how relieved I am,' Julian insisted over his fifth pint. 'Stella is a complete and utter pain. Seymour's welcome to her. She's neurotic, tricky as hell, a nightmare on legs. She may think she's clever, but she hides it well under all that drifting about like an overgrown fairy. Now Lynn, there's a chick with sense, don't you think, S-S-Simon?'

'The way she d-d-dealt with that fire and Gerald, it was impressive. I l-l-like that in a woman. We c-c-could invite her over?' said Simon.

'Fancy her do you, S-S-Simon mate? I could myself. Any port in a storm.'

'Perhaps you could stop calling me that.'

'Calling you what?'

'S-S-Simon.'

'But I've always called you that, mate.'

'And I've always loathed it.'

They stared at the dregs of their pints.

'Last orders!' cried the barman.

Julian stood up. 'Another pint?'

Simon looked at him quizzically.

'Another pint to see out this shitty old year? Simon?'

'Thanks I will. *Jules*.'

Chapter Fourteen

'Why don't you drive?' John holds out the keys to his daughter.

Like a grumpy child bribed with an ice cream, he can see she's tempted. Wrapping her fingers around the chilly bunch of metal, she walks to the driver's side of the car.

'You'll have to tell me how to get there,' she grumbles, 'I don't know where she lives.'

John gets into the passenger seat and does up the belt. He smooths the skin around his mouth and looks out of the window. Amy finds his anticipation appalling.

'Drive past Murphy's Pets towards the hotel, then left,' he says.

She has passed the estate of mock-Georgian houses many times before. The tidy front gardens and short garden paths. There are no pedestrians, only cars with iced-up windscreens in driveways where perfectly round Christmas wreaths of fake leaves hang from identical front doors.

Her father tells her to stop the car. They are outside a house she finds even more horrible than the others. For in the bay window stands a teddy bear and it is dressed as Father Christmas.

'Vi, this is Amy,' says John.

'Hallo Amy, come in. Happy New Year.'

The woman's curls frame her face like a helmet. Her silvery-pink lips remind Amy of wriggling worms.

John stamps his shoes on the mat as though to shake off snow.

She follows the woman into a room. Christmas music is playing. On a comfy chair is a cushion crocheted in snowflakes. She indicates where Amy should sit, then settles herself on the sofa. She tucks silvery-pink painted toes under her bottom.

'Put that on, will you John? It's parky out there, eh Amy?'

John seems familiar with the electric fire. Rising warm air makes the Christmas cards on the mantelpiece tremble.

'Shall you get us tea and some of that lovely fruit cake, John?' Vi's nose wrinkles when she smiles. Amy suspects Vi thinks it looks appealing. 'I bet Amy would like some.'

'I bet she would. Amy? Would you like cake?'

John and Vi look at her. Amy's brain has ambled to a stop. It is as though she has crashed a private party, but no one has noticed she is a stranger. She forces her head to move up and down to save having to speak.

John disappears from the room. A kettle boils; she can hear the chink of china. From the corner of her eye she can see the back of the Santa teddy. Something in her waits for the bear to turn around and wink.

'How did Christmas go?' Vi asks.

Amy notices the pink cardigan that Vi is wearing. With a jolt she realises it's the same one that she is wearing, the one her father gave her, only hers is green.

'My niece and nephew were here for the day. We had *turkey*.' Vi's tone suggests she has said something utterly surprising. 'Then pudding with brandy butter. I don't like cream *and* brandy butter on Christmas pudding, do you?'

The constriction in Amy's throat is making it hard to breathe. Spit pools in her mouth. 'Yes, no, I don't, I …' she mumbles.

She is relieved when her father returns with a tray. He hands Vi a cup of tea. Amy looks away. She cannot witness their eyes meeting or their hands touching. A horrifying image of the two of them kissing flicks through her mind.

'And for you, love.' John offers his daughter a plate. 'Festive in here. Vi's made it nice, don't you think?'

The only other Christmas decoration she has noticed is an artificial Christmas tree on a box covered in wrapping paper. She says, 'um,' and then after a moment, 'yes.'

'So any New Year's resolutions, Amy?' There's a lamp that makes Vi's ears glow as pink as her lips. 'John tells me you're starting secretarial college in the spring.'

Mid-way through cutting himself another piece of cake, her father stops, knife poised, waiting for his daughter's reply.

'That was my plan,' says Amy slowly, 'but I've changed my mind.'

John jumps as though he's stabbed himself. The motion sends crumbs of cake scattering across the pale carpet. 'Oh shit. Pardon me, Vi! You what, Amy? That's news to me, I thought we agreed you'd fill in that ...'

'I've decided to stay in the country.' She surprises herself with the confidence her voice contains. 'I've been, yes, I've been offered work there. Seymour, that's Mr Stratton, the owner, has said he will pay me from January.'

A plan forms in her mind as she speaks. She will replace Mrs Morle on Monday mornings, saving the cost of her wages, and use the Christmas money she got from her father and an aunt to pay for driving lessons. She will pass the test. She will do all the errands that are required, so Bob, Helen, and the others can concentrate on building the cottage. Once the vegetable garden produces food and there are eggs from the hens and milk from Daisy and bread that she, Amy, makes, it will cost almost nothing to feed everyone.

'Like a commune then? Back to nature and all that?' Vi says.

At the same time John blurts out: 'Why didn't you mention this before?'

'It's what the young people want these days, John, and why not? Alternative life. Being a hippy. So is that what you are then, Amy?' Vi smiles.

'It's not what you think, Dad. We work hard and we have a plan,' Amy says proudly, 'and Mr Stratton is happy with what we're doing.'

Strange to remember how she'd first lied to her parents about Seymour living at the farm. She didn't realise then quite how often he *would* be there. Sometimes she wondered why he did visit so often. 'Of course he's not always at the farm. He's a photographer. He leaves us to get on with things. He *trusts* us. He likes what we're doing.' Her tone is defiant.

Vi says: 'Don't know if I could do that, live in a group. I like to keep my space just the way I like it, y'know. Sharing with everyone makes that difficult, doesn't it, Amy?'

'I'm not that concerned about tidiness,' Amy sneers.

But she is. She hates it when the men tramp in from the puddle-pitted yard tracking footprints all over the hall. She tries to forget the conversations they used to have about how men and women should share domestic tasks equally. Because it doesn't happen that way; she does everything in the house.

'I'm sure you don't mean to sound rude,' John says pointedly.

'Well I'm not.'

'Not what?'

'Concerned about tidiness. Nor am I meaning to be rude.'

'It just sounded that way then.'

'Well if it did, I'm sorry.' Amy does not sound sorry.

'No offence,' says Vi brightly.

'What does David's mother make of it all? That's your boyfriend isn't it? Who else is living at the farm?'

'I don't think she minds.' Amy has not given a moment's thought to what David's mother thinks about her son being on the farm. 'Why *would* she mind? For goodness' sake, Dad, it's his life! It's not her business.' She does not hide her scorn.

'Oh isn't it?' The young are as self-satisfied as religious zealots, John fumes to himself. 'You lot, you think you know it all …'

'We're living differently to all the … straight people. And we're going to change the world, Dad; live in spiritual harmony with nature and … all that.' She's tongue-tied, too angry to put her feelings into words and it's humiliating. Everything she says sounds a bit vague.

She stands up. 'I think we should go, Dad.' Looking down, she realises with horror that there's a gap at her bosom where the cardigan has pulled apart.

The day she travels back to Wyld Farm, she resists the temptation to dump the cardigan in the dustbin. Never know when it might come in handy. Anyway, it would be a waste of the world's resources.

Chapter Fifteen

Parting the curtain with a finger, Maggie squints from a sleepy eye. It rains a lot in Somerset.

There's a blissful stillness in the house. Perhaps it's early? If she'd wound up the wristwatch her mother had given her as a Christmas present, she'd know the time, but she refuses to be ruled by the clock. The bed socks David gave her on Christmas morning (their mother bought and wrapped them, she knows for sure, but it's the thought that counts, David told her with a nudge) keep her cosy from toe to knee. Maggie pulls the duvet a little higher over her head.

It takes her a minute to fix on a New Year's resolution. To make Simon fall in love with her; that's too obvious and anyway, it seems to be happening already. To work less hard. That's more like it. The cottage would have completely the wrong vibe if it was fixed by people who weren't totally positive at all times. Resentment would seep from the walls and ooze from the floor; bad karma. Maggie snuggles down into the bed and resolves to ignore all demands on her time today.

*

Falling in love with a person is one thing, but falling in love with a place, what does that mean? There is no body to moon over, no mouth to crave kisses from, no person to communicate with.

The exhilaration and euphoria which invades a person in love is absent from the love of place. But that strong sense that 'this is right', that 'this is as it should be'; this is the feeling when the place that resides within, which lifts and feeds the spirit, is cherished.

This is how Amy feels when she gets off the train at Taunton. With mounting excitement she boards the bus for Exmoor. Yet almost immediately she falls asleep. When she wakes sometime later, the bus is already speeding along what she thinks of as the 'top road'. One of her favourite views. The beech trees stand like soldiers atop stone walls, guarding the soggy fields which plunge away behind them. The white of the sheep occupying the steep-sided combes are slashes against the brown bracken. Yellow gorse flowers wink like sunbursts. Skeins of mist scud across the landscape.

There is relief to be away, gone from the house where she first raised her head from the cot pillow on a wobbling neck, where her stubby legs became strong enough to bear her weight, where her first tottering steps took her barreling into the table where, a few years later, she sat to first form the letters that spelt her name and later, to study for exams. Once a place of familiarity and comfort, her former home offers no future. She had hugged her father, promised to write, and hurried away.

Stepping from the bus is like leaving an old world. Around her father's house there are pavements and pylons. Here she is astonished by celandines and snowdrops which grow on the verge. She falls to her knees to cup their delicate heads in her fingers. The wind blows her hair into dancing fronds. The anxiety that has dogged her for days, clinging like a spectre, slips away with the departing bus. She rummages in her bag for an apple.

The occasional vehicle that passes does so at great speed, the driver only glimpsing the girl they fly past. From out of the grey, first the sound, then the sight of a farmer on a tractor whirring by at a more sedate pace. Straw from the trailer, food for his animals, flies out behind him like a hail of golden arrows. Amy waits.

Eventually a motorbike stops on the other side of the road. David calls her from the throbbing machine.

'Ames! Come here, I've missed you. How was Christmas and your father and how did ...?'

She runs over to her boyfriend. Tears prickle, but she's determined not to cry, not now, so instead she hums as she embraces him, a trick she learnt as a child. A tune that was playing at Vi's house; Bing Crosby singing that terrible saccharine song about Christmas. A car passes the embracing couple; there's the toot of a horn.

'Your beard, David, you've grown a beard. You look, I don't know, like a pirate! Oh God. I can't wait to get home.'

She buries her head under his chin, her favourite spot, and whispers into his jumper. 'David, can we call Wyld Farm "home"?'

*

Draughts no longer whisper through the cottage; the once ill-fitting windows and doors sit snug in their frames. And while the floors of concrete and stone walls are cold, they are not damp. Despite the freezing temperatures, Bob insists the work must continue. Julian calls him a slave driver, pretending he's joking, but there's bile behind his jibe.

Bob summons his workforce each morning by banging on the farmhouse door knocker, persistent knocks, enough to penetrate the deepest dream. Recently he's taken to putting on music. The Who on full power chivvies awake even the most sleep-fogged. Julian, David, Maggie and Simon grumble as they trudge over to the cottage.

But Amy will already be gone. Just after dawn, she slips from the bed to follow Daisy's swaying body from the field. Even when dry-mouthed and hungover, the thought of the cow waiting patiently, her udder ballooning with milk, drives Amy from under the duvet. For there is solace when her face is pressed to the cow's flank. Her fingers turning tingly-warm as they cover the rubbery teats. Her ears rejoicing in the ping of the milk hitting the pail. The curdy smell.

A time when she can grieve for her mother. A place where she can rail at her father.

*

Few people visit; the cold, it seems, keeps them away. So in the evenings, it's only the five of them who press up to the range, their feet fighting for space in the lower oven, squabbling about whose turn it is to put a record on. Even Gerald does not appear. When the hash runs out, they do not phone him; no one has the money to pay for more. David complains to her in bed that they're becoming middle-aged. There is a quiet rhythm to the dark mornings and early nights that Amy appreciates. She does not admit this to anyone.

A postcard arrives. It shows a sunny beach and a sparkling sea. It is from Seymour who is working abroad or escaping the winter; it is not clear. Addressed to Pepper, the message reads that 'they' will bring back a tropical fish for the cat to enjoy. Amy feels envious: who is he with? She props the card on the dresser and imagines Seymour on a hot beach. He will be turning brown in the sun.

Chapter Sixteen

'Take a right turn at the next junction,' says the examiner, making notes with his stubby pencil.

It is hard to tell the man's age for his terrible brown suit and shoes are at odds with his hair which just touches his shirt collar. His boss can't approve of that.

'Pull up on the left beyond the blue van and park up, please.'

Amy adjusts her skirt. It is the one her father bought her to wear at her mother's funeral; it has ridden up her thighs. She dressed carefully for the test; everyone had said she should. The instructor, a man in all likelihood, will be susceptible to feminine wiles.

So last Saturday, David let her drive the Land Rover to a jumble sale in a village some ten miles away. Amy rummaged through the heaps of clothes on the trestle table. She found a pale pink blouse with a small nick on the sleeve for a few pence and a boy's school mackintosh. Last night she washed her hair and slept with it in plaits so that in the morning it bounced with curls. Simon said she looked just like F-F-F-arrah Fawcett-M-M-Major.

The instructor gave her an approving look when he met her in the driving school office. She listened attentively to his instructions; she is determined to pass the test.

'Your three-point turn,' he says, shaking his head, 'was not strong. You didn't go for the full lock of the wheel. Hence it was a four-point turn.'

When he clears his throat, his Adam's apple moves up and down like a lift.

'Then changing down a gear, there is …' He reaches out to touch the gearstick and as he does, his hand brushes her thigh. '… more practice needed there, eh?'

She assents silently, her curls bobbing.

'Your command of the road is tentative, Miss Tinker, but ...'

She steels herself for disappointment. The examiner has turned to face her. Surely he is closer than is strictly necessary?

'Taylor,' she corrects and slips down in her seat.

'Of course, yes, apologies. Miss *Taylor*.'

He makes a mark on his sheet.

'I must inform you that, I have decided that …' and now he is smiling and she sees a piece of dried food on the edge of his mouth and she can't help staring as it moves to and fro. '… that you have passed the driving test. Well done.'

He leans back in his seat. 'Would you accept my invitation to a celebratory drink in the pub?'

*

'We're going to the village, Mrs Morle. Is there anything I can get you while we're there?' Amy calls from the Land Rover.

Those girls spend more time driving around in that vehicle than they do working on the cottage. Mrs Morle shakes her head.

She shuts her cottage door firmly. She does need preserving sugar for her marmalade, but she'll add it to the list she'll give to Andrew Bishop when he comes to say he's passing by the village shop. No doubt he'll be going in a day or two and there's no hurry.

The gutting knife and meat cleaver clatter as she puts them back into the drawer. She'd used the tools yesterday to gut three rabbits that Colin, a local lad they'd made friends with, left in the farmhouse pantry. Would have been a waste to leave the animals, heads and feet still on and not yet cleaned for eating.

'Aren't they beautiful?' Amy was pouring milk into a jug when Mrs Morle came in that Monday morning. 'I don't know what to do with these rabbits, Mrs Morle, do you? Colin said they're good to eat, but they need skinning and so on. But, I mean, how? Do you … would you mind showing me how to do it?'

Mrs Morle didn't like being in contact with Julian's lot. But she and Lynn loved a bit of rabbit and there'd be enough for everyone.

'Alright, I will. Harry, that was my husband, he always gutted rabbit out in the field soon as he'd shot 'em,' Mrs Morle said. 'They'll go off quick with their innards left inside. The dogs love 'em, of course, and it makes less mess cleaning them in the field. But these was only shot on Sunday and it's cold in the pantry, so they'll be fine for eating. You and the other girl, you come over to mine later and I'll show you what's what.'

With a small sharp knife, Mrs Morle sliced through the rabbit's thick coat, careful to cut only as deep as the abdominal cavity. 'If you go through that membrane, you'll hit the guts and taint the flesh.'

Amy stood at her elbow trying not to wince.

'Now I take the skin off the body.'

It required far more force than her words suggested. The animal's front legs flounced in a macabre dance as Mrs Morle dragged the pelt from the flesh, as careful as when rolling her stockings down her legs each night. It was like removing a jumper from a wriggling baby.

The white abdominal sack gleamed.

'Inside there are the innards and I need to get them out before they turn.'

Mrs Morle's fingers dove into the sack and wrenched out pink-grey organs that Amy remembered from school science lessons. She had always been fascinated by muscles and sinews and blood vessels. She quite forgot it was a pretty little bunny that was being carved up.

'Some folk eat the heart and liver,' said Mrs Morle, 'but these have been nicked by the bullet so they're mashed. I'll give 'em to the dogs. You want to keep this left hind foot? It's good luck if the animal was shot by a cross-eyed person at full moon. Who was it brought these to you? Colin? Well, he's certainly no beauty.'

The vivid pink carcass was now stretched out on its tummy along the cutting board like a diver about to plunge into a pool. Smack-crunch! The rabbit's head was severed off with a slam of Mrs Morle's cleaver, then the legs were chunked up into pieces.

'So that rabbit's ready for the pot. Maggie, you lurking there, are you, been watching? You're cleaning the next one, eh?'

'I'm a vegetarian, I can't …' Maggie had been hovering by the kitchen door, alternatively appalled and fascinated.

'You're telling me you're going to miss a delicious meal of rabbit? I doubt that very much, not when you smell 'em cooking.'

Amy gutted the second rabbit. A sensible girl and willing to listen, thought Mrs Morle, as she watched the girl skin and joint the animal. Not a bad cook neither. She brought two servings of stew over to the cottage that evening along with a nice bit of mashed turnip and potato. Mrs Morle had never tasted rabbit made with garlic before but had to agree with Lynn that it tasted very nice.

Still didn't make sense though, Mrs Morle thought the next day as she swept out the Rayburn. What was a townie like Amy doing at Mr Stratton's house? In fact, what were any of them doing here, pretending to be builders and smallholders and the rest of it?

It was time they went back to where they came from. Mrs Morle's cup of tea had gone cold, but she drank it anyway.

*

Although her treasured book on self-sufficiency advises it's the season to scatter parsnip seeds, it is to the four winds the seeds fly rather than the soil. The morning is a fiasco.

'How could we ever be self-sufficient if we can't even get seeds planted?' Amy bursts angrily into the cottage.

High up on a ladder in a room that reeks of paint, Helen is whitewashing the ceiling. With her arms raised, her rounded belly is obvious. The woman is pregnant.

'Oh dear, difficult morning, Amy? Where would we be without frozen peas?' Helen smiles down at her. 'There's plenty to do inside if it's too wild for gardening. Maggie's painting the bedroom. You could help her.'

'But I'm meant to be growing the food and …' Amy grumbles.

She wonders if she dares to ask Helen about the baby. She always feels a little uncertain around her. It's not that the woman isn't friendly; it's more that Amy feels gauche and inexperienced by comparison. Amy kicks at some discarded paper. 'Alright, I'll see what Maggs is up to. How are you anyway?'

A grin splits Helen's face. She comes down the ladder and puts the roller in a tray.

'I'm going to sit for a moment.' She massages her neck. 'I get tired these days. Don't know if you've noticed but, well, I'm expecting a baby. I've known for a while but didn't want to say anything to anyone. It's due mid-July. Summer baby, just like me.'

'That's wonderful. Is it alright for you to be working like this?'

'I'm fine and what am I going to do – stop? I'm doing what I've always done. Not smoking as much as before and I'll probably stop before the baby's born. I did have a bit of morning sickness in the first month or so but after that, haven't really noticed apart from my trousers are getting tight.'

What does Bob think about it? He already has two children from a previous relationship. They live with their mother some twenty miles away. Amy's heard him moaning about giving money to his ex-wife.

'Bob's getting used to the idea,' says Helen as though she's read Amy's thoughts. 'Wasn't that happy to start with, mind. But I think he'll be cool when he sees the baby.'

Neither woman speaks for a few moments, then Helen climbs back up the ladder.

The cottage is slowly taking shape. There's a damp course beneath the newly-laid floors, the electricity and water supplies are connected, and the warmth from night storage heaters is drying out the fresh plaster. But it's some way from habitation …

She finds Maggie in one of the bedrooms. She's bobbing around to the music on the radio, a paint-laden sponge in each hand. It's obvious she's on speed; the building team, as they call themselves, insist it's the only way to get through the work. Maggie gestures towards a folded piece of paper on the mantelpiece. Amy doesn't resist; the day's been too frustrating. She snorts the white powder and rubs the remaining crystals onto her gums.

'You brought anything to drink? I'm dry as a bone,' Maggie says, without waiting for an answer. 'What do you think of it? Of what I'm doing. It's called sponging. I read about it in an old book on traditional decorating techniques.' She beams at Amy.

Yellow and cream blobs of paint have been dabbed here and there on the walls like puffy coloured clouds.

'Like the breath of daffodils! I love it,' giggles Amy.

'What will the Master think?'

'Seymour? Oh, I think he'll be fine. It's different and quirky and ...'

'I'm going to paint the window frames like my most favourite dessert. Bet you can't guess what that is ...'

Before Amy can respond, Maggie shrieks: 'Neapolitan ice cream! So I'll paint stripes of yellow and pale pink and brown around the window. Just gotta find the perfect colour for chocolate. It will look ... delicious!'

Amy sits back on her heels and watches her friend who is fizzing with energy. The day is improving. She can feel her spirits lifting. When has life ever felt so free?

Chapter Seventeen

Seymour is parking the car when Amy and Maggie burst out of the cottage. In paint-splattered overalls, they make a refreshing contrast to the moody passenger he's driven down from London. Eleanor, who he'd met on a shoot in Martinique where she was the local fixer, is the woman he is occasionally sleeping with in town. A girl with grit but a tricky one, too, with a list of things she doesn't enjoy, the countryside being one of them. So why she pressed to come for a weekend at Wyld Farm he cannot fathom.

'Hallo, you two. Let me guess … you've been painting! Maggie and Amy, meet Eleanor.'

'Hi.' Maggie nods at the woman in dark glasses who has not moved from the car. Another female that the London Lothario expects them to welcome.

'Hi, I'm Amy. Pepper got your postcard, Seymour. He says, you haven't been down in ages and where's his present? You're still a bit tanned.'

Through the barely-opened passenger window the woman's voice sounds agitated. 'Seymour, I must lie down immediately. Take me to the house. Is there mud out there?'

'A few puddles, I suspect, Eleanor. I told you that this is a *farm*. I'll show you where to step. Look, could you two be angels and bring in our stuff from the car? I'll administer appropriate attention to our delicate visitor.'

A foot encased in a high-heeled fur boot emerges slowly from the passenger side followed by a woman with spiky crimson hair. She allows Seymour to guide her towards the path and the house.

'He looks pleased with himself,' Maggs grumbles as she lugs a bag of shopping and a suitcase from the boot.

'I thought he looked a bit miffed,' says Amy. She take a bunch of lilies and two bottles of wine from the back seat and follows Maggie into the kitchen. She puts 'Tupelo Honey' on the turntable. A few minutes later, Seymour appears.

'You are both total treasures. Thankfully our hothouse flower is tucked up in bed.' He collapses into a chair. 'Eleanor has a headache. I can only find laxatives and one old Elastoplast in the cabinet. Apparently neither will help. In my opinion, a glass of wine is what the doctor orders. But Eleanor insists on pharmaceuticals. I don't feel like driving to the chemist.'

'I'll take you Seymour,' Amy says, 'I passed my driving test, you know. Give me a minute and I'll change.'

Seymour has not seen Amy wearing anything but dungarees for months. The fitted cardigan shows off her figure and the flowery skirt swirls around her narrow ankles. The girl is wearing espadrilles laced up her shapely shins, a tightly-belted mackintosh and beret set on her head at a rakish angle.

'We're not going anywhere special, you know. You look sharp,' he says admiringly.

'I can't drive your car in welly boots, can I? Dad bought me these shoes for … for Mum's funeral. They're fine for driving. I got this coat in a jumble sale ages ago. Anyway, I haven't been off the farm for a while.'

It's strange driving the low-slung car. Amy is used to the Land Rover where the driver's seat is high up and the vehicle moves at a comfortable lumber. Now she's in charge of a slinky creature that will, with the wrong command, streak off at speed. She prays they don't meet another car on the narrow lane and she has to reverse. The amphetamine is helping her confidence.

Seymour tries not to wince when she crunches the Jaguar's gears and misjudges the ferocity of the brakes on the first few corners. By the time they reach the main road, Amy is driving more smoothly. Seymour gives directions to the chemist's shop and returns with several purchases.

'Pills Eleanor can swallow to her heart's content. Now I'd like to order the Sunday papers from the shop by the canal. You lot ignore what's going on in the world, but I don't.'

Amy protests as she switches on the headlights. 'It's not easy when there's no telly and we don't get a daily paper. I listen to the radio sometimes but ugh, the news is so horrible. That terrible bomb at the Post Office. Anyway we're more interested in living in the present, in the moment.'

He directs her to a shop she hasn't noticed before and she parks. The lighted interior reveals tinned and dried goods, soft drinks, kitchenware and toys. Nothing of interest. But she follows Seymour inside, buoyed up by her success at driving.

'Hallo, Naresh, how are you?' Seymour shakes hands with the man behind the counter. 'I hope the family is well? This is my friend, Amy Taylor, who is staying at the moment. Amy, this is Naresh Rao.' He turns to Amy: 'His son Sunil is training to be a solicitor. He's completed one year so far. Where is Sunil?'

'Been to the football and on his way back now. A break from his study today. It's hard work, but he is doing well. He's a good boy. When he passes his exams, he'll be needing to find articles in a legal practice.'

'I know someone who might be able to help. When the time comes, let's talk again. You must be proud of him, Naresh.'

Amy has never seen Seymour out of the environs of the farm before. She knows he is charming and has a knack for making life exciting. But now she sees another side. A man able to put others at ease. He makes Naresh feel special. Perhaps it's what makes him a good photographer.

The men discuss the political situation in a part of India with which they both seem familiar. Will she ever have the chance to travel so far afield? She'll never have the money. Anyway she's not sure she'll ever want to leave Wyld Farm. It's where she belongs.

How sorry she feels for all the people who live in towns and cities and have boring routine jobs. They might be able to cope with the crowds and bustle. But she can't; she will not! Her father accuses her of escaping life, of being unrealistic. But he's just straight. She and her friends are creating another way of being, a better one. They will show everyone that life can be different.

While the men dissect the failures of a local football team, she wanders around the shop. In one corner there are joss sticks and scarves and ointments. She picks happily through the stuff on display.

'Why don't we get these for Eleanor? It says this salve is good for "tensions of the heart" and the tea "enhances harmony and well-being".'

'I'm not sure they're the sort of things Eleanor likes. Eleanor's got her drugs from the chemist. But I'll get them for you if you'd like, Amy. And some of those delicious Indian sweets, Naresh.'

Outside, the thinnest sliver of the moon sits in a velvet sky encrusted with stars. She pauses for a moment to look up.

'What a stunning evening. Do we have to go straight back to the farm?'

'No, I suppose we don't. Why don't we drive to Exmoor? I know a pub. A quick drink.' Taking her elbow, Seymour guides her to the passenger side of the car. 'I'll drive now.' He gallantly opens the door and she dips her head in assent.

It is exhilarating to be pressed back in the leather seat as the car accelerates along pitch-black lanes. Seymour switches on the radio. The liquid tones of a woman, singing of her beloved's face, fills the car.

'Roberta has a perfect voice, doesn't she?' Seymour says, turning up the volume.

She closes her eyes and loses herself in the music.

After a time, the car slows down. 'A proper old pub,' Seymour says, and he swings the car off the road.

The murmur of voices and crackle of burning wood. Seymour indicates for her to sit while he goes to bar, returning with glasses of whisky. They chat for a while, then he asks: 'Haven't seen you since Christmas. How did it work out?'

'It was strange, Seymour. We always used to open our presents sitting on Mum and Dad's bed. But Mum wasn't there. We didn't really know what to do. And the turkey. Dad bought one that was much too big. It sat in the fridge almost untouched, a horrid daily reminder that there are only two of us in the family now.'

She's aware he's listening closely. She's not used to such attention; David would have accused her of being maudlin by now or, worse, neurotic.

'Then I asked Dad if I could meet her … his girlfriend. That was weird. He let me drive his car to her house which he's never done before. I didn't like her. I don't know why, really. She was … too normal.'

The remark makes Seymour laugh.

'And then it became obvious that Dad had bought us both the same item of clothing for a Christmas present.' Amy indicates the cardigan she's wearing.

'I hope she looks as fabulous in it as you do,' he says. That makes her laugh. 'But now you're back at Wyld Farm.' He lightly presses her arm.

'What did *you* do? I know you went away somewhere sunny after New Year.'

'Had to get away. I'd describe my Christmas as just a tad *fraught*. I'll get us another drink.'

He comes back with another round of whisky. 'Put it this way, I made some pretty stupid mistakes.'

'Such as?'

'Well, you see, I made a mistake. I had an affair, well no, actually, only the briefest of flings … with Stella.'

He watches for her reaction. She toys momentarily with the idea of appearing surprised, then says: 'I spotted it right away the night you arrived with her and the decorations. Discretion is not your strong suit, Seymour. But did Julian find out?'

'He did, unfortunately. Then she went and revealed everything to him, silly girl. I didn't mean for them to break up, did I? Anyway, I'd already hightailed it back to London when all hell broke loose. I gatecrashed one of my dearest friend's Boxing Day lunches and got so drunk that I fell into the tree and broke a very fine table.'

She couldn't help finding it all very funny. 'And now you're with Eleanor?'

'Or Eleanor is with me, I'm not sure which. '

'One for the road, then.' At the bar, Amy searches for the pound note she squirrelled away for emergencies. The little leather purse is worn and curled at the edge. It once belonged to Shirley. She can hear her mother whispering in her ear, urging caution, but she ignores it. She buys two whiskies and a packet of peanuts.

'To us,' she says, and they chink glasses.

She insists on sharing the nuts equally and that means splitting one in half. Is it flirtatious to hold his bit in her palm? Their eyes meet. He lifts her hand to his mouth and, with a languorous lick of his tongue, picks up the nut.

'Here's to 1973,' he says.

Chapter Eighteen

Amy handles the seedlings with careful fingers. Only days ago she sprinkled tomato seeds onto bare soil. Now slender green plants have appeared as if by magic. Although many greenhouse panes are missing or broken, enough remain for the sun to heat the air beneath; she's drowsy in the warmth. Idling against the door frame, she is submerged by new foliage and old memories. Of red fruit dangling beyond the reach of her chubby toddler's arm, of biting into warm flesh, of juice running down her chin like wine. Of her father's voice, his arms of contentment.

The phone ringing penetrates her reveries. She ignores it; there is no one she wants to speak to. Then into her mind floats an image of her mother. Perhaps it's Shirley calling her? In a mad moment, Amy wonders if somehow her mother has come alive. Taking no chances, the girl pelts into the house, down the corridor and slams into the office.

'Hallo, hallo!' she gasps, her heart leaping with hope.

'It's Mr Stratton for you. Hold, please,' an efficient female replies. Disappointment is replaced by excitement. Amy imagines Seymour's secretary's red-nailed fingers pressing buttons. A few minutes later, Seymour's voice is on the other end.

'Hallo? Who's that?' he asks as though it is she who has called him.

'It's Amy.'

‘Amy, how lovely to hear you. Have I dragged the green-fingered goddess from her garden on this glorious day?’

‘Oh, I’m just planting out the tomatoes … How are things in London, how are you?’

‘All the better for hearing your sweet tones and hurrah, this summer we’ll have provender. Now, I was thinking of having a party this weekend. I want to bring some friends down. What are you all up to?’

It is obvious the party will take place: Seymour only ever gives the illusion of choice. It is disappointing that he is bringing London people; she rather hoped to spend some time with him alone.

‘The thing is,’ he continues, ‘I was thinking of quite a *big* party. So we may need, in fact, we will need the bedrooms in the house for guests.’ He paused, letting the implications sink in. ‘The cottage is almost habitable now, isn’t it? I was thinking … Isn’t it time you lot moved in there, at least for a while? You have a few days to get it ready. What do you think?’

Seymour had often talked about the farm as a place where friends would escape the ‘wonderful stink of the city’, where artists could replenish themselves. ‘We all need the buzz,’ he’d say, ‘but sometimes it has to be from a distance.’

The cottage was part of this plan, apparently. A place where people could stay or even live for a while. Amy adored it when Seymour talked like this; she hung on every word though she never dared ask how she fit into this scheme. She had never envisaged the world where such opportunities might exist and here she was - part of it. A place where people could work and express themselves and … just *be*.

Seymour continues: ‘Be a darling and have a chat to the others, Amy?’

'Okay, I will. It sounds fine.' She does not mention all the work that's still to be completed.

'Good girl. You'll need furniture. Ask Julian to show you the stuff in the barn. Must dash, a call on the other line. See you around teatime on Friday. Do make some of your marvellous bread, Amy, could you? Bye …'

*

The next day when David and Amy are out running errands, Julian takes Maggie and Simon to one of the barns. It is full of furniture, much of it draped in sheets or in boxes and crates.

'Stuff Dad inherited from Granny,' he says, unlocking a padlock, 'though I can't imagine that all of it was hers. I know this was from the Chelsea flat and some of it was from Mum's house, too, I think.'

'Wow. I n-n-ever knew all this w-w-was stored here. It's an Aladdin's c-c-cave.'

Julian sits on a white leather sofa while the other two explore. He thinks back to the Chelsea flat where he lived with his parents. A seven-year-old boy kneeling up on the sofa to watch from the window as they went into the drugstore opposite their flat. Girls in purple catsuits slipped in and out of the place that was known for its famous clientele. The place where his parents would stay until the small hours of the morning, unaware their son waited and sometimes wept, too frightened to fall asleep alone in the flat. The boy's dread when he heard them agreeing over supper that it was 'alright to leave him since it's only for a quick one'.

'Look at this, Julian.' Maggie pulls a dust sheet off a side table and a stack of chairs. 'Can we take these?'

Julian is brought back from painful memories; the feelings of loneliness remain. 'Oh that'll be fine,' he says quietly.

'I've found a w-w-wardrobe, but it's too massive to get up the c-c-cottage s-s-stairs,' calls Simon from behind a cupboard. 'But there are iron b-b-bedsteads and bedsprings and m-m-mattresses that will fit.'

Maggie points to a chest of drawers. 'I could strip it back to the wood and leave it bare. I can't believe we're going to live in our own place!' She straddles a child's rocking chair. 'I mean your Dad is cool, don't get me wrong Julian, but to be on our own ...'

'You s-s-sound so ungrateful, Maggie,' Simon says, 'and after Seymour's been g-g-generous to us.'

She shrugs: 'I don't mean to. It'll just be nice to think we'll be on our own, that's all. Do you think your Dad will let us stay as long as we want to? What about his talk of turning this place into an artist's retreat?' Her tone is slightly mocking.

'Maggie, you're being a b-b-bit unkind, you know,' Simon says gently.

'Piss off.'

'I don't think that idea will come to anything. Seymour and his plans ...' Julian replies.

Simon wanders into another part of the barn.

'I'm just glad you don't mind with being kicked out of the farmhouse. What a hassle. Where are we all going to sleep, anyway? There aren't enough rooms. Unless you and Simon share, of course,' Julian says. He watches her react.

Maggie ignores him. Instead she kneels down to unfurl a carpet. Though its colours are faded, the twisting repeated patterns remain distinctive. 'This is cool. It would go in the sitting room.'

'There *is* something between you and Simon, isn't there?' Julian persists.

Maggie glares at the floor. Has her brother been gossiping? It would be impossible to explain her and Simon's relationship to anyone else. Sometimes they sleep together, sometimes they don't. They do not talk of love and they don't own each other. 'We're friends,' she says firmly, 'and maybe more one day.'

When Amy and David return, a trailer is fetched and everyone helps to load it up with furniture. The white leather sofa, two comfy chairs (later they saw off the legs so the seats are nearer the floor), a squashy leather pouf and a glamorous chaise longue. Plenty of places to stretch out, essential for the laid-back life they plan on. Carpets, two cupboards, a wardrobe and an extraordinary length of embroidered silk to hang on the wall. A kitchen table and chairs. Bedsteads and mattresses for three bedrooms.

When there's a semblance of order, they light the oil lamps, roll a joint and listen to *Mudlark*. It saves them having the quibble over who is going to have the single room and the single bed. Everyone knows it will be Maggie.

*

When she's taken Daisy back to the field, Amy walks on to a place she has found where the land dips into a gentle bowl. She spreads out her coat and yields to its comfort. Curled up like a comma, her ear to the ground, she listens attentively as though she might hear the earth breathing. Grass presses up to her eyes. Peeking between the blades, she pushes her gaze onwards into the dark places beyond, imagines she has shrunk so small that she can slip effortlessly between the towering columns of green to a place of quiet solace. The alarming pulse of blood thumping through her head subsides. As the evening light drops and the world exhales, her anxiety dwindles.

She thinks of Seymour. Since that night in the pub, they had little contact. Her bruised heart, craving connection, had been wakened by his kindness and attention, her spirits soothed by his support. But she was wrong, it appears, to assume this would continue. Seymour has been tied up in London, busy with friends or work. He has not visited Wyld Farm in weeks. The link, if they had one, is broken; perhaps it was never there?

She drifts back, back to her girlhood when, if she was upset by the careless treatment from a friend or a teasing gossip at school, she would seek the solace of her mother's lap. Soft as grass, her mother's lap. And Shirley would thread her fingers through her daughter's hair and run them, rhythmic as breath, to coax away the terrors and the tears.

She must do this for herself now. Rising slowly to her feet, Amy wraps her coat around her and tucks her hair into her hat. She meanders slowly back towards the farmhouse, the place where she must find the ease that she craves.

Chapter Nineteen

Mrs Morle still charges Seymour for three hours of cleaning a week. Though Julian and his friends live in the cottage, that-girl-Amy still uses the farmhouse kitchen for jam-making and beer-brewing and vegetable-freezing. Needs a thorough tidy-up, for the girl doesn't seem to notice when the sugar drips or when bottling the beer leaves rings on the table. She drifts around as though she owns the place, her long skirts hemmed in mud from the garden. She's getting loopier by the day, concludes Mrs Morle, as she stirs oatmeal into a bowl of blood; she's heard her talking to the cabbages.

Now the girl has asked the boys to relieve themselves in a tin can she's put by in the yard. Whatever next? At least she hasn't asked me to do it, thinks Mrs Morle, because I would flat refuse. It's to make a 'plant feed', the girl explained, from urine and herbs she's bought from her hero horticulturalist, a man called Henry Doubleday. Load of tosh.

For the past two weeks it's been overcast. But today a weak sun shines through Mrs Morle's windows: goodness, they need cleaning. The builder has almost finished painting the outside of Bramble Cottage. He's working with that lad with the stutter. They chat while they dip their brushes in pink-tainted orange, the colour most of the cottages round here are painted if they're bought by outsiders. Ludicrous what these fools will pay for a second home and the locals only too glad to take the money and escape to a new semi near the shops.

Tonight Mr Stratton is having a party. Mrs Morle hopes it won't be too noisy or go on too late. Lynn has to get up on Saturday and work until lunchtime even if that lot can sleep in. Mrs Morle adds spice to the blood mixture. Two piglets were slaughtered yesterday for spit-roasting over a fire for the party guests. Cream turns the mixture pink. She spoons the congealing slop into a piece of animal intestine, crams her fingers down the flabby membrane, making it bulge and stiffen like … Mrs Morle blushes. There's no one to know what she is thinking.

Blood pudding is one of Mrs Morle's favourites and even if her apron looks like she's committed a murder, it's worth it for the rich aromatic taste; like eating iron.

Yesterday there was a terrible scream. Mrs Morle had assumed it was one of the animals sensing its end was nigh. Turned out to be that girl Maggie 'meditating' in the barn where the pig man started the killing. He hadn't seen her sitting cross-legged behind a hay bale and no wonder. What was 'meditating' anyway? Mrs Morle knew it involved sitting with eyes closed ignoring life, but it obviously didn't work because Maggie spotted the piglet's demise. Making a knot in the packed intestine, Mrs Morle drops three sausage-shaped puddings into a pan of boiling water and scrubs the potatoes for supper.

*

Simon teased her that it was her bible, the book on self-sufficiency she carries around with her everywhere. It warned her that carrot seeds were the trickiest to germinate. So she must have green fingers. Over the bare brown earth, feathery fronds of green now wave. David won't be interested but she'll tell Simon at supper. He'll be pleased, too.

A pulsing hangover makes Amy grateful for the excuse to kneel. Soil-stained pages advise that the seedlings need space to grow. A whiff of carrot accompanies the careful removal of orange threads from the soil, vegetables fit for a Lilliputian's table.

Last night it happened again. Amy had gone upstairs for a pee and heard a noise from the bathroom. She found Julian slumped against the airing cupboard. When he noticed her in the doorway, he became agitated and started to mutter about fairies in the garden stealing her vegetables. She had resisted the temptation to slip away and leave him. It was all a bit tedious and, if she was honest, a bit scary.

'Sit up, Julian, are you alright?' Amy tried to pull him into an upright position. He was pale and sweaty.

Then Simon appeared in the doorway and she felt such relief. 'What's the silly s-s-sod done n-n-now?' he said.

Together they manhandled their friend upright with his legs sticking out in front. Simon draped a towel down Julian's jumper and balanced a basin on his lap.

'I think he's a little smashed,' Amy whispered.

'I think you're r-r-right,' he whispered back.

They sat companionably with Julian pinned between them. She likes chatting to Simon; about the garden, what she's thinking, anything that comes into her mind, really. He's funny, too, but you have to listen for it because he isn't bothered to claim his space in a conversation if others want to dominate. Not like the friends of Seymour or Julian who do and say loud things in loud ways. She's the same, really; unwilling to voice opinions that might sound naïve when that lot are around. And the women they bring are always glamorous or intimidating; usually both. She'd rather pad about making tea, hoping her silence suggests a deep intellect. Perhaps Simon is embarrassed of his stammer. She must insist the boys stop mocking him about it. Maggie's right; it's charming.

'When I first met David, I was just a schoolgirl starting my 'A' levels. A bit proper actually. I used to blush terribly when I first heard him swear. I wasn't used to it.'

'I've only g-g-gone out with a few w-w-women.'

'How's it going with Maggs?' A few nights ago Maggie had confided in Amy saying she still hankered for the French man Emile; exotic and strange. She wasn't sure Simon was the man for her. He was too … kind.

'She's g-g-great, you know. She just l-l-likes to have her s-s-space.'

Julian was beginning to fidget.

'If he's s-s-sick he'll feel b-b-better,' Simon said, and as though he had heard the comment, Julian began to heave. An arch of yellow and green bile splattered energetically into the bowl. The stink of vomit and alcohol filled the bathroom.

'At least he hit the target,' said Simon, opening the window.

Slithering to one slide, Julian snorted as though amused.

'Let's g-g-get you to b-b-bed.' Simon tried hauling Julian to his feet.

Amy took the other arm. 'David says that it's good for the soul to get smashed,' she said.

'I'm not so sure it's g-g-great for your b-b-brain, though,' said Simon, and between them they helped Julian to weave towards his bed.

*

I will always have a fireplace in my bedroom, Maggie decides; a fire brings romance alive. She hugs her knees, kisses each one individually, as she remembers her boyfriend's fingers strutting across her tummy and slipping down her thighs. The creak of the bed springs as their bodies flicker in the firelight.

On the walls that she'd scumbled yellow hangs a painting she found in the barn. Brooding clouds under which a man rowed a cloaked woman across a lake of mottled waters. She watches it as her boyfriend makes love to her, imagines it is she and him in that dramatic landscape, heading away towards the mountains.

Some nights she does not sleep with Simon. Life on the farm can be perplexing; the expectations, the rules she contravenes unknowingly, the currents of emotion she cannot fathom. The narrow bed and white walls of her room are her route to composure. The figurine of a Hindu god that her mother gave her this Christmas helps her meditate.

Maggie skips down the staircase. She should be helping to prepare for tonight's party. She wanders over to the farmhouse. The kitchen table has already been dragged into the field and straw bales are in a circle around an open fire over which is suspended a pole. It's been rammed through the mouths and anuses of two little pigs. She looks away. The dogs whine as the smell of roasting meat drifts around the party field.

It tantalises the taste buds of those pitching tents or shaking out sleeping bags in anticipation of inebriation reducing their competency later in the evening. Others, less concerned about their sleeping arrangements, are hoping perhaps to occupy a sofa or the floor. They sit about drinking and chatting. If Julian has slipped them a little white pill, they might already be responding to the chemicals reaching their brains. Seymour's friends, fresh from bath or bed, drift from the house clasping glasses of good wine. Some carry a cushion or a rug so they can get comfy on the ground.

When the country ballad that booms through speakers is replaced by *The Velvet Underground*, the party begins.

Few notice that the sun is setting. But Amy does. Soft light caresses the contours of the garden. She wanders between rows of vegetables. Try as she might, she is not in the mood for socialising. There are going to be people at the party – she has seen them already when she peeked from her bedroom into the yard – whom she hasn't met since her mother died. It bothers her that they won't mention Shirley's death. She is already hurt and angry about something that hasn't happened.

She had tried to explain her turmoil to David. But he had taken speed and it always made him snappy.

'Come on Ames, not now! You're being neurotic and just a bit *staid*.' He pushed her on the bed and slid his fingers into her knickers. Being 'staid' was the worse insult anyone could receive, at least in David's eyes. 'We're having a party tonight and no one wants to talk about things like that at a party now do they.'

She wiggled out from under him. Perhaps he was right; who could be miserable on such a beautiful evening?

Snappy *and* annoying. Amy watches David weave his way round groups of people they know and many they don't, making jokes and poking fun. Offending people, perhaps, and she'll feel beholden to make amends. I'll do it later, she thinks, picking up a bottle of wine, or perhaps I won't bother. I haven't seen Seymour all evening. Where is he? She wanders over to a spot where the fire's light fails to reach and decides to get quietly drunk.

'Hallo Amy. Do join me. Do you want either of these?' Gerald is sitting in the shadow propped against an upturned box. He has a bottle of whisky in one hand and a cushion in the other.

'Just the cushion, thanks. I'm drinking wine.'

She doesn't want to sit with Gerald, not when she is sober

anyway. She is never as tongue-tied with anyone else. Despite this, she settles on the cushion and makes a fuss of his dog. 'Jackson is so elegant and cool. Does he like parties?'

'He does if his master can secure sufficient drink. I was born a few drinks behind most people,' he says, swigging from the whisky bottle, 'so I have to level the playing field.'

He's told her this before.

Friends and guests flicker in the firelight like they're on stuttering celluloid.

Gerald continues: 'So how do you like living here in Seymour's hippy hideaway? Being pranksters. Are you having a good time?'

'We are, yes, it's wonderful. I want to live here for, I don't know, *forever*. In harmony with nature, close to the land, grow food, tend animals ...'

'You've become quite the country mouse. I couldn't live anywhere else either. London's fine for a day or two but ...'

'We've just got to find a way to make it work. To be fully self-sufficient. I mean, we can bake bread and brew beer but we'll ...'

'Start a little business? You wince but you could always grow, I don't know, cannabis. Seymour's got outbuildings, hasn't he? Rig up some special lighting and heat. Amy, the girlie dealer. Has a certain ring about it.'

'Business – not me? A co-operative, maybe.' She's a little drunk now. She cackles. 'I do have green fingers, though. What would Seymour think? Where is he, anyway?'

'In the house, I think. You're off to find him, are you? Just don't reveal your drug-growing plans to him. Seymour prides himself on being a renegade but he's as uptight as they come.'

A cheer goes up. She slips unnoticed past Julian and David who stagger under the weight of the pole of pigs they have lifted off the fire. They flop the charred bodies onto the table. Party guests gather round, fascinated by the spectacle of crackled skin being hacked off the roasted bodies, even those whose appetites are suppressed by chemicals. Others salivate, eager to cram the meat into their mouths.

Lynn is standing in the shadows. Spotting a space, she slips in beside David. He wields a large knife with exaggerated bravado, providing entertainment for anyone watching him carve.

'Lynn, hallo,' David grins. 'Let me give you some of this.' He pinions a piece of meat on the tip of the knife.

'The music kept me awake so reckoned I might as well see what was happening. Mother can sleep through a storm. Thanks, I will have a bit.' Lynn's eyes flutter as David slides the pork between her lips. Painted red with lipstick, the pig grease makes them shine.

Last time she'd seen David, he'd come to the office to query a charge made on some building supplies. She'd had to find the paperwork. Rifling through the filing cabinet, she watched him talking with Aaron the Oaf, as she called her boss. David was confident and relaxed; he commanded the space as if to say: I know what I want and I'll get it.

'Delicious, eh?' He offers Lynn another piece. Taking the meat in her fingers, she pushes it in her mouth, looking at him as she chews. Slowly, she licks her fingers.

The party ratchets up a level; everyone is hard at it now. No one cares that the speakers buzz or that broken glass is being ground into the grass or that night is turning into morning. People are in the mood for intoxication. They drive for the place where rules are determinedly abandoned.

Impulses judged prudent are cast aside; it would be illogical to resist temptation. It's summer, it's a party, it's beholden on people to be fun and have fun. Alcohol and stimulants make bodies ricochet and brains race. Someone dumps an armful of straw on the fading embers; the fire flares into life like the flames of passion. There's a roar and a cheer. No one notices who's doing what with whom. If one of the hosts disappears into the shadows who is there to ask what he is up to? Who cares?

Chapter Twenty

'You are the sexiest girl I've ever been about to ravage.'

Seymour's muffled voice leaked from under Amy's dress. He pooled his tongue in her belly button. She ignored the stones of the wall gouging into her back and arched herself in offering. Seymour peeled down her leggings, exposing her white thighs and the nub of her sex.

'It's chilly,' she squealed as quiet as a mouse in a trap. 'I've missed you, Seymour, I want you ...'

'I'm going to have you now, my lovely girl, I've been thinking about you all night ...'

Their love-making was frantic. It had to be. It was the day after the party and David and Julian would be returning from taking back the hired wine glasses and plates. Simon was chopping wood. The sound of his axe on wood ricocheted like gunfire round the buildings, while Maggie was, perhaps, sleeping off a hangover. They didn't care.

As is the wont of lovers in the dangerous first flush of an affair, their drive to be together overwhelmed any scruples that might linger. Thrilled they had torn time from the fabric of life, frustrated it must be brief, they were tantalised by what they had yet to discover about each other. They hurried to the safest place they could think of, the barn. With his hand clamped over her mouth to smother her cries, they fucked against the stone wall.

Amy slithered to the floor, sated. Seymour re-arranged his clothing and watched her crawl, giggling and bare-bottomed, to collapse on a pile of hay.

'Seymour! It's the phone for you!' Maggie's shout came from the house.

'I'm coming!' Winking at her over his shoulder, Seymour disappeared, leaving her weak with laughter.

This was the second time she had slept with him in one day. Last night, sneaking away from the bonfire and up to Seymour's room, she'd had the best sex she'd ever dreamed of right across the corridor from the bedroom she shared with David. What would happen if he found out? David always talked about wanting an open relationship. Now he had one. She pulled up her leggings, straightened her dress and headed for the house. It was time to make soup. It always helped her to think straight when she chopped vegetables.

*

'So help me, dearest Amy.' Julian's eyes narrow against the smoke that curls round his head. 'He'll never find it growing. He says he likes the farm but does he ever actually go around it?'

Julian was right. Seymour sometimes asked Amy what she was growing in the garden. He praised her for the vegetables and fruits she produced for the table. Complimented her on the delicate aroma of early broad beans, the delight of dousing artichoke leaves in melted butter and scraping off the tender flesh, the joy of nibbling new potatoes cooked with mint. But how often did he walk along the rows of beetroot and spinach, cabbages and carrots that she hoed and weeded? Once he started to help her pick the runner beans that dangled so profusely from the trellis that it had partially collapsed. But then the phone rang and he slipped away.

He was very unlikely to visit her greenhouse though the warm air, laden with the intoxicating scent of ripening melon would have enthralled him. Why would he ever suspect *cannabis sativa* plants might be growing there, too?

Seymour would not be happy about Julian growing grass, of that she was sure. Occasionally he mentioned a concern about the amount of dope his son was smoking. Once he said that having the four of them living at the farmhouse meant Julian was less likely to get out of his head. Clearly Seymour was unaware of what they all got up to. Amy felt their presence fuelled Julian's habits.

That afternoon, Amy and Julian pressed seeds into little pots of soil and set them at the back of the greenhouse. Something in her hopes they will not germinate. But within weeks, delicate serrated leaves appear and the marijuana starts to grow.

*

The steel cord attaching the metal box to the tractor snaps. The fastening whips through the air with a hiss like a snake under attack. Twisting past Simon's eye, the metal bolt slices into his curved brow. A fine line of red blooms; the scar gives him a rakish look, Maggie later teases him.

They are collecting hay bales from the top field. David is chucking them onto the trailer while Maggie and Amy struggle to lift and stack them. It is back-breaking work; the bale strings cut into fingers and the dried grass slices uncovered skin. But it's glorious to be out on the Common where the air is fresh and the view is of green and gold patchwork fields that slope down to the coast. Until Simon's holler of pain shatters the peace.

'What's happened?' Blood is pouring down Simon's cheeks. 'Oh my God, it's not your eye, is it?' Maggie cries out.

Jumping up onto the tractor footplate, she begins to dab his face with her skirt.

'Be careful …' Simon's voice is muffled by her ministrations.

'Here, use this!' Amy hands over her scarf.

It had been chosen carefully this morning to complete the 'peasant girl' look Amy was after. The long skirt, the lace of a petticoat peeking out at the hem, the knotted shirt revealing just a flash of belly, the little boots. Amy studied herself in the mirror knowing Seymour will like it. He is expected back around tea time having been in London with Julian buying food he said was not available locally; fresh coffee beans, mozzarella, spices and virgin olive oil. David suggested cynically that the real reason was neither man could face the hard work involved in bringing in the hay. Amy said he was being mean. She wondered if he was right.

'I think it's only a deep cut. Thank God, he could have been *blinded*! The wire wasn't fastened on properly. Was it you that fucked up?' Maggie looks at her brother accusingly.

'I'm f-f-fine, honestly.'

David says bullishly: 'He's alright, isn't he?'

'But it might have been worse. You have to be careful around machinery, you fool.'

'Okay, okay. Don't worry about what *might* have been, dear sister. Be 'in the moment'. Isn't that what your guru teaches?'

'Don't patronise me,' she hurls back.

'Calm down, big Maggs. Why not do something more useful like fetch a plaster or something? Simon, you alright, man? Do you want me to take over?'

'No, I'm c-c-cool. I'll d-d-drive this load b-b-back to the barn.'

'Honestly, Simon, I don't know why you're not furious with that git.' Maggie glares at David as she and Simon whirr past.

Amy and David follow behind on foot.

‘It’s Seymour’s crap machinery that’s the problem,’ David says. He passes her a joint. ‘Try this, babe. Gerald brought it over the other day. It’s amazing grass, get you high as the hills.’

‘Perhaps you didn’t secure the fitting properly. You … you weren’t smoking this morning, were you?’

‘Oh for fuck’s sake, Amy, you sound so po-faced. You sticking up for Seymour again?’ he snaps.

‘Why are you always getting smashed?’ she retaliates.

In the distance, Andrew Bishop is on a tractor winnowing the cut grass in another of Seymour’s fields. Turning it over speeds up drying, he explained. His family had farmed in this valley for three generations. His father, Michael, bought land from Seymour when he wanted rid of a marshy field. Mr Bishop had never met a man who preferred owning a sports car to land. But London people were a strange breed. Once drained, the land provided fine grazing while Seymour’s metal possession disintegrated in the yard. Michael will hire out his son’s services if Mr Stratton will pay. The cash will buy a new concrete floor for the pig pen.

David insists the bales are left to be unloaded the next day. ‘You should rest, mate, after your accident. Let’s have a smoke. Come on, back to the farmhouse.’

‘Clean the cut for him!’ Maggie shouts as they leave. She turns to Amy. ‘How can you stand living with David? He’s selfish and lazy and never takes responsibility for anything that doesn’t suit him.’

‘He was really worried about Simon. He just felt a bit defensive,’ she says.

‘I’m not sure he cares that much. Or, frankly, sees what’s going on right under his nose.’ Maggie stares at her. ‘Just as well, eh?’

*

If only Eleanor had come with him. Seymour assured her that 'the hippies', as she called them, would not be hogging the bathroom or spread-eagling themselves across the sofas. For they lived *across the yard in the cottage*, he emphasised. He didn't mention Julian was still in the farmhouse. He couldn't force his son to live in that crowded little cottage.

But Eleanor refused. If she was there Seymour would not galvanise himself to have 'the conversation' that needed to be had with 'the scroungers'. Eleanor could be forthright, cruel sometimes, but she had a point. If Julian's friends dreamed of living off the land, let them go and try it for themselves without the 'shield of Stratton'. Did they not realise that the 60s were long gone?

Less necessary was her quip that having them around allowed Seymour to indulge a fantasy that he was their age. Cruel of her to reiterate the difference in years.

Perhaps she was right. Jars of jam lining the larder shelves and the freezer packed to the hilt with frozen beans sealed with the suburban twist were domestic signs he could tolerate. But when he found his records filed in alphabetical order that was different. Seymour disapproved of disapproval, of course, but order – or more precisely – *someone else's order* – was not the way he wanted to live. Julian's pals needed to move along.

Now the cottage was habitable, Bob was free to take on the next job; building a darkroom for Seymour, a space where he could work in peace. Then perhaps he'd think about improvements to the farmhouse. Eleanor might be persuaded to visit more often if the place was tarted up.

Seymour opens a bottle of red wine and pours himself a glass. He puts on a live Randy Newman album to help him think. He'll have to let Amy down, of course: he'll be gentle. Perhaps it had been wrong of him to start sleeping with her? But the girl had had such a difficult time, losing her mother and so on, and his attentions seemed to help. She said it was comforting to talk to him. He couldn't imagine why. What the young failed to realise is that everyone makes mistakes; age simply provides experience in covering them up.

Despite her rose-tinted chatter about creating a new society, he likes Amy and is obsessed with her body. But he has felt this way about other women he has had to 'bid farewell' to. From long experience he knows the feelings pass.

It will feel uncharacteristic but he will talk about *money*. He is a man of magnanimity and generous impulse, not an accountant. But penury will be his excuse. He'll tell Julian's four friends that that he needs to rent the cottage out in order to raise cash. Sorry and all that, but they'll have to find somewhere else to live.

At seven o'clock, Amy appears in the kitchen. She has dressed carefully. She wears David's white shirt over tight jeans and clogs she's painted silver. Her hair is pinned up high; a few pale strands trail her neck. She feels good. She's missed her lover. She brushes his lips with her fingers as she wafts past. They're alone. Everyone else is in the cottage getting smashed.

'You're glamorous,' he says, 'and just so you can cook supper. I'm flattered. Wine?'

'Yes, thanks. You know everything we're eating tonight was grown here,' she says with pride. 'Spinach and Daisy-cheese pie with tomatoes, then berries and yoghurt for pudding. I think more and more people will want to live together communally to buy and grow their own food, don't you?'

'I don't know, sounds a bit unlikely to me. Anyway, the grapes in the wine – they aren't ours – though if what those climate scaremongers say is right, soon I can have my own vineyard ...'

'... and I'll squish the grapes between my thighs,' she says suggestively.

She's hard to resist. 'You're so sweet,' he replies, licking her ear, 'and you make a very good housekeeper.'

She ignores the remark.

When she opens the oven door, the warm air lifts the hair off her face. He sees she's troubled.

'My father wants me home for his birthday next month. He's even sent money for the train fare. I don't want to go. I'm dreading it.'

He's seen this sudden switch in mood before. It's baffling how can she be cheery one minute and grim the next, but of course, she is young. 'Your father hasn't seen you in a while. I'm sure he's missing you,' Seymour says.

'He's got the lovely Vi, hasn't he?' she replies grimly.

Maggie comes into the kitchen with a handful of wildflowers. Simon follows behind.

'Hi Seymour,' they beam, and begin to set the table and light the candles.

Then David arrives with a bottle of wine that Seymour knows is sold in the village shop and will no doubt see charged to his account.

'Great to see you, man,' David says, clapping him on the arm. 'Good time in London?'

'Something smells good.' Julian slips into a seat at the table.

Dishes of food are passed around and they eat and talk. They're charming and clever kids, thinks Seymour. The stuttering Simon, the languid David and the lovely girls, the candlelight bouncing off their shiny faces. He's going to feel mean kicking them off the farm. The wine mellows his determination. He'll do it in stages, let them down gently. He'll start by suggesting they need to find jobs.

But not tonight. Right now, he's wondering if he'd be able to slip away with Amy. Her boyfriend looks particularly dopey. If David starts playing guitar, which he does interminably, it might just be possible to go to the barn for what could be called a *digestif*.

Chapter Twenty-One

Next morning, Seymour goes out and returns several hours later towing behind the Land Rover a 1920s ringmaster's wagon, the kind once used by travelling circus performers. He'd seen an advertisement in the paper. Wood-panelled walls, fitted cupboards, cut-glass mirrors, a wood-burning stove and a snug double bed, the caravan would make a quirky place for guests to stay.

David, Amy, Simon and Maggie are woken by the sound of a vehicle in the cottage's back garden. They emerge from the cottage bleary-eyed.

'Afternoon!' Seymour says. 'Beautiful thing, isn't it? I couldn't resist buying it.'

At the same time, Julian appears. 'Hi Dad. Where did you slip off to this morning? Hey, that's cool.' He nods at the wagon.

'I'm glad you're here, too. Let's get a cup of tea. We need to talk.'

He looks shifty, Maggie thinks, and not only because he's wearing that Rod Stewart *Every Picture Tells A Story* t-shirt. Does the man not know he looks ridiculous?

They crowd into the cottage kitchen.

'Now that the work here is finished, there are a few changes needed at Wyld Farm.'

It was out of character for Seymour to sound so serious. David stops stirring his tea. 'Really? What do you mean? Why?'

'Things aren't going so well for me at the moment. A bit tough. I haven't mentioned this but … I'm not able to fund everything anymore. It's time we talked about work. You lot need to find employment, get jobs. Make a contribution, I suppose.'

It's bizarre. Seymour never talked about money. 'Alright. Of course we can try. It might be tricky …' Amy ventures.

But Julian blurts: 'God, Dad! I can't believe you're being so heavy. My friends have been doing the right thing here. This is a bit out of the blue.'

'Yes, of course, and I'm grateful for what you've all done. But the cottage is finished now. I'm thinking about the future.'

'The future? What's this about, Dad? Has Eleanor put you up to it?'

'It's nothing to do with her, Julian. It doesn't seem unreasonable for you and your friends …'

'Oh doesn't it? Well I don't agree. We've been doing what you wanted. And suddenly you just announce it's all got to change. I'm not staying here to listen to this nonsense, I'm going to Gerald's. Anyone coming with me?'

Seymour says: 'Don't go over there, Julian.'

'I can't talk to you when you're like this! You're impossible.' He bowls out of the cottage; they hear a car driving off.

Seymour looks at the four of them and shrugs. 'That's how it's got to be.'

The rest of the day is peculiar. They sit by the unlit fire in the cottage; no one can be bothered to chop wood. Amy offers to heat up some leftover soup, but no one is hungry. When David starts to play the guitar, Maggie barks at him to stop. A bit later, someone suggests they go for a walk. As they cross the yard, Seymour is getting into his car.

'I'm going back to London,' he says, shutting the door.

Amy fights the impulse to stand in front of the car to stop him. Seymour needs her. What's he's hiding?

*

It was a perfect job. Near enough to cycle on the old-bone shaker and only part-time so home by mid-afternoon. Cruel start to the day, though. She has to be at the stables by 7am.

Maggie lies against the sun-warmed bricks and rolls a surreptitious cigarette. Malcolm, the 'head groom' as he calls himself – though why she couldn't imagine for she is the only other person working at the animal sanctuary – told her smoking was forbidden. A fire risk with the straw and hay.

Slipping the burnt match into her jeans, she draws the smoke down deep. The work is tough, but the animals are brilliant: six horses, four ponies and Donny the donkey, grumpy as a hornet but appreciative when his scarred ears were scratched.

Malcolm has really come down in the horsey world. You have to feel sorry for him. Two years ago he'd been working as a groom in a big racing stables somewhere near Newmarket. A fall from a skittish young stallion out 'on the gallops', his foot caught in the stirrup. Malcolm got dragged along the ground. The accident left him with concussion, a smashed pelvis and a leg broken in three places. He spent six months in hospital on his back, his plastered leg held up in a hoist.

There was fun to be had flirting with the nurses, he leered, alluding to kisses stolen on the night shift while the Sister wasn't watching. But lying flat had stopped his 'bowels moving'. Not until the day he was hauled to his feet by two strapping auxiliaries did things 'start to move'. Maggie gagged on the graphic detail he provided. Malcolm couldn't be more than twenty-eight years old.

With a lurching limp, his dreams of being a jockey were smashed.

The sun broke over the roof of the barn opposite; the dazzling light made Maggie's eyes pinch. One more minute in the rays and she'll get on with the routine. Watering the animals, mucking out the stables, sweeping the yard. It is easy in fine weather, horrible when it pours. She is learning stuff, too. Now the spring grass is growing, the horses and ponies have been 'turned out' in the fields. (That was the lingo, Malcolm told her. Turned out meant the animals lived outside all the time). All except Kelpie. The pony has to be brought into the stable during the day.

'Why, Malcolm? It seems a bit unfair. It's the summer and he'll be lonely without the others,' she complained.

'But he'll get laminitis, what you'd call sore feet,' explained Malcolm dismissively. 'On summer grass, that pony gets too fat.'

'And he'll limp like you!' she joked. Malcolm didn't laugh.

Maggie applied for the job. Seymour's outburst was a bit of a hoot and anyway, she was sick of being short of cash and it might be a way to meet some new people. When the man called to tell her she'd got it, said she was lucky, given her lack of experience, that she'd beaten the other candidates, she wondered if there were any. Still, nice to know she succeeded at something.

Carefully stubbing out her roll-up on the concrete, Maggie heads into the field with a halter. Kelpie was easy to catch if you offered him a treat. You just had to be careful of the other animals, especially that greedy horse, Dart.

*

It was a terrible shock. Any shred of respect that remained for Seymour Stratton vanished when Mrs Morle found the letter. It said the cleaning job she had done for the last fifteen years was finished. Seymour could no longer afford to pay her; Amy was going to be the housekeeper. Mrs Morle had done him proud, he wrote, he was sorry, he wrote, but it was over.

Mrs Morle flung the note across the sitting room; it hit the wall and slipped behind the settee. She wouldn't cry, not because of him. Him in his fancy car with his fancy friends, buying that ridiculous gypsy caravan, having all those parties for all those people. He could afford to pay for his house to be cleaned. He just didn't want her anymore.

*

'I didn't think Seymour was such a bread head,' says David, 'He can't make me get a job. I'm signing on. I need time to write music.'

So when David's giro arrives each week, Amy cashes it at the post office when she's doing the weekly shop. He also put a card up in the village shop offering guitar lessons. Now every Saturday he teaches a local school boy how to play. Simon has shifts in the pub and is doing up Seymour's wagon. Julian works on his father's Morgan. There is talk of selling the car for a great deal of money.

Amy is the housekeeper. Now she cleans the farmhouse as well as doing the washing and cooking. Sometimes she envies Maggie the chance to leave the house, even if her friend assures her that Malcolm and the animal sanctuary visitors are of limited appeal.

But at least being in the farmhouse gives her time to moon to music perfect for her mood; Carole King's *Tapestry*. Loose-limbed, powered by the sexual energy Seymour has ignited in her, she dances as she dusts, relishing what they've found in each other. One day there will be all the time in the world to linger with their limbs linked. Until then they must be cautious.

She's not cheating on David; they are exploring different ways of living and soon she will tell him about her lover. As Seymour says, no one should be hidebound by convention. That's why last weekend, Seymour came down with Eleanor. The woman sashayed into the house like a queen while she, Amy, dragged the washing off the line. Soon, Amy thought, folding the pillow cases, everyone will know the truth. Although Seymour has never said it in so many words, he too longs for the time they will live together openly. They just have to wait for the right moment.

Last Saturday, he propelled her into his bedroom as soon as David left the house to give a guitar lesson. He made love to her frantically.

'I love having you right *here*,' he panted.

It was obvious what he meant.

Chapter Twenty-Two

'It's good to see you, love,' says Amy's father from the driver's seat. John's come to meet her off the train. He pushes open the passenger door and she slides inside.

Amy has felt uneasy all morning, as though something terrible is about to happen. The car draws up outside the house where she grew up. The street looks subtly different although when she glances up and down, she cannot see anything has changed. She feels she's being watched and, from the corner of her eye, glimpses a face hiding in the hedge of the house next door. But on closer inspection, the face disappears. Perhaps it was only a leaf glinting in the sun. Grabbing her bag off the back seat of the car, Amy hurries to the front door.

The hall is dark and pinched as though the light has been sucked out. She feels apprehensive, that she must run away. But her father is right behind her, closes the front door with a click. The sound reassures her somehow that it is safe for her to walk into the kitchen. Her father begins to collect cups and saucers for tea; the rattle of china hurts her ears.

'So how are you?'

He pours milk into the jug her mother always used. He did not appear to notice that the floral pattern on the china has begun to twist and grow over his fingers. *Them's cornflowers, campions and ivy*, says Mrs Morle. Her voice has been churning around

Amy's head since she woke at dawn. It's annoying, sometimes frightening, but it won't stop.

'You haven't forgotten it's my birthday?' her father says lightly, but he sounds concerned.

'Course not, Dad.'

She digs in her bag for the card she'd bought in a rush at the railway station and hands it to him. There is the dirt etched like spider's webs on her hands. She carries the farm with her.

'And I made this for you.'

She pushes something wrapped in brown paper and decorated with coloured dots to make it pretty. It's a jar of pickled onions, his favourite.

'Thank you, love. I'll open these later. Vi's coming over here to celebrate. We'll open a bottle of wine, perhaps. That's alright with you, isn't it?'

It is not a request. The tea scalds her throat.

'I've got some news, Amy, and I hope you'll be happy for me.'

She stares fiercely, willing him to stop speaking.

'I didn't want to tell you on the phone.'

Nervously he fingers the envelope she gave him.

'I've asked Vi to marry me and she's accepted. We're engaged. To be married. Maybe next year, I don't know when exactly.'

The words, proud and solid, hit her one by one like physical blows. Her throat constricts. His mouth is moving, producing words and phrases that she only half-registers. Something about there not being bridesmaids, a ceremony 'in a register office but it will be nice'.

'But it's hardly a *year* since Mum died, Dad. How can you forget her so quickly, fall in love with someone else and get married? It's … it's wrong.'

'Why can you not be happy for me?' he replies hotly.

'How could you?'

Choosing each word carefully, searching as though if only he could find the perfect one to fit, he would make her understand, he says: 'I have not forgotten your mother, not at all, Amy. But what you do not know, can't know, is how terribly lonely I have been without your mother.'

'How can you talk such rubbish?' she roars back. 'Don't spoil everything. Mum loved you. That should be enough. There were the three of us, our family and that's just the way it should stay.'

Her father shakes his head. He tears at the envelope and opens the birthday card. A picture of a fried egg and across the yellow yolk are written the words, 'Dad, you're a good egg.'

'You don't understand,' he says quietly.

Her lips buzz like they've been stung by a thousand bees. The room, once blurry round the edges, comes into such sharp focus that she jumps.

'You don't know what you're talking about,' he repeats dully, his face in his hands.

Amy begins to hum fiercely. Outside the window, she senses the world has not stopped. A car drives by and a skipping child flashes by the window. Through her finger-clamped ears, her father is talking.

Amy lurches from the room. She runs upstairs, flings herself on to the bed and screams into the pillow.

*

Lynn has finished the milking. She takes the pail of milk to cool on the larder shelf. She likes being in the farmhouse. Amy asked her to do the milking. The cow is awkward, Amy explained, won't let down her milk for a man.

'Don't blame her, men are all fingers and thumbs. I'll do it for you,' Lynn had said. 'She'll get mastitis if it's not done proper. Then you'll need a visit from the vet and that costs a bomb. Mr Stratton won't like that, will he? Not on his economy drive.'

Lynn heard someone moving about behind the half-open door of the sitting room. Some might think it inappropriate for her to have peeked inside. She did not. And if the person in the room asked Lynn to come and join him, what earthly reason would there be for her to refuse? Music, wine and a little conversation are ways to fill a lonely evening. Some might ask why Lynn was in the farmhouse for so long, returning to the cottage long after her mother, assuming her daughter was asleep upstairs, turned out the cottage lights. But who was there to ask?

Chapter Twenty-Three

Amy counts again on her fingers. The bleeding should have started five days ago. She winds the mechanism on her jewellery box; the ballerina pirouettes but the music does not play. She will call Seymour after 6pm when calls are cheaper and before her father returns from work. She wonders what Seymour will say.

*

The assistant drops the light diffuser umbrella and picks up the ringing phone. 'Reception says it's Naresh Rao for you on line two,' he says.

Seymour points to the sleeve of the model's jumper. 'It's in shadow,' he hisses, then beams at the model. 'Give me a mo', darling, I must take this call. Don't move, you're looking wonderful. Hallo, Naresh. How are you? Yes, in the middle of this and that. Sunil passed his exams? That's fantastic news.' He winks at the model. 'Naresh, I have a friend with a law practice in Norwich. Not talked to him in a while but I'm sure he can help, perhaps get Sunil articles in his practice. I'll call him later, alright? Good. No hassle. Now, sorry about that, love. Turn to the camera. Smile …'

*

Dart pulled tourists in a carriage around Bath for years. But when the black gelding could no longer manage the hills, his owner abandoned him. The half-starved horse was found by the RSPCA. It took almost a year at the animal sanctuary for Dart's belly to round and the sores from the ill-fitting harness to heal. His mood, however, remained unpredictable. If another animal was offered a treat, the horse became envious.

So when he sees Kelpie being given a carrot, he retaliates. His kick lands with such a thump that the human holding the treat is flung backwards. The horse rears up, remembering from his past that aggression such as this is followed by a lash.

His front hoof catches the human, even as it is falling. The crack of a bone, the body twisting as it falls. A whimper. The human lies without moving.

Dart gallops away down the field.

*

When the shop manager calls to say the parts are ready for collection, Simon and Julian drive into town to pick them up. As they walk back to the car, Simon says: 'You're l-l-low Julian, what's up?'

'It's Seymour. It freaked me out the other night, him talking to you all like that. I can't work out what's eating him. My father does my head in. Let's not go back just yet, man. Cool?'

Simon has rarely heard Julian criticise his father. He follows him into a shop. 'It was a bit w-w-weird, him saying all that. L-L-L-ike we'd done something *w-w-wrong.*'

'He's uptight, that's all.'

Julian greets the man behind the counter by name, then charges a packet of Rizla papers, crisps and chocolate to his father's account. Simon wonders if Seymour minds.

'Bye Mr Rao, nice to see you again,' Julian says as they leave. 'My father needs to get himself together, work out what he *wants.*'

A short distance down the canal path, they see the gang. Boys with shaved heads and heavy boots clustered like flies on rotting flesh around a person who they are thrusting between them. Julian recognises Sunil Rao, the shop owner's twenty-year-old son. Hemmed in between the canal and the bank, the young man is trapped. His cry for help is smothered when one of the skinheads leaps on his head. He crumples to the ground. The gang screech triumphantly.

'We've got to help him!' Simon shouts and hurtles down the path. He is not aware that Julian is hanging back.

Gravel ricochets off the path as the gang's boots thud into the victim's body. As Simon approaches they scatter briefly and Sunil, taking his chance, scrambles up onto the bank and vanishes into the undergrowth.

The skinheads see Simon is alone. Fanning out across the canal path, they form a wall of flesh and start to move towards him. He isn't aware that Julian is watching from a distance.

'What's your problem, mate?' calls a skinhead who moves to the front like a general with his troops. 'What you looking for? Your darkie friend? Scarpered off, has he? Like your other friend wants to do.'

The boy grins without smiling. He's so close Simon can see every spot on his face.

'I j-j-just wanted you to stop b-b-beating up that b-b-boy,' says Simon.

'Coo, don't he speak posh! But he can't say nuffing r-r-right,' mocks a tall boy with narrow eyes. 'What's your problem? Gotta s-s-stammer, have ya?"

The boys skirt around Simon, blocking his escape.

When a woman starts walking her dog down the canal, she sees what is happening, whistles for her animal and disappears.

A bird lands clumsily on the verge. A boy lashes out with his boot; the bird flaps away, indifferent and lazy, and settles a little farther away. A cloud passes over the sun.

Simon says: 'Get out of my way, p-p-please.'

The boys are fifteen or sixteen years old, one gangly from a growth spurt; the rest retain remnants of boyhood. Their fathers could probably make them cry but here the boys bounce with bravado.

'I sees you going into that Paki's shop. You got a big motor, ain't ya? Giss the keys then.'

The tall boy grabs Simon's sleeve with one hand and thrusts out the other. Tattoos decorate his knuckles.

'Leave him alone!' Julian's voice is faint.

'Come on, h-h-hippy boy. Your boyfriend over there ain't going to defend you. Your wimpy f-f-friend is leaving you to us.' He stamps fiercely and hoots when Simon jumps.

There's ringing in Simon's ears. Everything is slowing down.

'I'm taking the keys, mate. I'm finding them for meself and you can't stop me.'

'Get off me!' Three boys pin Simon's arms to his body while a fourth digs in his pockets, thudding his boots into his shins as he does. Simon grunts with pain.

The fifth boy jigs about on tiptoes taking dainty dashes like a nervous ballerina rehearsing her entry.

The leader crows: 'We're going to get your motor, mate … Got 'em!' He dangles the keys above his head.

A yowl of triumph.

Almost as an afterthought, the spotty boy smacks Simon in the face. Blood sprays from his nose. Simon keels slowly backwards.

He sees Julian hovering near the canal entrance, an inhaler clamped to his mouth, before canal water closes over his head.

Screaming, the skinheads race past Julian and shove him spiraling backwards into the undergrowth.

By the time he's struggled to his feet, Simon is clinging to the canal edge.

'Fuck, fuck,' he groans, spitting out green slime and blood. 'They're g-g-going to n-n-nick the Land Rover. What's Seymour g-g-going to say, oh C-C-Christ …'

'Who fucking cares?' Julian gasps.

Saliva pours into his mouth. The last time he witnessed overt violence like this was in the psychiatric hospital where he spent a month in the last term of university. A patient flipped out when someone used his towel and attacked one of the nurses. He has never told his friends about the problems he faces; his mental health is private.

Julian's body has gone into overdrive. Sweaty and faint, he can only think of running away but anxiety makes him weak. The canal, once a verdant place of peace, has become terrifying.

'I've got to get away,' he whispers, 'please help me.'

Both he and Simon are panting.

'Okay Julian, we're safe. They've g-g-gone. C-C-Can you walk?'

They stumble towards where they parked the Land Rover. No sign of the boys. Then they see the vehicle and by it Naresh waving what looks to be a set of keys.

Next to him are two policemen.

Like a shot, Julian takes off across the green. Fear fuels his feet. The policemen, perhaps suspecting the fleeing figure is one of the skinheads, give chase. They split up, driving the suspected criminal towards a cul-de-sac.

Julian doesn't spot the trap. Hemmed in by houses and neat

front gardens, he's cornered. He becomes hysterical, gasping for breath, mucus bubbling from his mouth. When he won't respond to the policemen's request for identification, they search his pockets. They find a small piece of hashish wrapped in silver paper.

Simon watches his friend being marched back across the green and bundled into a police car. His last glimpse of Julian is of his white terrified face.

The shopkeeper tugs at his arm. 'We must call Seymour.'

'I don't have his number …'

'Come with me,' says Naresh.

*

On the train to London, her period starts. Amy feels both relief and disappointment when she sees the blood in her knickers. Last night, she'd been unable to reach Seymour on the phone. After trying his studio number and finding it engaged, her father arrived home from work. Half an hour later when John left to meet his fiancé for a drink, Amy tried again, but no one answered.

Amy fetches a sanitary towel from her suitcase and sorts herself out, stuffing the bloodied pants in the bin. She'd slept poorly, alternatively fretting about pregnancy and fantasising about motherhood and life with Seymour. Leaning against the carriage window, she falls asleep clutching the scrap of paper on which is written the address of Seymour's studio that the helpful woman from Directory Enquiries gave her.

*

It takes Malcolm back to see nurses rushing about the ward in their white caps and sensible shoes. He is shown into the day room of the ward; the nurse says he can see 'his wife' once she's settled in bed.

'She's not my wife,' he replies, but the nurse has gone. It was an odd morning, finding Maggie lying unconscious in the field with a bloodied slash across her jaw and her eye all puffed up. He called the ambulance. By the time it arrived, the lower part of her face had swelled too; she didn't look pretty anymore.

He slipped into the back of the ambulance so got a free ride to the hospital. Though the girl seemed to regain consciousness, she was babbling nonsense. He didn't bother to ask her if there was anyone he should phone, the nurses would find out soon enough. You have to take the rough with the smooth when you work with horses, he thought. Accidents happen. Perhaps the tea trolley will be around soon, he could do with a cup.

*

Julian tries to recall what the nurses taught him in hospital; to release his breath as slowly as possible as a way of controlling panic. He knows it helps as it has done before. As long as he can keep his eyes closed, he won't see the holding cell into which the custody sergeant marched him.

It's not the emptiness of the room, cold and smelling of disinfectant or the bars on the high window which makes his stomach clench; it's knowing that the door of the room is locked. A locked door reminds him of the secure wing of the psychiatric hospital where he spent one long, traumatic and terrifying week. He buries his head in his arms.

Hanging onto every atom of the air for as long as he possibly can, he exhales. Simon will find a way to contact Seymour, to contact Seymour, to contact Seymour, he repeats.

*

David is bundled up in a coat and wears fingerless gloves. The sun warms the farmhouse steps where he's sitting, strumming his guitar. He's feeling good. The song he's been tussling with for ages finally works. The lyrics will need changing but that's fine. The phone rings. There is no way he's going to answer it. He is focused on work, just as Seymour directed.

*

The stairwell smells of incense. Amy climbs two floors. An engraved sign on a metal-studded bright red door says *Seymour Stratton, Photographer.* Someone from an office or flat above rushes past; their footsteps crescendo, then fade. For a moment, Amy waits, not daring to knock. She is in half a mind to leave; will he mind her turning up unannounced?

But she cannot resist the chance to see him. To tell Seymour everything: about her father's planned marriage, the whole terrible business. He will understand. She knocks on the door. Her knuckles make no impression on the shiny surface. She presses on the buzzer.

'Who is it?' says a voice she recognises but cannot place. Other voices, too.

'Who is it?' the woman says again and Amy realises it is Eleanor.

The door flies opens. Amy steps aside as a tall girl with a high-cut fringe and an orange coat bowls by. 'Go on in,' she says, dipping her head, and runs lightly down the stairs.

Low-slung grey sofas and tubular chairs in bright colours cluster around a glass table. A lamp like a long-necked insect arches from one corner to hang over a tower of shiny magazines. Amy sees

Eleanor slip through a gap between two partition walls. Displayed on it are black and white fashion photographs. And a huge portrait of Seymour.

When Eleanor appears in a different doorway and sees Amy, her expression turns chilly.

'Amy! It's you. What a surprise.' She does not sound surprised; she sounds annoyed.

Amy nods.

'Is Seymour expecting you? He's in the middle of a shoot.'

A woman's voice rises over the partition wall. 'Phone call for Seymour, Eleanor.'

'Who is it?' Eleanor replies sharply. She examines Amy coldly, up and down, moving only her eyes.

'The man wouldn't give his name, says it's private,' calls the woman, 'says he must talk directly to Mr Stratton.'

'Let me take it.'

'You can try,' says the woman, sounding exasperated. 'I'll put the call through on line two'.

Eleanor turns away. 'Wait here,' she says over her shoulder.

Amy is desperate to pee. When a girl rushes past, Amy taps her on the arm and asks where the loo is. The girl indicates with a flick of green-painted nails at the gap through which Eleanor went.

Amy follows a corridor past filing cabinets, girls at desks and racks of equipment. Eleanor is stretched out on a white leather recliner talking on the phone. She does not notice Amy tiptoeing past. On the other side of the vast studio, a girl stands under brilliant lights. Several people dressed in black fuss around her. Seymour is bent over a camera on a tripod.

'Seymour! Sorry, darling but you have to take this call, he won't talk to me!' barks Eleanor.

As Amy slides into a bathroom, she sees Seymour shake his shoulders in annoyance.

✷

David looks up. A police car is pulling into the front yard. He stands, then sits down.

'Is this the property of Mr Seymour Stratton?' says one of the three policemen getting out of the car.

'It is,' replies David strumming a chord, 'but Mr Stratton is not here.'

'We have a warrant to search the property,' says a second policemen. 'Is there anyone else living here at present?'

For the next hour, two policeman search the farmhouse, cottage and outbuildings. A third man stands near David; it's unnerving that the policeman looks the same age as him.

He is cold. When the phone rings, David does not move.

'Aren't you going to answer that?' asks the policeman.

The phone stops ringing, then starts again almost immediately.

'Is there someone you *don't* want to talk to?'

'No, not at all.' David jumps up guiltily. As nonchalantly as he can, he walks to the office followed by the policeman. 'Hallo?'

'Hallo. Am I speaking to David Bond?'

'Yes, it's me. Who's this, please?'

'This is Sister Sarah, from the hospital. It's about Margaret Bond who is your sister, I understand?'

'Yes, she is. Why, what's happened?'

'Your sister was involved in an accident this morning. A horse kicked her in the face. She's been to X-ray and now she's in my ward with concussion and a badly-fractured jaw. She's comfortable, not quite awake yet but coming round. You can visit tomorrow afternoon between two and four o'clock.'

'I see. Oh my God, this is an awful shock … You say she's alright? I must phone our mother. What ward number is it? Please send Maggie my love. Say I'll call Mum and I'll be in to see her tomorrow.'

When David comes off the phone, he sees the policeman has been listening.

'It's my sister,' he says. 'She was kicked by a horse and is in hospital with a broken jaw.'

The policeman grimaces. 'I've got a sister. Wouldn't like that to happen to mine. Bit of a tricky day for you, all in all, eh?'

It is fortunate that one of the policeman searching the property has a fondness for dogs. Seeing Molly in a pen with her pups distracts him. When his superior calls the team together, the sergeant does not admit he has not completed his part of the search. The marijuana plants growing among the tomato and cucumbers in the greenhouse remain undiscovered.

*

'Hallo?' says Seymour.

He hopes he does not sound as irritated as he feels. He didn't want to do this low-rent catalogue job in the first place. Photographing leisurewear on second-grade models was not how he wanted to spend his time. But increasingly few design departments had the big budgets required for major fashion shoots these days. He wanted the job finished by mid-afternoon. Which was not going to happen if he was constantly disturbed.

'Seymour, hallo. It's Naresh.'

'Naresh? Oh, hi man. I haven't had time today to call my lawyer friend, I'm busy doing –'

Naresh interrupted: 'I'm not calling about Sunil. It's about Julian.' Naresh speaks in a measured way. 'He's been arrested. His friend Simon and I saw him being taken away by the police. And Simon was beaten up. He's here with me at the shop.'

'What? What?' Seymour stares at the receiver in his hand. 'Hold on a minute, please.'

Eleanor, hearing the tone of his response, is moving towards Seymour. He stalls her with a raised hand.

'Eleanor, I have to leave for Somerset immediately. I'll tell you everything later.'

He heads off her question as she opens her mouth. 'No questions. Stay here. Help Andrew complete the shoot.'

He nods at one of the young men dressed in black, who stands up a little straighter.

'The shot list is planned, the models are booked. This project must be finished today. Andrew and Eleanor will see that it is. Now excuse me.'

That's when he sees Amy on the far side of his studio. He shakes his head in frank disbelief, dips into a side room and shuts the door firmly behind him.

'Hi Naresh, I'm back. Listen, can you or Simon get down to the police station? We need to get a message to Julian. Tell him my lawyer will be there as soon as possible. Until then, Julian should say *nothing* to anyone. Assure Julian that I'm on my way. And thank you. I won't forget this, Naresh. '

Seymour leaves a message for his lawyer. Then he gathers his jacket and car keys and leaves the studio.

Amy is pressed against the sofa as though she might melt into it.

Eleanor glowers over her. 'You never answered me, Amy. Why are you here?'

'Getting a ride back to the farm,' she says, jumping up and piling down the stairs after Seymour.

CHAPTER TWENTY-FOUR

Her favourite female singer is on the radio. Melanie's girlie voice is celebrating roller skates and her quirky song fills the car as Seymour edges it though the traffic. People on the pavements could be wearing skates, they whisk along so quickly. Amy sings along.

'Turn off the radio,' Seymour snaps.

She glances at the crowd. At least she's not part of that frantic melee. She's riding with her lover who, even if he's grumpy, makes her feel like a starlet. She dismisses the memory of Eleanor's last daggered look.

Seymour's eyes dart from driving mirror to side mirror, trying to spot a gap in the stream of cars. He grumbles when another driver pulls up too close behind him.

She wants to stroke his neck. Instead she says: 'I've just been to see my father.'

Seymour changes down to a lower gear, accelerates and then slams on the brakes.

'There's so much I've got to tell you, Seymour. You'll never guess what. Dad's getting married!' Amy tries to sound jokey but tears are swelling. 'Married? Seems a bit bloody sudden to me.'

'You should be glad your father's found someone. You'll get used to the idea soon enough. He'll be happier with a wife.'

Was it a mistake to switch off the radio? Seymour wonders. At

least the girl wouldn't babble inanely. Can she only think about herself?

'I can't see what he sees in Vi. I mean she has this thing for *teddies*,' Amy sneers. 'Dad told me he'd buy me a dress for the wedding, as if that would make me feel better.'

Though it would be nice to have a new dress, she thinks.

As the traffic clears, the car picks up speed. Houses and flats and factories and shops whizz past. She considers it all with sympathy tinged with distaste and the warm glow of satisfaction that the life she's chosen (or has it chosen her, she sometimes wonders) is the right one.

These people will one day benefit from what she and her friends are doing, exploring a new way to live. One day they will understand that it is possible to live communally, to escape from the relentless clutches of consumerism and greed and to address the problems of the world in a spirit of love.

She does not say any of this to Seymour. 'What's happened, darling? You seem a bit uptight.'

'It's Julian. Naresh Rao called, the man I introduced you to in the shop. Apparently there was a scrap with the local gang, and Julian got mixed up in it in some way.'

'Julian? But he's such a gentle spirit.'

'I'm not sure why but they've taken him to the police station.'

'Police? What are you saying?'

'I understand he's been arrested. Could he have had something on him?'

'What do you mean?'

'Do you think he might have been carrying dope?'

'Julian doesn't smoke *that* often. I shouldn't think so.' She did not quite believe what she said but hoped it was true.

'He should stick to drink, more dependable in my view and

it's legal. I've talked to him about drugs, you know, what with his history and everything.'

'His history?'

Seymour doesn't reply.

The car crawls through lunchtime traffic in an area swallowed up by urban sprawl. A smell of fried food makes her stomach rumble. But then she sees the faces of the workers, men with short hair and women in sensible shoes, queuing for their lunches. She is not a person who could manage a dull conventional nine-to-five job. She disregards the fact she is an unpaid housekeeper, cleaner and gardener.

'What do you mean by 'his history'?'

'Julian – he's got mental problems – challenges, I think they call them. That's why he had all that time off from university, of course. Ended up in a loony bin, probably fucked up his exams. Where did you think he was? I assumed you lot were keeping an eye on him. That's partly why I got you all down to Wyld Farm.'

Seymour is angrier than she's seen him before.

'Look after Julian? I didn't know he was troubled! I was at school and living at home with Mum and Dad.'

Seymour spots a gap and swerves the car into it. Someone parps a horn.

'Would it have made any difference? Come on, Amy. You're too busy being an Earth Mother, playing at some hare-brained back-to-nature fantasy to worry about anybody else.'

'What do you mean? You asked us to stay at the farm. You seemed to like what we were doing. Seymour – why are you being like this?'

'This isn't working.'

'What isn't working? What are you talking about? You mean, you and me – us?'

‘Us? What about *us*, Amy? It was just a silly little fling. A fuck between friends.’

His eyes briefly meets hers. They are cold.

‘No. What isn’t working is you lot living at Wyld Farm. It’s over, Amy, your little dream is finished.’

She’s read in books that a character’s blood runs cold. She’d always discounted the description as exaggerated. Now she knows it’s true. Her arteries and veins run with ice.

‘What are you talking about?’ Her voice quivers. ‘What do you mean?’

Out of the window the sky is filled with strange colours; streaks of lemon and pink as the autumn sun begins to sink. Skirting the horizon is a dark blue band of sky that seems to girdle the earth. If only she could open the door and fly away to land there, gently as a feather, then everything might be alright again. She fights the impulse to hum.

It was always obvious to him that the girl had a penchant for dramatics; she should have been an actress. It’s partly what attracted him, her capacity for abandonment and drive for oblivion. Made love-making thrilling, fucking her on his bed just yards from where her boyfriend snored, too smashed to know what was going on.

Amy whispers: ‘My period’s started, Seymour.’

When he doesn’t respond, she says it again.

‘Your point is? Most young women find they menstruate each month.’

When she doesn’t respond, he says in a cross voice: ‘What are you saying? Was there some doubt about it starting?’

Where is the Seymour she is in love with? Amy fights the urge to touch him.

‘Yes, I thought I might be pregnant,’ she bursts, and she can’t keep the happiness from her voice, ‘and I was thinking that it wouldn't be so difficult. I could have a baby and stay at the farm with you and we could raise it together. Our country baby, our child …'

Seymour decelerates behind a delivery van. 'Jesus – what is this fool playing at?' He rams on the brakes and the gearstick into first gear. Flicking a glance at her, he explodes: 'God, you must be crazy, Amy, totally out of your fucking mind. There is no way *on earth* we should have a child together! Amy, I have a son your age! I *do not* want another child. And if I did, it would not be with *you*!'

Amy's throat constricts. It feels like she's choking.

He throws off a bitter laugh: 'Thank fuck you're not pregnant. You mad silly girl, what were you thinking?' He swerves round the van and they speed off again. 'Just listen, can you? When we get to the farm, tell the others to start packing. It's over, Amy, it's all over. Do you hear me?'

A physical sensation of implosion makes her gasp. Her hands fly to her chest as though to hold intact the bruise inside that threatens to spurt blood all over the car. The wound created when her mother left her, mutilated again when her father said he would marry, has never had the chance to heal. Seymour's harsh words rip off its thin scab.

Her head droops, rebounding only when the car hits a bump on the road. The physical jerking confirms she is alive. She feels dead.

When the car turns near off the road by some cottages for the steep descent towards the place that she will cherish forever, she drives away thoughts of her garden and plants, her life among the animals, everything that she cherishes and everything that she dreams of. She must be honest with this man though it will seal her fate.

'You accuse us of being selfish. But it is you – you - who is selfish, Seymour. Julian is your *son*! Why don't you take some responsibility for him and care for him? You've *never* looked after him, never been there for him. And he needs you, he really does. Love him Seymour! Love your son. Or Julian will be lost.'

The car screeches to a halt in the farmyard. 'Why don't you shut up and go away?' Seymour roars.

Flinging open the door, he springs from the car. The geese (which she recalls with scorn he insisted on calling Alarm and Fusspot; at one time she found it charming) start to weave towards him. But even they sense his dangerous mood for they veer off, protesting and flapping their wings.

David is on the front step of the farmhouse step, strumming his guitar. He glances up casually. 'Hiya dudes, you just missed them.' He studies the fretboard to form a chord.

'Who? What you talking about?' Seymour demands.

'The police, they've just been here.'

'The police? Here? For God's sake, why?'

'Search me. Well, they didn't actually.' He laughs. Amy can tell from his languid eyes that he's stoned. 'But they did search the farm. Didn't find zilch, nada, nothing. Chill out, Amy, what's up with you, babe? You're pale as a ghost.'

'David, tell us what happened,' she pleads.

There's a hash pipe and burnt matches on the ground near where David is sitting. Surreptitiously she nudges the stuff into the flower bed with her boot.

'You two seem a little uptight. Chill out, eh? All that happened is that three pigs showed up. I don't know, perhaps two hours ago, it's a bit of a blur. They waved their piggy search warrant and they went through the place. Poked their noses here and there. But they weren't very clever, were they? Cos they didn't find the dope plants.'

'The *what*?' Seymour is horrified.

'Oh, man, I forgot. You didn't know ...'

'Only a few plants. Not many, honestly,' Amy interjects hastily. 'It's only that we didn't have much money ...'

Seymour is shouting now. 'What? Growing dope here, on my farm? That's it. You're all out of here, this charade is over! Pack your bags – David, Amy – and get off my property. You're leaving today!'

A taxi swings into the yard with a flourish. Simon gingerly crawls from the back seat. Strips of plaster run from cheek to cheek across his nose. One of his eyes is closed due to swelling. His torn trousers flap as he limps towards them.

'I'm so r-r-relieved to b-b-e home. It's been t-t-terrible. I g-g-got attacked on the c-c-canal. I've been p-p-patched up at the hospital, thank God. J-J-Julian was on the c-c-canal, too. He ran off and the police ch-ch-chased him. He's been taken to the st-st-station, I'm not sure w-w-why.' He starts to breathe more calmly. 'Amy, D-D-David, hi Seymour. You're b-b-back? But ... where's M-M-Maggie?'

He digs in his pockets, then looks up sheepishly. 'Anyone g-g-got m-m-money for the taxi fare? W-W-Why do you all look so w-w-weird?'

Part Two

Chapter Twenty-Five

Sunshine bounces off the lawyer's designer glasses: '… and I leave Bramble Cottage in equal parts to Simon Webster, David Bond, Maggie Bond and Amy Taylor. The remainder of my real and personal property whatsoever and whosesoever is left to my son Julian …'

The five people mentioned are stunned; Julian because he assumed he would inherit the whole of his father's estate and the others because they cannot imagine why Seymour Stratton, who kicked them off Wyld Farm twenty-five years ago, would leave them a cottage.

'I was right to assume the information contained in Mr Stratton's will is unexpected,' says the lawyer, Sunil Rao. The name is familiar to some of the benefactors though no one can quite remember why.

Mr Rao pushes his glasses up his nose. 'Mr Stratton senior updated his will some time ago when he was first diagnosed with the condition from which he eventually died. He cannot have been aware how much the property would increase in value in the intervening years. Bramble Cottage must be worth …'

'But we won't sell it, will we?' blurts Amy.

There hadn't been time to check out how the years had exacted their toll before the five of them were escorted into the lawyer's office. But now there is. Time had not been unkind.

Maggie, whose tresses once cascaded down her back, runs her fingers through spiky salt-and-pepper hair. Long earrings dangle over a baggy dress; she wears biker boots. She exchanges glances with her brother. David no longer sports the beard and long hair so fashionable in the 1970s but is clean shaven. He has a rock-a-billy quiff and wears a battered leather jacket. He shrugs and looks at Simon.

Amy's husband has retained his boyish looks though he frets that his hair is thinning and his waist thickening. He is right on both accounts. 'Surely we can t-t-talk about that l-l-later?' he says and wonders how owning the cottage will affect their plans to buy property in France. 'Don't you think so, d-d-d-darling?'

'Sure,' Amy nods.

They file from the lawyer's office into the hall where a male receptionist sits behind a desk typing.

'Is there somewhere we can smoke?' Julian asks.

The man struggles out from behind his desk, his rucked up cardigan exposing an overhang of flesh at the waistband. He unlocks a door. 'Out there. In the yard. There's a bin.'

The evidence that other smokers have calmed their nerves here pepper the ground. Surrounded by slumped buildings, the shadowy yard does not benefit from weak March sunshine.

'Oh my God, can you believe it! Me, us, we own the *cottage*! I can remember every nook and cranny,' Maggie says.

'That's because we repaired them with our bare hands. Mine took years to recover,' jokes David.

Maggie tugs a jacket round her shoulders. 'Fancy Seymour remembering us in his will. I thought he was glad to see the back of us. It's freezing out here. Merry, up!' A little dog leaps onto her lap.

Simon says: 'I'm so s-s-sorry about your dad, J-J-Julian. When d-d-did Seymour p-p-pass away?'

The air of ease and entitlement that had once emanated from Julian has disappeared. Dark shadows flicker across his face. 'November. Horrible time of year, I've always loathed it.' His grey hair is tied back in a ponytail and his beard is carefully clipped along his jaw. A ring dangles from one earlobe. He looks like his father, Amy remembers. Perhaps it's the wizardly shape of his nose?

'Cigarette anyone?' Julian asks.

There is an awkward pause while Julian and Maggie smoke. The others rock from foot to foot and rub their hands, wondering what happens next.

'I hope you don't mind the cottage being given to us, Julian?' Maggie voices what everyone is thinking.

'Course not,' he replies quickly.

'I didn't know what to expect when the lawyer's letter asked me to come,' David says. 'I'm blown away, Julian. Your father was wonderful to remember us. I'm so sorry he's no longer with us.'

'Perhaps he felt he owed you lot something? I don't know, he never told me what was in his will. All I know is that I'll miss him terribly.' Julian sighs and flicks his cigarette stub into the corner, missing the bin. 'Seymour could be difficult, as you well know. But we became close over the years. We lived at the farm and he cared for me there. I'm not sure if you heard but … I had a breakdown. Several admissions into hospital, actually, and …'

'I always thought you were a bit loony,' Maggie says.

One of the things about Maggie, Amy remembers, is that the part of her brain where the faculty of restraint should reside is missing. She always said exactly what wandered into her head. This clearly remains the case. 'We were all rather wild at the time so it's no wonder,' Amy quickly says.

'It's all a bit of a blur, to be honest. I was doing a lot of drugs.'

'We all were, Julian,' says David.

Another pause follows. Then Simon says: 'Seymour was always so g-g-generous. It's th-th-thanks to him I have an interest in C-C-Claret and an appreciation for the f-f-finer things in l-l-life …'

'… and he had impeccable taste and panache,' says Amy.

'I never thought I'd find knowing how to plaster a wall useful but I have to say it's come in handy,' adds Maggie.

Everyone laughs. Though it feels forced, they are grateful for levity.

'Oh, it was a magical time. I honestly thought we'd change the world. Seems a bit naïve now, silly even, doesn't it?' Amy looks around, but no one catches her eye. 'It was a tough period for me, when I was living there, and I sometimes think it saved me. My mother dying and Dad getting married again. I don't know, being there in the garden, with the plants and animals, with you all. Looking back I can see it helped me recover. Does that sound weird?'

'Only a bit,' Maggie touches Amy's arm. 'I'd forgotten how fucked up your life was then. So Julian, what did for Seymour in the end?'

Julian rolls another cigarette. 'He was diagnosed with cancer a few years ago. Then last summer he got terribly ill. Miriam, that's my wife, she looked after him with some help from the hospice nurses. He died in the farmhouse, it's what he wanted. Might be hard to believe but Dad became more reclusive as he aged. Left London and started to work on different sorts of photography.'

He lights the cigarette. 'Shall we carry on this conversation somewhere warmer? You'd probably like to see the cottage. Come back to Wyld Farm. I'll call Miriam and tell her we're on the way.'

'Can someone give us a lift? Merry, David and I came by train,' Maggie announces as though they should be impressed. 'I always use public transport,' she adds, getting into the Webster's family estate.

‘I’ll ride with Julian,’ David calls from the dilapidated Jaguar. ‘He says to follow us if you’ve forgotten the way.’

And they do because they have.

*

The five of them had not met over the past twenty-five years. Wyld Farm consumed (or destroyed) any interest they’d had for each other. Life took them in different directions. Their time together became a tale they might tell to amuse others, not something to be re-visited. Better left as a hippy dream, the more glorious perhaps for being ephemeral.

Chance brought Simon and Amy to the same party five years after they left Wyld Farm. At first they moaned about the way Seymour had treated them before grudgingly admitting that they might have been an annoying group of hedonists with idealistic undertones and questionable domestic habits. The more they reminisced, the more their Garden of Eden fantasy seemed funny. They often said it was a shared sense of humour that made them fall in love. When they invited Julian to their wedding, they did not receive a reply. Eighteen months later when Chloe was born, life and parenthood became too absorbing to paddle in rose-tinted nostalgia.

*

Curiosity calls them to Wyld Farm. The track to the farmhouse is still full of potholes. The cars bounce and squeak over the bumps. Green shoots dot the ploughed fields. The soil, the colour of bruised meat, is heavy with rain. The farmhouse appears through skeletal trees. A lighted window and smoke curling up from a chimney. A wooden gate now blocks the entrance to the yard. As David opens it, dogs race out to mill around his legs like spinning tops.

They park the vehicles. Over a bramble hedge stands the cottage of the same name. It's bizarre to be back back at Wyld Farm.

'We lived in Bramble Cottage when we got married,' Julian says. 'But when Seymour got ill, we moved into the house, Miriam and Peter, our young son, and me. Seymour couldn't be on his own. Go inside and have a wander. It's not locked.'

The hall is cramped. There's a smell of cold and of woodsmoke. The sitting room where Amy spent so much time, high and happy, is gloomier than she recalled. The windows admit little light and even the few pieces of furniture make it feel cluttered. Signs of a family are evident: newspapers stacked under a table, children's books, a toy train; they might have just left.

Up the narrow stairway is the bedroom Amy once shared with David. Did she paint the wall this soft green? The marble-topped washstand seems familiar. Is there evidence on these creaking floorboards that her bare toes trod here? Exposure of memory to reality reveals discrepancies, but she cannot place where the errors lie.

Over the past years, she has often thought about Wyld Farm. Sometimes she judges she had been thwarted by powerlessness. That's too simple, she decides. There was hurt but there was healing too. A face she isn't expecting to see stares back at her from the mirror. Cross-hatched lines furrow the skin around her eyes and her hair, once ash-blonde, is dull brown. Things are better out of focus, she decides, folding away her glasses. She heads for the stairs.

Maggie is in the room she sometimes shared with Simon, the man with the affable manner who is stammering to her brother downstairs. What was it about him, the man in deck shoes and chinos that once had made her spirits sparkle? She had not always been happy at Wyld Farm, that's for sure, but at least she'd had choices. Unlike her life now. Her interest in pummelling English into the heads of students is dwindling.

'I could do with a smoke.' David says to Simon, rolling a joint. 'I suppose it's being in this cottage, I associate it with good times. Join me?'

Simon is resisting the temptation to touch the crumbling plaster by the cooker. 'Not p-p-part of my lifestyle, thanks. I'm a management consultant, did I say? I suppose for you musicians it's p-p-par for the course. Amy says you're in a b-b-band? Anyway, we have to h-h-head homeward shortly; recalcitrant teenage daughter to k-k-keep track of this evening.'

David does not mention he works as a designer for a packaging company to pay the bills and child support. The band is his hobby. 'Alright, next time we're down here at our *country cottage.* What an incredible piece of luck, eh? Good old Seymour. This will be a perfect place to bring my son, get away from the city. Marco loves to kick a ball and there's not much space where he lives with his mum. Amy, you want some of this?'

'Thanks, I will,' she giggles. She remembers how David used to make her stomach flip. Reminded her of Jim Morrison.

His wife has not laughed like this for ages. Simon watches her reach into the cupboard, her dress pulling tight across her bottom. He feels a frisson of desire.

Triumphantly, she turns to shake a cup at him. 'When we lived here, do you remember, darling? I used to think it was glamorous to drink from cracked crockery. I suppose we should be getting back home soon. David, can we give you and Maggie a lift back to the station?'

*

Miriam cannot go and see the cottage full of its new owners. Julian's so-called friends, the people who were scarce for so many years when he needed their support. To witness them in her home, judging her possessions, tainting her things with their glances, she can't bear it. Instead she does what makes her feel better when she's anxious. She potters. Habits that restore order restore equanimity.

There was never time to tackle the chaos of Seymour's house when he was ill. Even though the hospice nurses came in twice a day, by the time Miriam was home from work and made supper, put Peter to bed and pushed the buttons on the washing machine, she was too exhausted. In the last weeks of life as Seymour slipped in and out of consciousness, she'd taken compassionate leave from work and sat, day and night by his bedside, keeping him as comfortable as possible. Pandemonium mounted.

Today she'll make a start. Miriam switches on the larder light. The one tiny window is covered in dense mesh; the air is still. Jars of pickled vegetables line the shelves like specimens in a museum. It's impossible to read the faint writing on the pot labels. It's probably stuff leftover from those halcyon days when the group tried to be self-sufficient. She sweeps the jars into a bin. But even the satisfying smash of glass cannot obliterate the question that swirls in her mind. Why did Seymour leave Bramble Cottage to them?

Chapter Twenty-Six

The cottage bulges with its new owners. Simon, Amy, seventeen-year-old daughter Chloe and, so she won't be moody about being 'stuck at the end of a mud track', her best friend Tilly. There's Maggie and her terrier, Merry, oddly named for the dog with a tendency to snap as he did at David's six-year-old son, Marco, a lover of football but a hater of mud on his treasured boots. They decline Julian's invitation to join Miriam and Peter for a drink at the farmhouse. Instead the group cram around the kitchen table for lasagne.

Simon stands. Forks hover. 'Can I p-p-propose a t-t-toast?'

Amy remembers how shy he used to be about public speaking. She sometimes wonders if he uses his stammer as a way of making people listen.

'To the gathering t-t-together of dear old friends in this b-b-beautiful c-c-cottage and to absent f-f-friends.'

'Absent friends.' They raise their glasses.

A brief lull indicates a respectful nod to Seymour. The adults appreciate being remembered in his will but they can't forget he treated them shabbily. Being at Wyld Farm brings it all back.

Chloe finds the dinner difficult for other reasons. It is beyond her why the grown-ups are so pleased to be crammed into a cramped cottage 'full of old grey things – and that's just the furniture!' she whispers to Tilly later.

All her parents and their funny friends do is reminisce. With laughter and veiled innuendo, their stories make her wither. To make things worse, they play terrible music. Rod Stewart was tolerable but Maggie's favourite 'prog rock' band, Yes, made a horrifying sound.

'Why weren't the band named 'No'?' Chloe says, collapsing dramatically onto the mattress she and Tilly have been told is where they will sleep. 'God! Are we really meant to stay here?'

There's a knock on the door. David sticks his head around the door. 'Sleep well, girls,' he says.

Even though he's old, David is not completely uncool; her mother mentioned he played in a band. The quiff is unfortunate, but it's better than Maggie's hair which looks as though it's been chewed by a rat. Apparently Maggie is a teacher. Chloe wonders how someone so tetchy can work with students.

'Thought I'd mention that Julian once slept in this room,' David says. 'He heard a ghost. But I wouldn't worry, I'm *sure* it's gone by now.'

Chloe who has successfully maintained her sangfroid expression all evening, bursts out laughing.

'We'll send the ghost up to *your* room,' she retorts, 'so prepare to be spooked.'

Her parents, washing up in the kitchen, are pleased their daughter is being friendly at least.

Announcing that she wants the single room 'because it has the right vibes,' (Simon raises his eyebrows in derision but says nothing) Maggie stands by the bathroom door with her wash bag and towel.

'David, you take the bedroom with the fireplace, the one Simon and I used to have. There's enough wall space for you and Amber to hang your instruments.'

This is the first time David's girlfriend had been mentioned.

'Which leaves the other double room for Amy and Simon. It's where you used to sleep, Amy. Though you were with David then, weren't you? How things change, eh? Alright, I'll be as quick as I can. But I do like a soak.'

She closes the bathroom door behind her.

Half an hour later Maggie finally vacates a steamy bathroom. David is already in bed after a pee in the garden and a wash in the kitchen sink. The Websters use the bathroom. Simon ignores the green mould behind the loo.

By 11 o'clock, the cottage is quiet save for the giggling of the teenagers. Renovations made a quarter of a century ago did not include sound proofing. Maggie bangs on the floorboards of her room above where the teenagers lay.

'Shut up can you, Chloe and Tilly? I want to sleep!'

There is peace in Bramble Cottage.

*

Over the next few weekends, the new owners arrive as early as they can on Fridays. Re-establishing relationships and talking about old times is fun when combined with fine weather, tents for the teenagers, ear plugs and plenty of wine. Tolerating other people, their children or animals, is eminently possible when one can escape for a walk in the glorious countryside. Irritations are mollified when the scent of flowers blows in through open windows. Idiosyncratic behaviour is a delightful indulgence when viewed from a hammock.

But on the third Saturday afternoon when the weather turns overcast, Amy finds dog excrement in the carefully-prepared vegetable patch again, Marco scribbles over the Mandala poster that Maggie had hung in the kitchen, Simon leaves a pan caked with scrambled egg unwashed in the sink and David rehearses one guitar solo again and again, the honeymoon period concludes.

'Utopia d-d-does not happen without organisation,' Simon says. 'Let's have a d-d-drink and blue-sky how we're going to run the cottage.'

Maggie snorts with derision.

Amy says: 'You're not at work now, darling, people don't use words like that, not in real life. Simon simply means to say let's talk things through.'

'I'll put Marco in front of a Marx Brothers video,' says David.

'Now that sounds fun,' says Maggie.

Simon brings out a bottle of claret, noting it's the third one he's shared that weekend. They'll need a budget for cottage wine as well as household stuff. Though Maggie professes not to drink alcohol, she pours a fair amount of it down her throat.

Amy fetches chairs from upstairs, suppressing irritation when Maggie does not help but lets her dog lick her mouth, a habit Amy finds revolting.

'Having a rota would work for me. I'd like to come here with my girlfriend and band so we can rehearse,' David says.

'I'd like to bring Dad and Vi down for a weekend. I was thinking we could plant a garden, perhaps some fruit bushes. Would people like that?' Amy asks.

'Do you really w-w-want to look after another g-g-garden, darling? Especially if we do b-b-buy a p-p-place in France.'

'Merry needs space to run around,' says Maggie.

'And Marco will want to play football. Not sure there's enough space,' David adds.

'Okay, so just grass in the garden. A lawn will need regular cutting though. We'll need to agree who does what and when. And while we don't need rules, not *exactly* …' Amy looks at Simon for support, 'there might be certain things that aren't, that wouldn't be allowed.'

'Like what?' says Maggie.

'I don't know …'

'Is this about my dog?'

'Well, I'd have thought it best if Merry doesn't do his business in the garden.'

'*I* call that a rule,' Maggie complains. 'My dog should be able to poo where he feels moved to do so.'

'But not in my … I mean the garden,' Amy replies.

'Alright, alright. But if we're making rules, I've got one. My Buddha statue. It must be given respect.'

'It's a bit c-c-creepy,' Simon mutters.

'My Buddha is not creepy, Simon, my *Buddharupa* is special.' Maggie is bristling. She notes the years have added rigidity to her former boyfriend's attitudes. 'Someone has been moving it. Where I put it should be where it *remains*.'

She bought the statue on a trip to India over twenty years ago. A visit she often referred to (some students think rather too often) when teaching the basics of the English language.

'It's a Meditation Buddha and will bring serenity to our cottage.'

Simon looks askance.

Amy says quickly: 'Fair enough. No one is to move the Buddha. So, repairs to the cottage. Perhaps we should start a fund, pay in regular amounts. Anyone like to manage that?'

No one speaks.

'I mean, there are d-d-damp patches behind the c-c-cooker and toilet, the bathroom tap's leaking and …'

'It all sounds rather expensive,' David says.

'But necessary to do, surely?' Amy wonders if David is still tight with money.

'I'm not loaded like you lot. Child support and all that.'

'We're not loaded,' protests Amy.

'You drink nice wine,' says David.

'Which we're h-h-happy to s-s-share ...'

'... and you're buying a cottage in France,' David adds.

'We m-m-might one d-d-ay.'

'I hope owning Bramble Cottage will be a *positive* thing,' Maggie says drily.

The atmosphere has stiffened. She's put into words what everyone is starting to wonder.

'A t-t-top-up anyone?' says Simon brightly.

No one demurs.

'I'll need another bottle then. Oh dear, there doesn't seem to be one. Does the pub sell wine?'

*

'Wave to Amy,' Miriam says to Peter as they drive past the cottage on Monday morning. Her neighbour is in nightclothes standing in the porch staring glumly at the rain.

Miriam has been up for almost two hours getting herself and her son ready for work and nursery. She will drop him there on the way to the office.

There is still a frisson of pride as she dresses each morning. Two years of night school and weekend study snatched when Peter napped to prepare for the accountancy exams was worthwhile. Her promotion and the accompanying rise in pay were welcome, particularly as she is the main breadwinner for the family. Miriam waves to the man on the tractor who drives by. In reality she is the *only* breadwinner.

Julian has never had a job as far as she knows, and that situation did not change when they married five years ago. He keeps himself busy with his cars and machines, fixes fences and chops wood; he does not earn cash. She manages the family finances. The means by which food finds its way onto their table is never discussed.

'Peter, see the cows in the field. What do cows say?'

'Moo,' the boy responds dutifully. He slips his thumb between his lips, hoping his mother won't notice in the mirror. She says it is a babyish habit, but she doesn't know how delicious it tastes.

Miriam kisses her son goodbye and drives on to the firm where she works. It is the first time one of the cottage's owners has stayed on into the working week. Julian told her Amy is a freelance writer; women's magazines apparently. Miriam does not read such magazines. She noticed Simon and the miserable teenage daughter leaving the cottage on Sunday morning, no doubt driven away by the steady drizzle. That's life in the countryside for you; you have to be resourceful, come rain or shine.

Amy might be lonely, Miriam thinks, as she settles at her desk. But there definitely aren't enough leftovers from Sunday's roast to invite her round for supper.

When Julian found himself proposing marriage to Miriam within four months of meeting her, he was almost as baffled as she. Miriam was like a lifebuoy; round and unsinkable. Comfortable in flat shoes and anoraks, she was the unlikely partner of a quirky man like Julian. But his previous girlfriends, exotic in name and character, would not have provided the steadiness he needed. Whether conscious or not, he knew she offered what he needed.

Neither was Miriam the sort of woman that Seymour admired, at least initially, for she was not beautiful. But her inscrutability intrigued him. Seymour came to acknowledge, if not to understand, that something she offered was crucial for his son's stability. The night he invited her to play Scrabble, they all knew what it signified; acceptance. Miriam usually beat Seymour at the game and, though he minded, it was not tremendously. When Seymour became very unwell, he announced that Miriam was allowed to give him bed baths; no one else. She had something he needed, too.

Chapter Twenty-Seven

Amy closes the door as Miriam drives past, wondering vaguely why she feels as though she's been caught doing something naughty. She makes a pot of strong coffee and sets up her typewriter in the sitting room. She had always imagined the cottage would be the perfect place to write her column of gardening tips for housewives who could curl up on their clean sofas and fantasise about what they would one day plant, certain in the knowledge they would never put hand to trowel. Today she must write an article on the 'seven vegetables you can grow that children will love to eat'. Needing more light, she runs upstairs to fetch the lamp.

She's like a string bag drawn tight. She fingers the walls and touches the surfaces as though they might disclose something hidden; looks in drawers and behind doors. If she'd been asked to explain what she was searching for, she could not have said. Only that having been ripped prematurely from here, the place to which she had given total commitment, she always assumed returning would be revelatory. But it's disturbing.

Pragmatism forces her to her typewriter. By one o'clock, the article is written. She puts on a coat and a pair of wellies and leaves the cottage.

Outside it seems a grey veil had been slung from the sky. The geese give a half-hearted hiss, then waddle pigeon-toed back into their hut. The grass on the hill is greasy from rain. At the top she stops to catch her breath. Looking back down at the farm, she hopes she might, in some illogical way, see Daisy waiting by the barn and her garden abundant with vegetables. Why does it feel so dispiriting that there is no evidence that she or her friends had ever lived here? Now wheel-less cars crouch by the barn. A plastic bag caught on wire flaps erratically in the wind. A pile of logs blackens in the sibilant rain. The only sign of life is a shed light suggesting Julian is working or has perhaps forgotten to flick the switch.

She remembers an ancient path that runs between dry stone walls and wind-twisted hawthorn where tiny wild strawberries nestle in the crevices. Through a broken stile is the field where enormous shaggy parasol mushrooms used to grow. She'd cook them with butter and the star-shaped flowers of wild garlic. A hare bolting from the undergrowth makes her jump. Only when her heart settles does she walk on towards the head of the combe. She's searching for a sheep path that cuts down through ferns and stunted rowan trees to a tumbledown cottage at the bottom, but it takes her a while to find the boggy track. Down she slithers and slides, splashing through a stream where watercress could be found in the rippling shallows. But Mrs Morle would see it in her basket and tut. She mustn't eat it, there might be flukes in it. So many memories …

The village looks different; why is she surprised? Recession has blighted some parts of the country over the past few years but the homes she passes suggest their owners are more than solvent. Neatly painted exteriors adorned with burglar alarms, well-stocked tidy gardens and new gates with locks on the driveways suggest economic health. Where signs of life are indicated by parked cars, the vehicles are new. Peering in the window of the boarded up grocery shop, she sees bare shelves and a curling poster advertising frozen fish fingers.

Amy drops her article into the post box. It sounds empty.

The bell on the pub door tinkles. Three men in overalls drinking pints seem surprised by her arrival. A dog stretched out on the floor raises a lazy head, then grunts back to sleep.

'That's a nice welcome, isn't it?' jokes the bartender. 'Please come in out of the wet. What can I get you?'

'I think I caught the post. Cider and a cheese sandwich to celebrate, please.'

It is warm in the pub and nice to chat to the friendly young man. She is cheered by it all and finds herself chatting on, telling him about her long-cherished dream to live in the country. That now she has the chance to do that, even if it will mostly be at weekends and occasional holidays.

'Is your place nearby? I've been living here since last autumn so don't know the area well. Moved here from Portsmouth. From what I gather a lot of new people have moved in over the past few years.'

'I didn't think you were local. I live in a cottage that was part of Wyld Farm. I suppose it's second home owners like us moving in that changes things. How's the job going?'

'The pub's a bit quiet during the week, but the weekends are busy with locals. Visitors are starting now summer is coming. The owner wants to start offering fancy food, what they call a gastro-pub. Some of locals aren't sure …'

'It's the first time I've been in here since we moved in. Years ago there was a village shop selling everything you needed. Closed at lunch time – can you imagine that? The owner used to let me sell my jam for twenty pence a jar.'

'You used to live around here?'

'Me and my boyfriend came in the summer of 1972. Stayed for about eighteen months. Before you were born, I expect.'

'I was born in the summer of '74. My name's Aubrey, by the way. Can I ask you something?'

'Of course. What would you like to know?'

'I'm looking for someone who was living around here about that time. You might have known them.'

'Gave you trouble, did he?' Amy jokes. 'What's his name?'

*

David invites Peter over to the cottage to play with Marco. Miriam is doubtful that a sophisticated town boy will find her lad a good playmate but she agrees. The farmhouse is isolated and it's good for Peter to play with other children. She'd have preferred it to involve running about and tree-climbing but Marco has his 'Ninja Turtles' with him, David says. Miriam had no idea what he was talking about, but Peter's eyes lit up when he heard; described creatures with odd Italian names who fought baddies. It sounded most peculiar.

First stop, the bathroom. Every second day Miriam shaves her legs, a habit she developed at the age of fourteen following a visit to her cousins in the US. All the girls had long, brown, hair-free legs and hers, as little cousin Tommy pointed out loudly so everyone could hear, were hairy. Once hair-free, Miriam creams her legs and puts on her jeans. Usually she has to do the chores, domestic and personal, while keeping Peter amused. It seems not to occur to Julian that he might help, and somehow she can never find it within herself to ask. Parenting to him means eating together at meals, turning the television off, collecting the boy from nursery when Miriam has to work late and kissing the boy goodnight. No doubt it's to do with his upbringing. Perhaps things will change when Peter shows an interest in machinery. No sign of that so far.

Julian is sleeping off the effect of last night's visit to the cottage. From the sounds of smashing on the flagstones which woke her up at midnight, he was inebriated. His jacket, slung over the bannister, reeks of smoke. She hopes it is only from tobacco; the doctors suggested his medication prohibited him from smoking anything else.

Miriam did not go with him to cottage last night. She said one of them had to stay with the sleeping Peter. Unlike some parents she has read about, Miriam does not trust to baby monitors. She does not tell Julian she will not befriend 'the group', as she calls David, Maggie, Amy and Simon. She will be pleasant and helpful but that's it.

Miriam sweeps up the glass shards and fetches a bucket of water to wash the hall. It is still hard to refer to the farmhouse as 'home'; the place smacks of her father-in-law. It is as though they have carved out small runs through the forest of Seymour's life to scuttle between bed, bathroom and kitchen. Some parts, such as Seymour's darkroom, they do not enter. Julian locked it as soon as Seymour died as though the room contained secrets. But once the money from Julian's inheritance comes through, things will have to change. The place is tumbling down.

Chapter Twenty-Eight

She presumed the knocking was Andrew Bishop coming for her shopping list. So it was a shock to see Seymour standing there, a scarf wrapped around his neck like one of those African tribesman with an extended neck.

'Mrs Morle,' he said sheepishly, 'I have come to make amends and to beg your forgiveness. To apologise for my insufferable behaviour in foolishly suggesting I no longer needed your services. I could not have been more wrong. I've brought you these.'

He handed her a large bunch of flowers; the softest pink carnations, a sprinkling of tiny white rosebuds and feathery fronds. Despite everything, her arms accepted them.

'Mrs Morle,' Seymour said as she breathed the heady scent, 'is there any way you could come back to work for me and Julian? We would be so grateful.'

She peered through the foliage. She'd only occasional glimpses of the man these past six months when he drove in or out of the farmyard. There's been no sign of him or anyone at all over Christmas. Seymour's tanned face suggested a visit to warmer climes.

Since that police visit last September, Julian's friends had disappeared like a bad smell. Good riddance. She had asked Andrew Bishop what the police had been after but, despite his contacts in the local force, he couldn't find out. That-girl-Amy had not been round asking for chutney recipes and the one who picked dock leaves saying she'd use them as toilet paper, and the boys too, all vanished. The only people Mrs Morle ever saw were Julian and, sometimes, Gerald. City types never lasted long in the country and that was a fact.

'Would you come back as our housekeeper, Mrs Morle?' Seymour's tone was just this side of pleading.

When Seymour sacked her, Mrs Morle had quickly found two cleaning jobs. One for a family who lived in the village and another for a couple in the town. The three-mile walk to the village was manageable but the other job meant taking the bus. That was unpredictable and the journey tiring, especially in the winter. His offer was tempting. But Mrs Morle could not forget the insulting way Seymour had terminated her work, out of the blue and by letter.

It was as though he'd heard her mind working.

'I did not discuss with you properly my need to change your working arrangements, and that is unforgivable, Mrs Morle. But I hope you can be generous enough to see your way past my misdemeanour with my sincerest apology. Could you, Mrs Morle?'

Just then Andrew Bishop pulled up in his Cortina. 'Morning, Mr Stratton, cold enough for you? Anything you want getting from the shops, Mrs Morle? I'm on my way.'

'Yes Andrew, I do,' she replied. 'I'll just fetch my list.'

The most exciting item on it was a packet of sausages. Two cleaning jobs did not replace the money she had earned from Seymour and she had to be careful. No one was averse to economy, of course, but it would be nice to have a roast on a Sunday and not to worry about the electricity bill.

Seymour called out to Andrew. 'Morning. Are you off to town? Mrs Morle, let me save you the walk and take the list to Andrew.'

The man guffawed at something Seymour must have said. That infuriated her.

'Something wrong with your neck, Mr Stratton?' Why was the man trussed up like a turkey with that silly scarf? 'How is Julian these days?'

'He's fine. Missing you, though. Especially when I'm working away so much.'

'He always did, Mr Stratton. I suspect he misses his friends too. Haven't seen them about ...'

'Yes, well, that situation didn't work out the way we hoped, I'm afraid. There we are. I took him away on holiday for Christmas and now he's going to ...'

'I'll be off then, Mrs Morle, if there's nothing else you want at all,' Andrew Bishop called out.

'Give me a minute, will you, Andrew?'

It would suit her so much better to work for the Strattons. She did miss Julian, too. He was a queer boy but a good one. Her resolve melted.

'Get me a leg of lamb as well would you, Andrew? A small one mind. I'll settle up the extra money with you next week.'

She glared at Seymour. 'I'll start back at the farmhouse on Monday, Mr Stratton, and do three days a week. With a 50 pence rise in my hourly rate, mind. Drop the key through my letter box, there's no need to ring the bell. Tomorrow would be convenient day to start.'

And she shut the door.

Carefully laying the flowers on the draining board, she reached for the scissors. The flower heads danced in her shaking fingers. As she cut the stems, tears rolled over her cheeks. They dripped down her neck and soaked into her cardigan. She cried hard for several reasons: because Seymour had treated her badly, embarrassment that she'd caved in and done what he wanted, relief that she had her job back. But most of all because of the gaping hole that had been left by her daughter's disappearance. What had become of Lynn?

*

Gerald called in to see Julian only because he did not see Seymour's car in the farmyard. The man could be snippy. Gerald parked his Mini and went into the farmhouse. The office was empty and there wasn't a fire in the sitting room grate. The kitchen sink was piled with unwashed dishes and there was a half-cut loaf on the table.

Then the back door shut. Julian came through the boot room door, his hair flattened from wearing a hat, his nose red.

'Chilly out there. Hi Gerald, thought I heard a car. How's things?'

'Went out this morning early, it was beautiful. Jackson chased a rabbit right across the hill. Runs like the wind that dog, it's a wonderful sight. I just came to see if there's anything you were after? Now Daddy's gone.'

He shoved aside a pile of clothes on the bench and sat down. 'How are things here? Ever hear from your pals? Troubadour Dave? The loopy ladies?'

Julian nodded. 'There was a postcard from Amy a while ago. The cat pooed on the envelope which seemed apt. I haven't heard from anyone else. Not sure what they're up to.'

'Explain to me what happened. Seymour got aerated about them being here or something? But I thought that's what your father wanted? A rural escape, a hippy commune …'

'Seymour. You know how he is, how he changes his mind.'

'Quite. Parents come from a strange land. My dear boy, if you need anything at all, just give me a tinkle, yeah?'

'Of course. You've been away?'

'Just a little trip. To Morocco and a farm near Katama.'

'Cool.'

'Indeed. I've found a farm in the foothills and the guy there grows some good hashish, he's pretty together. I've persuaded him to deal with me directly in future, provide me with regular consignments. It's a better deal for him and for me, cuts out the local fixer. The plan is to hide the stuff in a car and drive it through Spain back to England.'

Julian listened. 'Wow. You'd need to find the right sort of car. If you like, I could start looking out for one, maybe do the modification. I'm pretty good with a welding torch …'

'Great, sounds like you're on. We can talk terms as things progress. Is there anything I can give you now? A little whizz? You can pay cash or put it on tick …'

Chapter Twenty-Nine

Maggie wobbles along. It is not her bicycle; that is double-locked outside her flat. This bone-shaker has been lent to her by Julian. The handlebars make her sit like a schoolmarm and with no basket on the front (where is one meant to carry one's dog if there is no basket?); she fears she might flip head first over the front wheel if she brakes too hard.

Still, it was nice of Julian to pump up the tyres and the lanes are quiet this early on a Saturday. Within half an hour of leaving Bramble Cottage, she is in the market square. The stall holders are starting to trade.

She had planned to do several errands. But discovering she has limited cash in her purse puts an end to that. The town lacks a 'hole in the wall' and the bank is, of course, closed on a Saturday. Maggie wanders around the stalls, wondering what she can afford for supper. There is little food on 'her' shelf in the cottage kitchen cupboard save for oil, rice, tea and a wizened clove of garlic. A few vegetables and a pint of milk will have to do.

She follows a different route home. It goes past the canal entrance and just there she sees a shop she's not noticed before with a candy-striped awning. Unexpected for this little town, she's intrigued. The shop is a cornucopia of jewellery, glassware, carved wooden boxes, ceramic bowls, candles and baskets, all tastefully displayed. Packets of spices and dried fruits spill from a chest.

Maggie digs around in her bag. 'Can I have this dried mango, please?' she says to the Asian woman who emerges like a vision from a Bollywood film. She's wearing a lustrous blue silk top over trousers edged in silver embroidery. 'Your *salwar kameez* is wonderful,' Maggie says, feeling lumpen in her jeans and army jacket.

'You know the name of my clothing! I'm glad you like it,' the woman smiles. 'It is so comfortable for working in. Your reaction is not the usual one I am expecting from my customers. How do you know *salwar kameez*?'

'I travelled around India once. Goa, oh it was years ago.' Maggie sounds wistful.

They talk about India, a country the shop owner said she had first visited herself only four years ago. Her parents, who have retired there, left the shop to her. Her brother, Sunil, has no interest in commerce.

So now she regularly travels to India to buy things for her import business. The shop is only part of her plans, the woman explains. She is going to sell to shops in London. Buyers at Liberty are interested, she says proudly.

'This cushion would look wonderful in my bedroom.' Maggie strokes the tiny embroidered flowers that are scattered across the white silk. Lines of pale green stitches make stems for appliqué leaves.

'Would you like to buy it?' the shopkeeper asks.

Maggie nods. 'I would. But I haven't got enough cash and my cheque book is back at the cottage. It's too far to go and get it. Anyway, I couldn't carry it on my bike.'

'You cycled here? You are brave. Where are you staying?'

'Not far, the village near the Old Mineral Line. I'll buy the cushion next time I'm down.'

'I know that village. My brother and I often walk there. If you like, I could bring you the cushion in the car tonight after the shop closes.'

Maggie's plans for the evening do not extend beyond cooking the vegetables and taking Merry for a wander.

'I couldn't put you to any trouble,' she says half-heartedly.

'It's no trouble for me, it is not far. I'll come about six. Is that suitable? Write down the address. My name is Indu Rao, by the way.'

Buying things often makes Maggie cheerful.

'Alright then. I'm Maggie Bond. I'll see you later. The sign to Wyld Farm is a bit hidden behind leaves but it is nailed to the tree. You should spot it. Bramble Cottage is in the yard.'

As she is leaving, Indu calls out. 'I remember your village, Maggie. When I was a schoolgirl, my parents used to scare me with stories of wild hippies who used to live near there.'

'Oh really?' Maggie replies. She will not admit she had been one of them. It would be too humiliating now she has turned out so ordinary.

'Indu is not the sort of person I expected to meet around here,' Maggie tells Merry as they lay on the bed that afternoon. She scratches the dog's tummy hoping she is forgiven for not taking him on the shopping trip.

Being in the cottage is bringing back so many memories. How ecstatic she was when they moved into the cottage, how defiant when she let the sheep escape from the field and how lust-filled when she ended up in Simon's bed. And even after that horrific accident when the horse's kick smashed her jaw, she was unbowed. She went to India as soon as she could escape the doctor's scalpels.

She used to lead life firmly by the nose. Now it has her cropped and contained, scuttling between the staff room and her classes who struggle with their verbs. The lethargy of lesson preparation, the tedium of teaching.

Maggie lets Merry out into the garden, making a mental note to clear up the mess later. Then she begins to tidy up. The muted mismatched furniture and the faded carpet are hideous and Indu has such exquisite taste. What will she think?

Digging around Amy's drawer, she finds some tea lights. The sitting room will look better in candle light. She'll stoke up a fire, too. She will not take Indu into the kitchen. The cracked lino floor and melamine cupboards are so outdated. But sharing a house it is difficult to decide what to replace.

Maggie runs a bath. At least she doesn't have to queue this time. She nicks some bubble bath from the bottle on Amy's shelf and sinks into the soapy bubbles. Her eyes trace a crack in the ceiling. It will be nice to have a visitor and a new cushion.

✷

Indu steps out of her car in jeans, a leather jacket and high-heeled boots.

'Hi Maggie,' she calls as she takes a parcel from the back seat of her car. 'I found the cottage, your directions were fine. Here's the cushion!'

She tip-toes across the yard, avoiding the puddles.

'Hi,' Maggie says. 'Come inside. This is very kind of you. I've only just moved in so I'm not really set up for visitors. Did I say? I share this place with friends.' She has put on the only other item of clothing she had at the cottage; a baggy dress. She'd like to reveal the butterfly tattoo on her shoulder but it's too chilly not to wear a cardigan.

The women sit either side of the fire. Though Maggie feels awkward, her guest appears at ease for she chats away about her plans for expanding her business. Producing clothes in Indian workshops – 'ethnic chic' Indu calls it – and importing it to the UK. What did Maggie think of that idea?

Indu does not pause to find out. Local sales might never be high, but the shop will be a showroom for buyers to view the collection. Maggie is lucky to live in a town; it's where Indu wants to be.

Maggie watches Indu talk. She is probably a little older then Indu, who must be in her late thirties. Did Indu's parents expect her to marry and have children? At least Maggie's mother has finally stopped the pointed questions. Indu mentioned a brother, Sunil, who was a lawyer in a local practice. Was it he who sorted out Seymour's will? Indu said Sunil was soon to become a father for the second time.

Indu turns to Maggie. 'I have said enough. I chatter like a bird, my mother says. I want to hear about you now.'

It would be dull if Maggie were to talk about being a teacher. Though once she had been thrilled by the idea of teaching English as a way of travelling the world, this had not happened. Maggie has ended up living in a small town outside Bath. Though once a wild child who lived in a commune, her life is a conventional one. What happened?

So Maggie finds herself enthusing about her application to an international development agency. Of her determination to teach English abroad and her desire to 'make a difference'. (The fact that the form lies uncompleted on her bedside table at her flat is a minor detail.) Maggie speaks so convincingly that she begins to believe that soon she will be living abroad.

Indu nods encouragingly. 'You and I are so alike!' she says.

As far as Maggie can tell, the only similarity between them is what her brother teases her about – 'being well covered'. But Indu celebrates her body as though she welcomes its curves while she,

Maggie, hides them under baggy clothes.

'We're alike because we're both determined – nothing will stop us,' says Indu standing up. 'I should be getting back. This will be a lovely cottage once it's done up. In a nice quiet spot. Which is great if you like the quiet. I like the town.'

Chapter Thirty

It never failed to excite him, images emerging from the chemical soup. Seymour carefully lifted the paper from the developing tray, rinsed it and hung up it to dry on the line from which other photographs dangled: so many pictures of his son in his twenties, before he'd been knocked down by the various drug treatments various doctors said would help. The boy found it hard to cope with life; that was all. That was enough.

Seymour was leery of nostalgia. But his body tingled when he saw photos of Julian driving a tractor loaded with hay bales, Julian leaning against the Morgan with his hat at a jaunty angle, Julian playing with the dog they'd together agreed had got just too damn old. It was sad, the day the vet came over to put the dog down. They'd made that decision together, he and Julian, decided it was time to end it. Comes to us all, Seymour said to himself. Don't talk in clichés, old man, he scolded himself.

So many photographs from the 70s. That boy with the stutter, Simon, his arm around Maggie, the girl with the delicious big bottom. Squashed on the steps of that gypsy wagon, their smiles like sunbursts. Behind them that girl Amy pointing at the camera as if to say, I've got your measure. And one of her boyfriend standing in the doorway of a barn, his eyes glazed. What was the oaf's name? Been smoking with Julian, probably.

It wasn't just the grass that caused Julian's problems, Seymour thought, shoving the photographs into a drawer. He dipped another sheet of exposure paper into the tray. Smoking marijuana was an innocent enough pastime, fine if you could handle it. Made one a bit dull, perhaps, and prone to raid the biscuit tin. No, it was the chemicals and something in Julian's make-up that made him vulnerable. An image of Gerald emerging from beneath the developing fluid made Seymour recoil. Full-face to the camera, Gerald's fingers were resting lightly on his dog's head, the smoke from his cigarette drifting off as nonchalant as the man who released it, the person Seymour blamed for Julian's problems.

Was that fair? He asked himself. If Gerald hadn't circled around his son would things would have been so different?

Seymour dropped the photo as though it smelt putrid.

'I only give him what he asks for,' Gerald had said to him once. His voice was not raised: it was Seymour who was yelling. 'I'll go now, old man, keep it together now, Seymour. Just bear this in mind. Your son is the problem – not me.'

Seymour could not bear Gerald's presence any longer.

'How can you call yourself a friend when you don't help him?' he walked menacingly towards Gerald.

'Everyone has to help themselves, don't you think?' Gerald had retorted, mincing backwards down the hall, feigning fear. 'And you're never around, old man. Not much help. So keep your cool, eh? Come on Jackson, we're not wanted here.' Gerald spun on his heel and left.

✷

When Mrs Morle called him, Seymour was in his London studio photographing a politician. His client, a well-known woman, was highly displeased when Seymour said he must take the call. In the past few years, having a central London studio where celebrities and stars could be driven in their limos meant much of his work was now taking portraits of the rich and famous. Let no one assume that these people were any less vain or impatient than fashion models.

'I'll be right back,' Seymour promised, and hurried to his office. 'Look after her, will you?' he growled at his assistant and shut the door.

An hour later, having flattered the politician and jokingly promised her his vote in the forthcoming election, he handed her back to her chauffeur. Grim-faced, he set off for Wyld Farm.

Earlier that day, Mrs Morle had heard an odd sound at her cottage door. She found Julian collapsed in a heap, blood streaming from his head, garbling something about a car. She stepped round him and hurried to Andrew Bishop's cottage. The man raced off down the lane in his van looking for he didn't know what while Mrs Morle led an incoherent Julian into the farmhouse office. Pointing at a chair, she telephoned Seymour.

Julian had had an accident, she told Seymour. He was distressed and needed his father. Mention of his father's name sent Julian spiralling from the room. Mrs Morle asked Seymour if she should take Julian to the hospital or phone the police.

'No and no!' he barked. 'I'm on my way. Just stay with him until I arrive and don't let him sleep. Find his inhaler!' Almost shouting, he added: 'Only if he starts feeling sick or vomits should you take him to A&E. No police.'

In the kitchen she found Julian cowering in the corner and mewling like a tortured cat. The hairs on her arms stiffened. Mrs Morle crouched beside him and, though he flinched when she touched his shoulder, he clawed for her hand when she made to stand, trapping her in a most awkward position.

It was ages since Mrs Morle had been so near to the floor. Her muscles protested. Wincing as her knee banged into the flagstone, she twisted onto her side, landing with a bump on her bottom. Places in the kitchen she had never been able to see before came into view: under the settle were scattered crumbs and the torn edge of a cigarette box with what she realised with horror might be mice droppings. She'd put down a trap tomorrow if she ever got off this wretched floor.

Dragging a cushion off a chair, she wedged it under her bottom. At least the Aga was on. Leaning against the wall, she wondered what to do for the best. Right now this seemed to be what Julian wanted; for her to stay near.

The boy had seemed a bit odd in the year since his friends disappeared off the farm. But Julian was prone to moods, she knew that from his childhood. Snappy too, though that was less like him. However, she did not overly concern herself. Julian had come through strange phases before. Anyway, she had enough of her own worries.

His yelps began to grate. After a time, she could bear it no longer. 'Julian,' she said firmly, and though he did not look at her, his head swung vaguely in her direction. 'I've got to get up, dear. I can't stay here any longer.'

He seemed to accept this for as she struggled to her knees, he released her hand, the one he had been gripping. She hauled herself to her feet, then collapsed into a chair.

An hour passed. At times the boy keened and she was at a loss to know what to do. At other times, he was silent and she would peer down, careful not to get too close to whisper: 'anything I can get you, dear?' When would Seymour arrive to take over?

Someone with a head injury should not be given anything by mouth, she'd been told that. But surely the boy needed a drink, his lips so cracked? Slowly getting to her feet, she moved towards the sink. 'I'm getting you a drink, Julian.' Just a tiny bit of water in a glass couldn't harm, surely? He drank it quickly and held out the glass for more. 'Later,' she said, and sat down again.

Another hour passed. In between sudden outbursts of wailing, he was definitely settling down, no longer gibbering to himself.

'I'm going to fetch the ironing, love, might as well get on,' she said, and she fetched the board and a basket of dry clothes. The smell of hot-pressed material began to pervade the room. It smelt cosy. She gave Julian a little more to drink and switched the radio on low.

Finally she saw that he had fallen asleep, his head jammed against the wall, his face slack. Blood had seeped through the bandage on his head. She noticed a graze on his jaw and a deep gash on the hand curled in his lap. It was nice to see the boy resting at last; she was pleased for him and for herself. She sat in a chair and nodded off.

She woke with a start when the front door was flung open. Hurried footsteps could be heard coming down the hall.

'Where is he?' Seymour flung the question at her as he came through the door.

'There's no need to shout,' she said quietly. 'He's over here. He's sleeping.'

'I told you he shouldn't sleep!'

'You don't tell me to do anything …' she spat back.

Seymour knelt by his son and shook him. 'Wake up, Julian. Are you alright? What happened in the car?'

Muted grunts in reply. Seymour turned to Mrs Morle.

'Andrew says he found the car upside down in the field just along the lane, the driver door open and the engine running. He fetched a tractor and ropes and he's towed the car back here. It's a write-off. It's a wonder that Julian survived.' He turned back to his son. 'Come on, Julian, sit up on the chair. There's a good chap. Phone the doctor, Mrs Morle, will you?'

Later that afternoon, the GP made a house visit. She diagnosed mild concussion and said a few days' rest should suffice. 'Then tell him to come to the surgery for the appointment he missed,' she added.

'He had an appointment? What for?' Seymour asked.

The GP raised her eyebrows and shook her head. 'Perhaps you should ask your son.'

✷

Some people harden as time passes; they become fixed in their views and their ventures. For Seymour, it was the opposite. Like a piece of unhewn stone, the years had moulded him into a softer man, one that former friends might not recognise. Empathy and forbearance, qualities suffocated in the chase for fame and fortune, flickered into life. Though not the steadiest of flames, still they burned.

Few do not struggle with the demands of parenthood, the wrestling between self and selflessness. Most accommodate its joys and delights. But for Seymour, it was not until he'd spent hours by the side of his almost moribund son waiting for signs of sanity to return that he finally understood its power. If there was one thing to commend mental illness, it was this: it awakened in Seymour an untrammelled love for his son. Feelings he formerly judged in others as slavish adherence to social expectation, indulgent adoration or worse, biological determinism, now made sense.

Seymour fell in love with his son. There was no humiliation in being a laggard to the cause, he told himself; it was preferable to lifelong resistance. And if most parents stepped back as their children became adults while Seymour found himself moving in the opposite direction, so be it.

He was the same person, of course; sharp-tongued and easily bored. Not given to self-reflection, he sometimes thought back to that final fight with Amy. Her comments were, of course, inept and wide of the mark, the things a woman in the throes of rejection spits out. But as the years passed, he began to see her words contained more than an element of truth. If he was honest, they started to sting; they bit, they burrowed. At the same time, he was finding fashion models and celebrities more rather than less annoying. Demanding and petulant, they required amounts of admiration and flattery it was exhausting to provide. It left him feeling tainted. The day Julian was discharged from the psychiatric hospital for the second time, his mind was made up. Seymour closed his London studio. He instructed his lawyer to put the place up for sale. He moved to Wyld Farm.

Seymour began to photograph the shapes and patterns, forms and contours, that he saw while walking in the Brendon Hills. Aspects of nature that had been closed to him became captivating; the weather, the seasons, water moving over stone, vegetation growing and dying. He was energised, obsessed, inspired; driven to explore subjects he would previously have dismissed as dull and to pursue a perspective at which he would have sneered; abstract nature photography. The countryside was the only place to live, he told London people who sometimes called asking why he'd disappeared; it was rich and exciting. No commission could tempt him back to the metropolis. Time was short. Why would he waste it?

Domestically, life changed, too. Seymour cooked while Julian chopped; Seymour washed the clothes, Julian hung them out to dry; Seymour shopped, and Julian made lists. When his father explored the countryside taking photographs, Julian pottered around the farm, gardening or fixing machinery. And when Julian was crushed by bleakness or splintered with anxiety, Seymour was there through the bitter days and bleak weeks.

Music was their constant companion. To provide comfort, energy, consolation, distraction or entertainment, Seymour orchestrated playlists. He drew on the vast collection of vinyl already at the farm but added to it, too. Modern and classical music that he heard on the radio or read about in the reviews; he had it sent to the farm by post. Occasionally he took his son to see live music in a pub and several times to a local church where the choir was particularly good. If Mrs Morle found it maddening to work in the music-filled household, she accepted it was the way the Stratton men lived.

*

He barely acknowledged the diagnosis. It confirmed what he had suspected for some time: an uninvited presence resided in his body. He took the drugs, tolerated the treatments, and acknowledged with equanimity that they offered care rather than cure. There was much he needed to do and fighting the inevitable was not part of his plan. 'Thank you, doctor,' he said and, despite the pain, Seymour left the specialist's office with a spring in his step. He made an appointment with his lawyer, the son of his old friend Naresh, the shop keeper. Sunil Rao would impose legal certainty in a world of chaos.

*

'How did you manage it, Mrs Morle?' he asked her one afternoon.

Julian was in hospital again. He had become so unwell that despite Seymour's best attempts at musical and culinary therapy, his son had been admitted under section. The doctors raised the possibility of electro-convulsive therapy, a subject that made Seymour furious and devastated in equal measure.

Mrs Morle stopped buttoning her coat.

'Do what?' she said. Had Mr Stratton had been drinking? He looked terrible. Crumpled in a chair by an unlit fire, his head was sunk into his shoulders like an old turtle.

'Raise such a balanced child,' he replied. Exhaustion dragged on the skin beneath his eyes. She saw that he was suffering.

'I tear myself apart sometimes, asking myself if it is me who is to blame for Julian's troubles.'

'There's all sorts that goes to making someone troubled,' Mrs Morle replied, starting her slow roll towards the door. Then she turned around to face him. Taking a deep breath, she said: 'I ask myself the same question, you know.'

'You? But why, Mrs Morle? Lynn has done so well. You told me that she has a job, a boyfriend ...'

'Ah. That's all nonsense and lies. I haven't told you the truth, Mr Stratton. Didn't want to bother you, not when you had your own troubles. Don't go torturing yourself, Mr Stratton. At least your boy is around. I'm on my own. All alone.'

'What do you mean?'

'Lynn – well – the only thing I knows about my girl is this; she's gone, and I don't know where she is.'

'But I thought she was ...'

'I wait each day for a letter from her and I pray each day it will come, don't I? But it don't come. And I don't know where my lovely daughter is living or how she is doing at all.'

The nausea that plagued him over the past few months made Seymour belch. 'I do beg your pardon. Is all this true? Why did Lynn go? Where is she?'

Mrs Morle did not answer. Shuffling herself around, she headed for the farmhouse door.

Chapter Thirty-One

'Up you go, Chloe.'

'What time's he coming, Mum? Do I have to be there, too? It's so embarrassing, some weird guy from the pub.'

Chloe trails upstairs from the kitchen to Maggie's room where her revision books wait.

'Darling, I told you, Aubrey is coming for supper at 7pm. It'll be nice to get to know a local person. I'm popping into the town now and when I get back, I'll bring you a cup of tea and you can have a break. See you later.'

Amy had brought Chloe to the cottage so she could revise for her 'A' levels during reading week and escape the distractions of friends popping in unannounced. Conversations about exam panic, exam stress, lack of sleep. Girls could describe in forensic detail the colour and complexity of their revision schedules. But as for actually sitting down to study …

Amy parks the car in the market square. The butcher who said he knew the life and times of every animal displayed in his shop window sells her some lamb chops, and she buys two bottles of Beaujolais in the wine shop: she'll take one home for Simon. She posts an article she'd finished the previous day and while in the post office, asks for directions to the care home.

'She's in her room, prefers it to the lounge,' says the nurse. 'Watches the birds out the window. Sometimes she knows where she is, other days she talks a bit of nonsense. She doesn't get many visitors.'

Her name is on the door: Mrs Lily Morle. Amy had never known her neighbour's first name, the woman who had taught her so much. She had asked Julian about Mrs Morle's whereabouts, when she noticed the cottage where she'd lived now had new people in it. He was vague; told her she'd been admitted to a care home when she could no longer cope.

Amy knocks and slowly pushes open the door. She would have picked the woman out in a crowd. The same neat side parting, though the hair was white now, and pale pursed lips. Mrs Morle wears a floral dress and a cardigan over orange-coloured nylons that ride the bumps of varicose veins.

She is staring out of the window. There is a bird table, the feeder empty of seed.

'Hallo Mrs Morle. Do you remember me? I'm Amy Taylor. I used to live at Mr Stratton's farmhouse a long time ago. Do you remember me?'

The woman raises her eyes to Amy's face; it is like being clamped by pincers. 'Who are you?' she says in a not-unfriendly voice. 'Do you want a cup of tea?'

'Oh, that would be nice, thanks.'

Amy pulls up a chair next to Mrs Morle who fidgets with her cardigan buttons while gazing at the bird table. Amy glances around. A spoon-rest with the words, *Best wishes from Minehead,* sits on a small table next to a glass bird. A tin of talc on a doily. A pink shawl is folded neatly on the pillow of a single bed.

'I've brought you this.' Amy presses a lavender bag into Mrs Morle's hand. 'I made it. A little thank you, Mrs Morle, for everything you did for me when I was at Wyld Farm. You were so kind.'

The woman's fingers rub at the cotton bag. She nods at Amy. 'Lavender,' she says.

On the bedside table there is a framed photograph of a woman that Amy thinks must be Lynn. The hair has a few grey streaks in it, but the green eyes are unmistakable. Lynn is smiling at the camera and holds a little girl on her lap.

'That's Lynn, isn't it?' she says.

'My daughter,' Mrs Morle nods. 'I'll be fetching her from school soon. What's the time?' Her hand scrabbles around the handbag at her feet. 'Must get myself tidy.' She stands up and pulls a comb through her hair. 'I best be off now.'

A click of the bag clasp suggests she is ready.

Amy says gently: 'I don't think Lynn is at school today.'

'She always goes to school, never misses a day,' Mrs Morle retorts.

The door opens and a woman in an overall bustles in with a cup of tea.

'Tea time, Lily, here you are, and a biscuit. Sit down, Lily. Would you like a cup, dear?'

'Mrs Morle is talking about Lynn being at school,' Amy replies.

'She always does that, dear, about this time of day. She gets confused. Lynn isn't at school, Lily, she's grown up now. She doesn't live round here anymore, you know that, Lynn's been gone a long while.'

The woman's voice is raised more loudly than Amy feels is necessary.

Mrs Morle shakes her head and repeats fiercely. 'Time to go to school, must fetch Lynn, must …'

'You can take her outside for a walk if you like. It helps to calm her down. I'll bring the tea out.'

There isn't much to see in the garden, but it is pleasant to be out of the overheated home. Through the window, Amy sees into the lounge where residents, mostly women, sit around a blue rug like it is a pool of still water. Some are held in their chairs by tables pressed up against their stomachs. Others have been tipped so far back that the ceiling is the easiest thing for them to gaze at. A television chatters.

Amy gives Mrs Morle a biscuit. 'The birds might like this,' she says.

The woman begins to crumble the biscuit between stiff fingers. Both became mesmerised by the sweet dust as it drifts in the air.

'Feed the birds,' Amy croons and Mrs Morle sings along in a moment as light as a butterfly.

Back in her room, Mrs Morle washes her fingers at the sink. Above it hangs a framed photograph of a man in working clothes.

'Who is that?'

'My Harry,' Mrs Morle waves her damp fingers. 'He's out on the farm, be back soon enough for his tea.'

She carefully folds the towel and sits back in her chair to wait.

*

When Aubrey arrives, Amy is standing on a chair and chopping the hedge.

'Let me do that, Mrs Webster,' he says taking the shears from her.

Within minutes the hawthorn is trimmed into a shape. Aubrey rakes the cuttings into a heap.

'Where do these go?' he says, holding out the tools.

'Thank you, Aubrey, that's helpful. Prop them by the door. Shall we have a drink outside before dinner? It's still nice out. I'll just call my daughter. Ah, here she is. Chloe – this is Aubrey.'

Her daughter is standing at the back door. For a reluctant supper guest, Chloe has made an effort. Fitted white jeans and sparkly earrings, her hair is caught up in a casual twist. She looks fabulous even if the set of her mouth suggests petulance.

'Pleased to meet you,' Aubrey says, wiping his hands on his trousers. He wishes he'd changed his shirt after his shift at the pub.

Amy says: 'I'm glad you could come. It's nice for us to get to know local people, isn't it, Chloe? I'll get some wine.'

'Yeah,' says the girl. She is horrified by the man's sandals and knitted tank top. Her annoying mother insists on being friendly with everyone and she has picked a loser here.

'Your mother tells me that you're revising for exams?' the man says.

'Yeah.'

'How's it going, the studying and everything?'

'I'm a bit stressed, actually.'

'Of course. I was relieved when mine were over.'

'You didn't go to university?' Amy appears with glasses and a bottle of wine. She turns to her daughter. 'Aubrey works in the local pub.'

'I know, mother, you told me,' Chloe sighs, picking her fingernails.

'I finished my Masters last year and I've applied for funding for further study, a PhD.'

'Really? I didn't realise. Look, please call me Amy. It seems a bit formal to use my married name.'

Chloe splutters: 'If you're clever, why are you working in a pub? In this out of the way place? No shops or cinema or other people or bars. Nothing to do. Unless you like *walking*.'

'I do like walking and the countryside is beautiful. But there's another reason why I've come here. I think I mentioned it,' Aubrey looks at Amy. 'I'm searching for someone. My mother.' He is pleased to have finally captured the girl's attention.

Chloe is transfixed. 'You don't have a mother?'

'I have two mothers actually.'

'*God* … two mothers! Appalling thought. Just teasing, Mum. How can you have two mothers?'

'I was adopted at birth. So I have a birth mother – whom I've never met – and the mother that brought me up. After I finished my study, I decided that before doing anything else, I would see if I could find her. Maybe my father, too.' He shrugs.

'I know people who are adopted often want to do that at some stage of their lives,' says Amy sympathetically. 'Were you able to talk to your mum and dad about it?'

'Yes, of course. They've been open with me about being adopted from when I was about eight or nine. They weren't keen on secrets.'

Something niggles at Amy, a memory she cannot recall. 'I'll just check the food.' She pokes at the chops. Standing by the cooker, she tries to work out what's bothering her.

Outside, Chloe is telling Aubrey her mother is 'an old hippy' and did up the cottage with all her weird friends in 'the old days' before either of them were born. She is making him laugh.

'Come inside you two, it's time to eat. Bring your glasses.'

When they have started eating, Chloe says: 'Do you mind me asking, Aubrey? How do you begin to look for a mother? What did you do?'

Aubrey puts down his fork. 'It was a bit haphazard. You see when I was adopted in the early 1970s, record-keeping was rudimentary. I contacted the agency that arranged my adoption and they gave me this flimsy cardboard file with a few scraps of paper in it. It included notes from the agency worker who arranged my adoption and other stuff. I don't know what I was expecting but it wasn't that.'

'God, how weird,' said Chloe. 'Did anyone go along with you?

'One my friends did offer to come but I wanted to go alone. The woman at the agency was really nice, actually. She explained that when I was adopted, unmarried mothers giving up their babies were told to think of it as a 'clean break'. That's what the woman arranging my adoption probably said to my mum – that she and I should never meet again.'

'It's hard to imagine that now. It sounds so … punitive,' Amy says.

Chloe adds: 'Harsh, yeah. But weren't you a bit angry with her for giving you away?'

Amy winces. Her daughter is so direct.

Aubrey shakes his head. 'Why? I presume there was nothing else she *could* do. For all I know she was forced to give me up. No, I'd like to thank her for her brave decision – and tell her that I'm fine.'

Amy is impressed; Aubrey seems so mature and sanguine about his past.

'But how did you end up round here?' Chloe says.

'That's strange. I found a note in my file, a claim for petty cash. The agency worker must have given my mother money for fares so she could get back home. The woman recorded the place, mentioned this village by name.'

'Wow.' The meal is far more interesting than Chloe could have hoped and, despite his terrible fashion sense, Aubrey is rather sweet. She decides to act the hostess.

'That's quite a story. Mum's bought a lemon tart for pudding. I'll fetch it. No, you stay there, Aubrey. You're our guest.'

*

'Morning, Chloe. You're up bright and early.'

The girl is already at her desk, books open and a pencil between her fingers.

Amy stifles a yawn. Her sleep was disturbed last night. What she had been struggling to recollect finally woke her in the early hours. Something Simon told her a few days after they'd decided to get engaged.

He had insisted she sit on their Habitat sofa, the one she hated as soon as they brought it home and realised the cheap foam filling was too bouncy to be comfortable. She had larked about, pretended to wobble off the sofa.

'What is it, darling? Why the oh-so-serious face?'

'I think we should be honest with each other before our special day,' Simon had said.

The phrase made her giggle.

'I can't believe it's that bad, darling! Have you robbed a bank? If so – hurrah – please can we use the money to buy a new sofa?'

'I'm serious, Amy. I think we should tell each other who we've slept with. We shouldn't have secrets.'

'Oh but I like a little mystery. It's naughty and …'

'Isn't honesty the basis of a good marriage?'

'Don't be pompous, darling, it's not *sexy*. You know about most of my boyfriends anyway. David, that French guy, Terence …' She reeled off the ten men she had slept with.

She did not mention Seymour. Clarity could be cruel. How could she explain to her husband-to-be that Seymour was the most important of her lovers? As the perfect storm of her life raged, mourning her mother, missing her father, Seymour and life on Wyld Farm had given her the sanctuary she needed. And though Seymour had hurt her terribly when he dumped her, trampled on her tender heart, it taught her something she had to understand; what she needed from love and a partner. For that she was grateful.

Simon divulged to her the three women he'd slept with. She pushed him onto the sofa in mock outrage, then teased him about his lack of sexual conquests.

Almost as an afterthought, he added: 'And there was Lynn Morle, too. One jolly evening at Wyld Farm, I crept off with her to the barn.'

His revelation barely registered with Amy at the time. But last night it sent her bolt upright in bed. She switched on the lamp. If Simon had slept with Lynn, could Aubrey be Simon's son?

'Mum, Mum!' Chloe is shaking her arm. 'You've gone into one of your trances. Listen, Mum. I'm really going to work hard today.'

'Good, darling. Last day before we leave for home so you can get lots done.'

'That's my plan. Because basically, yeah, I'm going out later.'

'Going out? But where can you go around here?'

A faint blush colours Chloe's face. 'I'm going for a walk along the Old Mineral Line.'

'But you don't like walking.'

'I do, Mum, just not boring walks like you and Dad go on. Aubrey is taking me. He's going to pick me up on his scooter. Could you collect me from the pub when he starts work at six? Will you, Mum?'

*

The road is long and straight. Aubrey explains it had once been a track for a tiny train transporting minerals from high in the Brendon Hills down to the coast at Watchet. Information that if her father had told her Chloe would have found tedious in the extreme.

But Aubrey has a way of describing things that makes them interesting. He is nothing like the boys she meets at school or at parties, 'lads' she calls them. They only talk of sport and spots.

Huge straight-trunked trees grow by the side of road. Plants with giant palmate leaves arch over their heads.

'Makes me feel like Alice, like I've shrunk in size. I'm in Wonderland,' Chloe whispers.

'Do you like that book, too? It's one of my favourites,' Aubrey whispers back.

They talk about the other books they like and music and the beach in the town where Aubrey was raised and the university she hopes to go to and where they'd like to travel. Then they walk in silence.

After a time, Aubrey says: 'I've decided to give in my notice at the pub. I'll leave after the weekend.'

'Really? What about finding your 'real' mother?'

'I've got a real mother and she's back at home with my Dad in Portsmouth. I've been living around here for a while and I haven't found her and I've decided I should just get on with my life. Talking to you and your Mum last night, I don't know, it helped me to see things clearly.'

He is holding Chloe's hand. Not much taller than she, Aubrey could see all the colours in Chloe's eyes. 'It feels right somehow,' he says, gently letting her hand drop.

'You sound like you know what you want.'

'I think I do.'

They start to walk again. After a few minutes, they reach the village cricket pitch.

'Let's sit here,' said Aubrey. He clears the bench of sweet papers left by a previous visitor.

On the other side of the pitch, a steep bank of trees sweeps up to the sky line. Gangs of birds trace the tree tops in flight.

Suddenly, Chloe is giddy with happiness. 'Thanks for taking me on the walk. I liked it. Mum will be shocked by that! She says I'm lazy.'

'I don't know about that.' He sounds serious. 'Can we stay in touch, Chloe? Would that be okay?'

She was hoping he'd ask. She tugs at his jacket sleeve. She doesn't mind that it's made of corduroy. 'It would be lovely. I liked being in Wonderland with you.'

'Did you? I liked it too. I like being with you.'

They are sitting quite close now, their hands almost touching.

After a time he says reluctantly: 'I suppose I'd better get going. I've got to set up the bar for tonight, and to tell the owner what I've decided to do and ... it's been ... Chloe – good luck in your exams. I'm sure they'll go well. You're clever.'

'Good luck to us both,' says Chloe.

She leans against him. He turns towards her and his long hair brushes her face. Too bad if anyone sees their kiss.

Chapter Thirty-Two

For more than twenty years, Mrs Morle hoped each day to see an envelope with her daughter's handwriting lying on the doormat. Precious longed-for words from her daughter.

But it's still a shock when the letter arrives at the cottage. Mrs Morle's knees crack like a gun when she bends down to pick up the letter. Gentle fingers slide cherished sheets of Basildon Bond from their envelope, the surfaces upon which her daughter's breath has fallen and where traces of her fingerprints might be. Mrs Morle raises the pages to her nose, sniffs long and slow, as though her child's scent lingers in the ink.

April 1995

Dear Mother,

I hope you will be happy to hear from me. Bob my husband says you will be even though it's more than 20 years since we last saw each other.

I had to leave you, what else could I do? Giving up my baby broke my heart. I have always hoped that my son found a nice family to love him and look after him. I will never know.

I sometimes wonder if you regret what you did, making me give him away. How much we missed, you and I.

When I ran away from you, I found a job in a hospital, first

in the kitchen and then as a cleaner on a ward. One of the nurses persuaded me that I should train. It was a good choice for me because it took me away from everything I knew and everything I had ruined. I did my nursing exams and I passed. I worked my way up and now all these years later, I'm a Senior Staff Nurse.

It was hard for me to live in a town. But I'm glad that I did for that is where I met my husband. Bob is a psychiatric nurse. He did not judge me as though I had fallen as a girl, and I began to see the world through his eyes and to realise that I was not bad because I fell pregnant. We got married and we are happy.

We had to wait eight years for our darling daughter. Daisy was born last April. She has brought so much joy into our lives, and every day I thank my stars that we have her.

Being a Mum has made me think of you and everything good that you and Dad did for me. On her first birthday, I decided I would get in touch. We cannot change the past but we can try to make the present better and the future hopeful.

Bob and me would like to visit, Mother, now Daisy is settled, to show you your beautiful granddaughter.

I have forgiven you – but have you forgiven me?

I enclose a photograph of Daisy. Her middle name is Lily after the grandmother that I hope will one day know her.

With love from your daughter, Lynn

Chapter Thirty-Three

Simon surveys the pile of letters on his desk. He recognises David's writing on one envelope. He hopes it contains a cheque for the 'cottage maintenance and repairs' fund. Last month, David admitted to Simon that he was 'a bit short' and asked if Simon could sub him the money? Simon was happy to agree. He opens the letter. He hopes owning this cottage jointly with David and Maggie will not be a recurrent administrative and financial headache.

He is not reassured. The letter not only asks for an extension to the loan but requests another to cover this month's contribution. As a postscript, David adds that he can't use the cottage this weekend; he'd forgotten his band has been booked for a gig. Can Amy shift the rota so he can go later in the month?

The front door to the house opens. Downstairs he hears Amy and Chloe coming into the house, dragging their cases. 'You c-c-could have stayed at the c-c-cottage!' He shouts.

The traffic sounds leaking through the open door drown his voice. He's irritated. Why didn't David call by phone to rearrange his visit rather than write?

Chloe stomps up the stairs past his office. She mutters, 'Hi Dad,' followed by the click of her bedroom door. The countryside has marginally improved her mood, it seems. At least she has acknowledged her father's existence.

'Did you say something?' Amy asks, kissing the top of Simon's head. 'How are you, darling? I've left the cottage nice and tidy for David's arrival tomorrow.'

'You needn't have bothered. He's not going down after all. He's got to rehearse for a *gig*.' Simon practically spits the word.

Over the years, Amy has noticed that Simon's stutter disappears, not when he is angry but when he is *very* angry. Her husband gestures dismissively at a letter.

'And David says, can you sort out a different weekend for him to use the cottage. And oh, can he have another loan? I'd forgotten he was an irresponsible nuisance.'

'Sometimes we are all faced with responsibilities we were not expecting,' she replies.

'That's a bit c-c-cryptic, darling,' Simon says. 'I always m-m-meet *my* responsibilities.' He gives her a quizzical look.

'Oh, do you? Then let me remind you of one you may have forgotten. The young man I met in the village pub – Aubrey? He came for supper last night with me and Chloe.'

'Very n-n-nice for you. How is this r-r-relevant, may I ask?'

She is annoyed now. How can he not remember?

'Aubrey told us about his past. How he was given away at birth and adopted. Now he's now searching for his mother who apparently used to live in or near the village. The village near Wyld Farm.'

'Yes?' Simon is still flummoxed. She is hinting at something, but he cannot imagine what.

'Aubrey was born in 1974. Have you forgotten creeping off to a barn for a bit of nookie in the hay? Lynn Morle, darling. Think about it. The dates match. What I'm saying is – could Aubrey be your and Lynn's son?'

For the second night running, she had barely slept. The thought that Aubrey could be her stepson was one thing, something she might come to accept, even welcome in different circumstances. He was a charming young man. But when Chloe had announced with glee last night that she was falling in love with him, it was horrifying. Incest was not something Amy wanted to grapple with.

Simon shakes his head. 'Silly g-g-girl, I was only t-t-teasing you!'

'Teasing? What do you mean?'

'I told you a l-l-lie about sleeping with L-L-Lynn. Of course I didn't s-s-sleep with her.'

'A *lie*? Why in hell did you say you had, then?'

'Because you weren't being straight with me. Remember? You kept things back from me that night. We were meant to be open and frank. But you kept something from me.'

She stares at the man she's been married to for more than twenty years.

'It w-w-was a little g-g-game I played with you.' His tone is serious. 'I wanted to t-t-test you, Amy. I knew you had been, shall I put it bluntly, s-s-screwing Seymour. It was obvious to everyone, except D-D-David, perhaps. I wanted to see if you would b-b-be honest.' He takes her hand. 'And darling, you were not.'

*

A dealer in Germany is interested in buying some of Seymour's work. For several days, her letter lies on the kitchen table. Miriam reads it again. The condolences in stilted English, the carefully phrased request to see 'more of the great man's work'. There are other letters, too; one from Seymour's agent. His book of portraits of models, politicians, actors, footballers and entertainers from the 1970s, is still selling well.

'We've got to start sorting out your father's affairs. A dealer wants to visit,' Miriam says.

Julian is checking his beard for toast crumbs. No point in reassuring him there are none. It's one of his tics. 'She must have seen the obituary in *The Times*. What are we going to say to her? Do you even know what's in the darkroom?'

'I haven't thought about it.'

'All the equipment, the stuff he was working on before he got too poorly. His archives, all those boxes. Shouldn't we at least get rid of the chemicals?'

'I've told you Miriam, I haven't thought about it,' Julian snaps.

A spoonful of cereal on the way to Peter's mouth stops in mid-air. The boy glances at his father and mother.

'You're right, Miriam. I just find the whole thing upsetting,' Julian adds quickly. Though he appreciates his wife's efficiency, he finds her persistence exhausting. 'Could you see what's in there? I suspect a total muddle. I can't bear it yet.'

Later that morning, she takes the key hanging from a nail by the darkroom door. The lock turns easily.

'Can I come with you, Mummy?' Peter stands against her thigh.

'I don't think … alright darling, stay by me.'

Miriam feels for the switch. A bulb emitting dim light hums into life. Mother and son shuffle into the room. Blacked out windows make it hard to distinguish what's there. The smell of chemicals.

Miriam feels along the wall for another switch. Two single bulbs hanging from wires now illuminate a ceiling-high stack of shelves and a row of filing cabinets. A desk, several chairs and tables are piled with cameras and other paraphernalia. A floor-length black curtain waves in the draught. Holding Peter's hand, she draws it back. A line of three deep sinks and arched taps. Trays of fluid in which photographs float like squid. Above their heads, other images dangle like bunting.

'Is this where Grandad lives?' whispers Peter.

'No, he's in the graveyard, do you remember, darling? He used to work in here. He took photographs. Look, here's one he took of you.'

Propped up on the draining board is a picture of Julian kneeling by Peter.

'Can I have it?'

'Of course you can. Sit here for a moment.' She lifts the boy onto a chair. 'I've just got to search for something in Grandad's office.'

Seymour had been more orderly here. In one drawer, there are invoices, bills and statements. In another, correspondence including two letters from the German dealer are clipped together.

It all needs sorting and she will do it at some point. She won't mind. Creating order out of chaos has a satisfaction. She flattens the paperwork to close the drawer but something is jamming it. She feels inside. Bent against the back wall of the drawer is a stamped envelope addressed to Seymour's lawyer, Sunil Rao. It's unsealed.

Miriam doesn't resist temptation, taking out the letter and reading it. She gasps.

'What is it, Mummy?'

'Nothing, darling. Just something that I must deal with.'

Chapter Thirty-Four

'I'm going to the cottage tomorrow.' Simon hands Amy a gin and tonic. A slice of lime and plenty of ice, just the way she likes it.

She wonders what he's about to say.

'Since our D-D-Dave isn't using the c-c-cottage, I called Julian and suggested we get together for a b-b-boy's weekend.'

'That sounds nice,' Amy sips her drink.

It is not clear why but since discovering her husband has known all along about her affair with Seymour, she has felt faintly ridiculous. She wishes she had been honest with Simon.

'Julian's up for it. He says M-M-Miriam's obsessed with s-s-sorting out the house at w-w-weekends. I'll leave t-t-tomorrow, be b-b-back Sunday evening.'

'But we've been invited to the Palmers for drinks.'

They exchange the glances. Neither wants to spend an evening drinking wine discussing neighbours who aren't present.

Amy goes to check the pasta. Simon follows her into the kitchen.

'Mum, when's supper? I'm starving,' Chloe hollers from upstairs.

'Chloe, can you c-c-come down if you want to speak to us. Amy, I'll c-c-call the Palmers and make our excuses, s-s-say something's c-c-come up at the cottage.'

'So I won't have to go on my own. That's great, thanks. Chloe, supper's ready! Can you come and lay the table, please? Forks and spoons for pasta.'

'I know what we need.' Chloe glares at her mother as she comes through into the kitchen. Grabbing a handful of cutlery, she plonks it on the table. 'Dad, Mum, I have to tell you something.' She eyes them defiantly.

'Set the table properly, please. And mats, too, Chloe. These bowls are hot.'

'God, Mum, you're so anal. Look, I'm spending the weekend at Tilly's. I'm eighteen. I should be able to do what I want and they're *my* exams. I'll study tonight and all Saturday, then me and Tilly are going to a party and her Mum is going to pick us up at midnight and I won't get smashed but I *can't miss this* party.' She has not drawn breath.

'Fine,' Amy snaps. 'Simon, we were living at the farm when we were her age with no responsible adults. It's up to you, Chloe.'

*

On Saturday morning, Amy wakes to an empty house. Odd to be alone and without any plans. The third time she finds herself straightening the tea towels, she knows she has to act. At the station, she buys a listings magazine and takes the train to London.

The pub is packed with people who are drinking and shouting. She walks to the back of the bar. Through a door is the place where the music happens. On a raised portion of the floor that does not justify the description of 'stage', four musicians manoeuvre like matadors between mic stands and amps. David's jeans and boots give him a certain glamour and the flame-haired saxophonist in a tight gold dress looks good, too. Another woman tunes her bass. A rotund accordion player in a trilby hat spits 'one, two, three' into a complaining microphone.

Amy goes to the ladies, pins up her hair and slashes colour on her lips. Buying a beer, she joins the fifteen or so other people standing around the edge of the music room as though avoiding a massive hole. Then the long unfamiliar intoxicating sound of electrically enhanced live music begins. Amy's bones jangle. Quirky songs that mix jazz, blues and Klezmer are sung by David with harmonies from the bass player. Some people dance. Those who do not, sway and swing. Amy is not the only person to whoop in appreciation when the set ends.

'Those familiar dulcet squawks. I knew it must be you!' David plants a sweaty kiss on her cheek. 'Thanks for coming. How did you find us?'

'It was brilliant fun, I really loved it. What a band!' She is genuinely enthusiastic. 'Simon got your letter. You said you had a gig tonight and as I was at a loose end, I came along.'

The next band is already trooping onto the stage. Five lads in big boots with short hair, are greeted by catcalls and shouts as their fans swamp the area by the stage. They lower the average age of the audience by many years.

'These guys are special, you should stay and listen,' David whispers as an ear-splitting roar of electric guitars crashes over their heads.

He pulls her to one side as more young people flood in from the bar, bringing smells of beer and sweat. Fast and furious, the band thunders through its set, the drunken lead singer continuing to carouse even when he topples into the drum kit. He is dragged to his feet by another musician. Raw energy out of control.

'This is fabulous!' Amy shouts as fans leap on each other's shoulders, each trying to spring higher than the next, shouting out the lyrics they know and making up those they don't. Worries about Chloe, confusion about Seymour, concerns about the cottage, are forgotten. More fun than she's had in ages.

A bouncing fan pushes her into David. Like a light switch, her body tingles at the feel and the smell of her first love. Reluctantly, she disentangles herself. He straightens his jacket and catches her eye. She finds herself gliding towards him.

'Hi,' a woman hisses in her ear. 'We haven't met. I'm Amber, David's girlfriend.'

✷

Amy just makes the last train. The taxi drops her home and she lets herself into the house. It was stupid of her to flirt with David. Thank goodness it went no further.

Just about to go to upstairs with a glass of water and two headache pills, Amy notices the answer machine light flashing. Miriam's calm voice explains that Simon has tripped and smashed his knee, has been to A&E and will be discharged from the local hospital in the morning. Is Amy able to drive down to collect him? Or should Miriam do it?

CHAPTER THIRTY-FIVE

Seymour settled down with a cup of coffee in the garden. Mid-April and with a blanket on his knees, Miriam was right: it was warm enough to enjoy the sun. Seymour had always been a sun-worshipper. And a connoisseur of coffee. Every two weeks a packet from Fortnum's arrived at the farm with a special blend of beans along with his favourite madeleines.

Seymour licked the sugar off a second biscuit. Where was Garfield? Had the postman retired? This generation of postal workers only deigned to leave their vans to shove the mail through letterboxes. Not the proper 'delivery' that Garfield had once provided, walking across the valley carrying the post in his bag.

Seymour flicked through a weekly political magazine. Before Miriam left this morning with Julian to buy sandals for Peter, she had settled him with a pot of coffee, a rug and his book. The garden could not be called beautiful for the flower beds hosted weeds and the hedges were unruly. But it was certainly pleasant.

'Ah, Mrs Morle. This is a surprise.'

It amazed him that at eighty-one years of age, Mrs Morle still worked for him. But not on a Saturday. So why was she heading towards him?

Clasped to her chest was a letter. A dramatic gesture he did not associate with her stolid temperament. Letters were the only way the woman kept in touch with the outside world. She refused to have a phone despite Seymour offering to pay for the installation.

'Lynn's letter has come!'

'A letter from your daughter? My goodness! This is unexpected. Sit down, Mrs Morle, you look exhausted.'

'Water. I need water.'

'Yes, of course.'

He slid over the glass of water that Miriam had left for him to take his pills. The tablets winked accusingly at him. 'What does Lynn say?'

Mrs Morle's eyes were glued to the letter as though the words might fly away.

'She's fine, she's married – *married!* And she had a baby last year. A little girl, Daisy Lily. Oh, that's such a pretty name. I can't believe it, Mr Stratton, not after all these years, her getting in touch. I hoped she would one day but …'

'So you're a grandmother? Congratulations Mrs Morle, that's wonderful.'

Taking Peter in his arms at only a few days old had made him swell with pride. It was a feeling Seymour had not anticipated.

'Daisy's got pretty eyes and lovely hair – see this photo! I can't wait to show Harry.'

Mrs Morle sometimes talked as though her husband was still alive.

'She's beautiful, Mrs Morle, takes after her grandmother, naturally. Does Lynn talk … about visiting?'

'She does. She wants to bring Daisy to meet me.'

'A reconciliation after all these years. You can plan a little party, a celebration. Mrs Morle, is everything alright? '

'There's something I must tell you, Mr Stratton. Something that happened to my Lynn all those years ago.'

'Really? Alright, if you feel you must.'

Mrs Morle patted her hair, slightly turned away. 'It's the reason we fell out, Mr Stratton.'

'We fell out?'

'Me and Lynn, I mean. You see, she got herself pregnant when she was just a girl, no more than eighteen years old. It was a shock. The day she told me, I didn't know what to do, I was beside meself. Wouldn't tell me who the boy was that done it, neither.'

She was taking in short, sharp breaths.

'Have a drink, Mrs Morle, please. You'll faint.'

'I was terrified about people finding out. What would they think of her – or me? So before the baby showed, I sent Lynn away to one of them special homes for unmarried girls. That's where she had it.'

She turned to him. Her lips were dry.

'I made her give it away for adoption, Mr Stratton. A baby boy, she told me when she came back home. But she said she couldn't bear to be with me no more, not after that. So she took herself off. She left me. I never heard from her again. I told you it was because she got work. But it weren't. Oh, I've missed her so much.'

Her head sagged. Her pink scalp showed through thinning hair.

'I'm sure you did what you thought was best, Mrs Morle.'

'Seemed the only thing I *could* do at the time, Mr Stratton. Best for her *and* the baby, I thought. But now, looking back, I think that I was wrong.'

A car drove into the yard. There were voices. Seymour's daughter-in-law talking to Peter and Julian. Seymour filched the glass from beside Mrs Morle and hurriedly took his pills.

'We can't change the past. Though you and I both, we sometimes wish we could,' he said deliberately. For a moment, his hand rested on hers. 'And you have Daisy to look forward to. Lynn wants to come and visit. It's good news, surely?'

'I've got regrets and there's nothing that I can do with 'em,' said Mrs Morle. She struggled to her feet. 'Best be on me way, eh?'

Chapter Thirty-Six

'I just don't want to spend money that we don't have on some poky cottage that you own with some old gits from the past, one of whom wanted to put her tongue down your throat last night!'

Amber's shouts ricochet round the car. 'It's our allocated weekend, according to her bloody rota,' Amber sneers, 'and we need some space and will you shut up David and drive!'

*

Maggie wakes. The town is quiet this early in the morning. She stares at the ceiling. Last night the lonely hearts contact – she couldn't grace the despicable person with any other label – did not show up at the venue where they had agreed to meet. How rude and unkind can people be?

In some moods, her bedroom is a place of tranquillity. Today the emptiness defines her.

She ties her dressing gown cord around her hips and waist. She lets Merry out in the garden. It's when she's going back into the flat that she sees the letter lying on the door mat. She's been expecting it for days. But seeing it for real, the organisation's stamp on an envelope addressed to her, is a shock.

She handles the letter like it's a suspicious package. Props it against the pepper pot while she makes tea. Ignores it while she makes a piece of toast. Opening it means facing rejection. Breathing slowly in and out, Maggie conjures up the voice of her meditation teacher telling her to abandon negative thoughts.

Chucking the toast in the bin, she rolls a cigarette and leans out of the window to smoke.

For the last few days, it's rained incessantly. 'That's summer over,' people have been saying from under umbrellas. Today the roof tiles on the house opposite glint in the sun. A plane's white tail drifts in the sky.

It's an omen. She prises open the envelope.

There's a knock at her door. 'Hi Maggie, sorry to bother you.'

It's one of the men who lives upstairs with his partner, the one who thrusts political pamphlets at her. Geraint or Gareth, she can never remember who is who. 'It's about the party,' he says.

She shakes her head. 'I don't want to join the party. I'm going to live in India.' She hasn't put concealer on her scars this morning. She doesn't care.

'Oh cool. I'm not calling about *that* party, actually. It's about the one we're having tonight. A celebration. It might be a bit noisy. Come along if you'd like to.'

Waiting for the coach, Maggie lists in her head all the things she must do before she leaves. What about Merry? Tonight she'll stay at the cottage. Even if it's not 'her weekend', whoever is down there will have to stuff it. She's about to leave the country for the next three years. Who knows? She might never come back.

*

The sounds of a saxophone and a bass guitar competing for volume blast from an upstairs window. Amy peeks through the half-closed curtains. Her husband is sprawled on the sofa, his plastered leg on a chair, a can of beer in hand. Next to him Julian balances Peter on his knee. All holler 'yeeesss!' at the television. Crisps scatter from the bag as the boy waves it about in celebration.

Amy pushes open the door of Bramble Cottage. It catches on the uneven floor; for a moment she is suspended between entry and exclusion. She goes into the kitchen.

'Oh, Amy, you're here at last.' Miriam's tone is clipped. 'I'm waiting for the match to finish. Then I'll take Peter back to the farmhouse.'

The volume of music coming from upstairs is such that she must raise her voice to be heard.

'Miriam, hallo.' Amy walks closer to the woman so she can be heard. 'Is that David and Amber? But he wrote to us saying he wasn't using the cottage this weekend.'

'I really don't know.' Miriam says dismissively. 'He and Amber were here when I got back from the hospital with Simon. I gather from the rather heated conversation that Amber doesn't like football. I think there was a disagreement, shall we say.'

'Oh dear. Well, thanks for collecting Simon. I came as soon as I could.' This is not strictly true. Amy had dropped back to sleep after the alarm went off, something to do with the effects of mixing beer and gin. 'Do you know how the accident happened?'

Miriam regarded her coolly. 'Simon and Julian had a party last night. I wasn't there, I had an early night. But at some point, I gather, Simon fell over and smashed his knee. He was in agony. They woke me up. I had to drive Simon to casualty.'

'I'm so sorry you had to get involved.'

'What did you say?'

'I said, I'm sorry you had to sort everything out,' Amy has to shout to be heard.

'What alternative did I have? Julian was in no fit state to drive,' Miriam bellows back.

A roar from the sitting room. The kitchen door flies opens. Amy expects to see Peter running in to tell his mother about a goal. But it's Maggie.

'What the hell is going on here? It's like bedlam!' she screeches. 'I came for some peace and quiet, for God's sake!'

She glares at Amy and Miriam, then runs upstairs followed by her barking dog. They hear her screaming at her brother, a door slamming, steps thundering down the stairs and then shouting from the sitting room.

'Since you're all unexpectedly at Bramble Cottage,' says Miriam, rising from her chair, 'I had better tell you what's happened.'

Chapter Thirty-Seven

It was like the day they moved into the cottage. When Miriam says she has an important piece of information to share and could they all please gather, Amy, Simon and his plastered leg, David, Amber, Maggie, Merry, Peter and Julian cram into the sitting room to sit, perch and lean among the crisp crumbs. They carefully avoid the Buddha.

Miriam stands centre-stage by the unlit fireplace. She says it is necessary because sitting worsens her back pain. Amy suspects the real reason is she feels more in control.

Everyone is exasperated. How long is this going to take?

Maggie is seething. She has come to the cottage to walk in peace with her dog and think about India. Not to huddle inside with everyone else. Owning this cottage is turning out to be a complete pain.

David is petulant. He has been hopeful of getting Amber into bed. Although his sister's undignified screaming threatened to spoil the mood, playing the sax usually makes Amber amorous. A foot massage will help. As soon as this is over, he will find the massage oil.

The itch under Simon's plaster is driving him crazy and his creeping hangover will only be mollified by another beer. If only he could sneak out to fetch the last can from the fridge. He distracts himself by thinking about that splendid cottage in Normandy and the details the agent sent.

Julian wants to smoke the roll-up in his pocket, but it is not allowed in the cottage and anyway, Miriam will give him the eye if he does.

Amy knows something unexpected is going to be revealed.

Peter is hungry.

Her training as an accountant lends Miriam's disclosure a methodical air. For her, the revelations are broadly positive. The weekend's chaos only confirms it is the right way forward. Better for her husband's health and their marriage certainly. She will not, of course, share this view with the assembled group. She enjoys the thought that her husband will be dumbfounded by what she imparts. He will admire her capacity to keep secrets. He will wonder what else she has not told him. He will understand her a little better and fear her a little more. She finds that erotic.

Miriam waits for silence to settle, then begins: 'After Seymour's death, Julian and I agreed that we must clear out Seymour's darkroom. As you may not be aware, my father-in-law continued to work until only a few weeks before his death. Some of his best work in my view. But he was finding administration an increasing burden. It was a task which he did not allow me or anyone else to help with.

'Perhaps that explains why when I started clearing out the studio a few weeks ago, I found an unsealed envelope addressed to his lawyer in a drawer. It carried a stamp. I hope you agree I did the right thing when the next day I delivered the letter personally to the addressee, Mr Rao. The lawyer who read out the will.'

She pauses for a moment to formulate her phrases and heighten the effect. Half an hour ago, it had been impossible to talk in the cottage. Now Miriam can hear the wind in the trees. 'Before I delivered it, I read the letter. Was I right to do that? It was not addressed to me. Be that as it may, I did.'

She clears her throat.

'The intention of the letter, written four months before his death, was to add a codicil to Seymour's will, the will written and now held in Mr Rao's office. The letter and codicil were signed in the presence of Seymour's hospital nurse, a Mrs Janet Norris. She used to come to the farmhouse to help us care for Seymour. We know her well. This codicil stated that certain clauses in the will should be modified.'

Those listening are mystified. What is Miriam saying?

'The codicil modifies the will in favour of Seymour's *second* son,' she says.

Julian starts. Miriam has not mentioned any of this to him. He has a *brother*? Julian had often longed for a sibling during childhood, and more recently when Seymour was ill, imagined sharing the burden with a sibling. He imagines what it might be like to have a brother. Wonderful, surely? It crosses his mind briefly that it could complicate things financially. The farmhouse and the land might have to be divided up.

Simon is not surprised to learn Seymour had fathered another child. He tries to catch Amy's eye, but she is staring at the floor. He looks at David. Both men shrug.

'The son's name is not given in the codicil because Seymour was not in possession of it. He did not have the person's name. But he was able to identify the boy as being the issue of him and … Lynn Morle.'

Maggie explodes. 'What? Lynn and Seymour? What was he thinking? The man was a *complete* sleaze ball. Sorry Julian, but really, couldn't he keep his dick …'

'Do you mind? Peter is here,' he says, glaring back.

'So he gives with one hand and takes back with the other. Typical Seymour,' she adds.

'Could you stop? It's my father you're criticising,' says Julian.

Amy feels a jab of jealousy. Had Seymour been sleeping with Lynn as well as her? She remembered their relationship as being passionate. She's more than slightly miffed.

'Shall I continue?' Miriam asks. 'The codicil requests that every effort is made to find the man. He was born in 1974 and, according to his grandmother, was given away for adoption in the first week of life. That being the case, Seymour instructed that Bramble Cottage and half the royalties from his books, Faces, should be inherited by the second son.'

'What?' Everyone is shocked.

'To reiterate, I took the letter to the lawyer that same day. I expect you'll hear from Sunil Rao formally to explain what has happened. However, off the record, my enquiries suggest this change will be upheld *if* the son can be found. He will inherit Bramble Cottage and some money. As it's only been a few months since the distributions were made, it's unlikely a challenge would hold. If any of you were thinking about that.' Miriam glances around the room. 'I'm sorry to be harbinger of bad news.' She does not look sorry.

She takes a bundle of photographs out from a leather tote. 'I thought you might like to see these. Pictures of you all when you lived at Wyld Farm. They were in a drawer in the studio. Seymour had labelled it – *Wyld Dreamers*.'

She puts some on a table and holds out others to Simon.

'Oh dear, p-p-pictures of us? N-N-Not sure I'm up for anymore s-s-shocks t-t-today.'

Amy takes them instead. They are of scenes and people she remembers and some she has forgotten. Parties and meals and walks, a picnic by a stream, one of her milking Daisy, the five of them in the vegetable garden podding peas. How young we were then, she thinks. How hairy and trim and dreamy and really rather luscious.

'Mummy, I'm hungry,' Peter says.

'Of course you are, Peter. Daddy and I will take you back for some food.'

*

The Strattons leave for the farmhouse. Amber says that the four of them must have 'stuff to discuss' so she'll go for a walk. She gives David the thumbs-up sign as she leaves the cottage.

'I need alcohol,' he says. 'This is all rather unexpected.'

'Easy come, easy go,' says Maggie, which irritates everyone for different reasons.

'Only one can of beer left in the f-f-fridge. Rest was finished last n-n-night, sorry m-m-ate. And my name's on it.'

'So our inheritance has been rescinded. Is that the right phrase?' David says.

'What about the pub?' says Maggie. 'Someone said they sell quite nice wine there.'

'God, this is a blow,' says Amy. 'Not owning the cottage. I think I'm devastated.'

'There's always F-F-France, darling, a cottage in N-N-Normandy like we d-d-discussed …' Simon says.

'Dirty old Seymour,' says Maggie. 'Never liked him.'

'It was proving to be a bit of a hassle,' says David.

'What was?' Amy says.

'The cottage. Expensive for a start.'

'You always were tight, David,' Amy replies. 'I've always wanted to come back to Wyld Farm again …'

'Well, I'm off to India,' says Maggie. 'Can't wait actually. Just got to find a home for Merry. I was wondering, Amy, if …'

'I'm skint. I don't have enough cash to buy another place,' David moans.

'We d-d-don't want a d-d-dog, Maggie, and that's f-f-final.'

'Simon, are you quite sure? A dog would get you out of the house each day and Chloe will be off to university soon. Empty nest syndrome and all that.'

'I guess I can go on tour with Amber now,' David says brightly.

'The boy has to be found *before* he can inherit the cottage,' says Maggie, 'I mean, he might be dead.'

'Maggie, that's a bit …

'We should tell them, Simon,' Amy says.

'Tell us what?' David and Maggie reply in unison.

'We know where he is.'

'Who?'

'The boy.'

'What boy?'

'Seymour's second son.'

'You do? Why didn't you say? Where is he then?'

'Shall we go to the pub?' says Amy.

Chapter Thirty-Eight

Amy told Julian and Miriam she would leave the church promptly after the funeral and return to Wyld Farm to get things ready for the wake. Mrs Morle had outlived the few friends she made in her life, but there are others who will want to celebrate her life: Andrew Bishop and his wife, the care home manager, and Sunil Rao.

They will join Mrs Morle's family, people she reconnected with only in the last years of her life. Because of her dementia, Mrs Morle was never entirely sure who Lynn was. But she liked the friendly lady who brought a delightful little girl to visit her in the care home. Mrs Morle looked forward to her husband's visits, too. She did not realise it was Aubrey, her grandson, who escorted her around the garden. It made her happy to think it was Harry, so like Harry he was.

Amy feels at home in the farmhouse kitchen. Her heels click on the flagstones as she fetches plates, chooses cutlery, and arranges slices of the *tarte tatin* she brought from France on the Minton platter that was Seymour's favourite. She can't help it; she listens for his voice as though her former lover might burst into the room at any minute, all ebullient fizz and energy. If she ever felt anger towards him, it has dissipated. Now she wishes to thank him. In the maelstrom of life at Wyld Farm, Seymour had, in his own way, given her stability at a time when she needed it most. It ripped her apart when he sent her away from her Arcadian dream in the

Somerset hills. But now she sees it was the best thing that could have happened. From him, she learned what she needed most from love. His rejection released her to go and find it.

The kettle boils quickly on the sleek new Aga. In the past three years, the farmhouse has been modernised. Stone floors glisten, drawers close with a swish, thick carpets and curtains keep the place cosy. The wild murals are gone, painted over in stylish taupe and vivid terracotta to set off big prints of Seymour's black and white photographs. Two of Julian's paintings hang too; abstract acrylics in bright colours. He has found the confidence to show the work he's started in the last few years. At last night's supper, Simon teased Julian and Miriam that Amy should write a feature story about their glamorous home for a glossy property magazine.

Despite the changes, the farmhouse still churns with dreams and gentle ghosts.

The sound of car doors slamming; there are voices in the farmyard. From the office window, Amy sees Aubrey talking to his mother, Lynn. The woman disappears into the cottage. It's where she's staying for the funeral; she must be fetching something. Aubrey takes Daisy's hand and tells his half-sister a joke; the little girl giggles. Julian and Miriam call for Peter and watch him hold open the gate so Simon can drive in. Everyone waits for him to park, then they walk together towards the farmhouse.

She is not ready, not yet.

Through the boot room and out the back door she slips into the garden. The vegetable patch has grown over and the fruit bushes are gone. Now there is a lawn, worn thin in patches near a football goal and a large trampoline. The flower borders are full of happy weeds. How gratifying to see the apricot tree is still here. She planted it against the warmest wall when Seymour gave it to her.

It's ablaze with blossom. A breeze lifts the shock white flowers into the air. Petals drift like snow.

Perhaps Chloe will eat its fruit this summer? Last night, as they stacked the dishwasher while their hosts put their son to bed, Aubrey confided in Amy and Simon. He said with a blush that now Chloe has finished her degree, the two have decided to start seeing each other again. That they are in love. That he wants to renovate Bramble Cottage. That Chloe will help him.

It made them chuckle, those plans of Aubrey's; had them in stitches when they were getting ready for bed. Did Aubrey have any idea quite how lazy princess Chloe was?

Other thoughts Amy does not share with Simon for she is not sure if her husband would understand. To her there's a kind of moral beauty that Aubrey now owns the cottage. Possessing it allowed them all a brief nostalgic sashay into the past. But that was over now, no longer relevant. How happy she is to think that Chloe will live for a time at Wyld Farm. Amy's link with the place will continue through her daughter and, though it is hard to understand quite why, it is gratifying.

She can hear the murmur of voices through the open kitchen window; the guests for Mrs Morle's wake. Amy heads back into the farmhouse.

AFTERWORD

In the 1970s, I lived and worked for a few years on a Somerset farm.

Photo - Edward Babbage

I fell in love with the landscape and the life, and the things I did there formed the fabric and foundation of my life. Some of those experiences have influenced what's written in this book but little bears direct resemblance to what we got up to. That's for another book, perhaps.

Author's Note

I recommend these inspirational books:
The Fat of the Land by *John Seymour*
Food for Free by *Richard Mabey*
Organic Vegetable Growing by *BG Furner*
Easymade Wines & Country Drinks by *Mrs Gennery-Taylor*
Perfect Cookery by *Marguerite Patten*
The Tassajarra Bread Book by *Edward Espe Brown*
The Secret Garden by *Frances Hodgson Burnett*

Songs, music and albums that inspired Wyld Dreamers:
Eric Clapton: *Layla,* **The Beatles:** *Here Comes The Sun*
Little Feat: *Little Feat*
Dusty Springfield: *I Only Want to Be with You*
Simon & Garfunkel: *Bridge Over Troubled Water*
Joni Mitchell: *All I Want*
Leonard Cohen: *Songs of Love and Hate*
Aretha Franklin: *The Moment I Wake Up*
Rod Stewart: *Every Picture Tells A Story*
Grace Slick: *White Rabbit,* **Rolling Stones:** *Sticky Fingers*
The Beatles: *Sgt. Pepper's Lonely Hearts Club Band*
The Byrds: *Eight Miles High,* **Lyn Anderson:** *Rose Garden*
March Bolan: *Get It On,* **The Who:** *Who's Next*
Van Morrison: *Tupelo Honey*
Roberta Flack: *The First Time Ever I Saw Your Face*
Leo Kottke: *Mudlark,* **The Velvet Underground:** *Loaded*
Randy Newman: *Live,* **Carole King:** *Tapestry*
Melanie: *The Rollerskate Song*

Acknowledgements

There are many people to thank for their support in the writing of this book, but I'd like to mention in particular: Greg Hodder, Sally Wilkinson, Hugh Constant, Michelle Fink, Richard Holmes, Toni Turner, Callum Holmes Williams, David Roth and especially Kipper Williams.

Thanks also to my agent, Laura Morris, and my publisher, Matthew Smith, for their constant good humour and continued support.

Wyld Dreamers is Pamela Holmes' second novel following the popular historical drama, *The Huntingfield Paintress*.

The mother of two boys, she lives in London.

'A genuinely original, utterly enchanting story'– *A.N. Wilson*

'A slice of Suffolk history brought beautifully to life'– *Esther Freud*

'An atmospheric and enjoyable story of a singular and free-thinking woman'– *Deborah Moggach*

Plucky and headstrong Mildred Holland revelled in the eight years she and her husband, the vicar William Holland, spent travelling 1840s Europe, finding inspiration in recording beautiful artistic treasures and collecting exotic artifacts. But William's new posting in a tiny Suffolk village is a world apart and Mildred finds a life of tea and sympathy dull and stifling in comparison. When a longed-for baby does not arrive, she sinks into despondency and despair. What options exist for a clever, creative woman in such a cossetted environment? A sudden chance encounter fires Mildred's creative imagination and she embarks on a herculean task that demands courage and passion. Defying her loving but exasperated husband, and mistrustful locals who suspect her of supernatural powers, Mildred rediscovers her passion and lives again through her dreams of beauty. Inspired by the true story of the real Mildred Holland and the parish church of Huntingfield in Suffolk, the novel is unique, emotive and beautifully crafted, just like the history that inspired it.

URBANE